**AN EN**

"Something w......."

Zach raked his gaze over a patch of brambles. He had the sense that something was amiss, but he couldn't put his finger on it.

"We not take long," Chases Rabbits chafed. "Raven On The Ground need us."

"We won't be any help to her if we're dead." Zach looked at the brambles again. Few would choose it as a spot to hide, what with all the thorns. The center of the patch was especially dense, which would also discourage anyone from crawling in. Almost too dense, he thought, at the same moment that Blaze growled.

Details came into focus with sharp clarity—a squat form that seemed to be part of the brambles, but wasn't; branches that were going every which way, when most grew straight up or at right angles to the main stems; and the dark eyes that were fixed on him with fierce intensity.

Zach snapped his Hawken up. In the brambles a gun boomed. He felt a searing shock to his shoulder, and then his right arm and fingers went numb. He lost his hold on the rifle. . . .

# WILDERNESS #65:
## *SEED OF EVIL*

# David
# Thompson

Dorchester
Publishing

*Dedicated to Judy, Joshua and Shane.*
*And to Beatrice Bean, with the most loving regard.*

DORCHESTER PUBLISHING

September 2011

Published by

Dorchester Publishing Co., Inc.
200 Madison Avenue
New York, NY 10016

ISBN 13: 978-1-4285-1153-8 (Double Edition)
E-ISBN: 978-1-4285-0930-6

The "DP" logo is the property of Dorchester Publishing Co., Inc.

Printed in the United States of America.

Visit us online at www.dorchesterpub.com.

# Chapter One

The sheriff and his deputies bristled with weapons. They crept through the muggy Missouri night following a trail an informant told them about. The trail ended on a hill that overlooked a valley. The valley was a black pit with a pair of glowing eyes at its center.

The sheriff and his men huddled. The sheriff could hardly see their faces. Several worked for him full-time. The rest were volunteers who lent a hand when he needed extra help. He needed it tonight.

"From here on out, our lives aren't worth a plugged coin," the sheriff whispered. "One mistake is all it will take. I don't need to tell you how dangerous he is. I shouldn't need to remind you that the cutthroats who ride with him are a pack of rabid wolves."

"What I want to know," said John Byerly, one of the regular deputies, "is why we're going to try to take them alive."

"They're entitled to a chance to surrender."

"Hell," Byerly said.

One of the part-time deputies cleared his throat. "You know as well as we do, Sheriff, that they'll make a fight of it."

"It will be kill or be killed," said another.

"We do this as the law says to do it," the sheriff insisted. "If any man wants out, now is the time to say."

"Hell," Byerly said again. "I'm not complaining. I

just don't like the notion of sticking my head in a bear's mouth and then asking the bear not to bite it off."

Several of them grinned nervously.

The sheriff fingered his shotgun. "All right. We've been through what to do. Remember the signals. Anyone gets in trouble, yell for help." He said the next pointedly. "Above all, we can't let Ranton escape."

"He's a bad one," Byerly said.

"That he is," the sheriff grimly agreed. "Wherever he goes, he sows seeds of evil. It's time to put an end to it. He has infested our state long enough." The sheriff stood. "Let's do this, men."

The trail was narrow and winding. Midway down, a deputy tripped. Everyone froze, but there was no sign their quarry had heard.

The sheriff was sweating. His mouth was dry. All his years in office, he'd never had to deal with anyone like Neil Ranton. If ever there was a man who came out of the womb born rotten through and through, Ranton was it.

The twin eyes were lights in windows. The two-story house was old, built by a settler years ago. It had been abandoned when the last of the family died. It was so far out that no one wanted the place, and it had fallen into disrepair. But the house was good enough for the use Ranton put it to.

Female laughter brought the sheriff up short. It was wrong, them sounding so happy. He whistled in imitation of a robin and his deputies spread out. They had two minutes to surround the place. Then it would commence.

The sheriff wiped his palms on his pants and thumbed back the hammers on his English-made shotgun. Both barrels were loaded with buckshot. He wasn't taking any chances. If anyone raised a gun to him, he would blow them in half.

Off in the night an owl hooted.

Without warning the front door opened and a man came out.

The sheriff crouched. He aimed the shotgun, but he didn't shoot. He couldn't give himself away until his deputies were in position. He wished he could tell who it was.

The lamplight inside briefly framed the figure. Then the front door closed and the man came down the porch steps, moving toward the outhouse.

The sheriff swore silently. He hadn't counted on this. But he was confident his deputies would take the man into custody quietly. They were well trained.

The outhouse door creaked open and shut.

By then the two minutes were up. The sheriff rose and advanced to within a dozen feet of the front porch and cupped a hand to his mouth. "This is the sheriff! We have you surrounded! Come out with your hands in the air! If you resist we will use deadly force! Come out now!"

The sheriff crouched, and it saved his life. In an upstairs window, a rifle cracked and the slug whizzed past his ear. The sheriff jerked his shotgun up and let loose with one of the twin barrels. The window exploded in a hundred shards, and a man shrieked.

Bedlam broke out. Everywhere guns blasted. Men cursed and shouted and screamed.

The front door was flung wide and out charged a heavyset man with a pistol in each hand. He fired at the sheriff as he came down the steps, and the sheriff let him have the other barrel in the chest. The buckshot lifted the man off his feet and slammed him against the porch rail hard enough for him to pitch over it.

As abruptly as it had begun, the firing stopped. A man wailed that he was hit and begged for help. A woman sobbed.

The sheriff reloaded. He was almost to the porch when Byerly rushed up.

"Deputy Hanson is dead."

"Damn," the sheriff said.

"It was the one in the outhouse. He left a knife in Hanson's chest."

"Did you get him?"

"No, he got away. But I did get a glimpse." Byerly paused. "Sheriff, I think it was Ranton."

The sheriff gripped the shotgun so hard, his knuckles hurt. "Hell in a basket. Fetch the dogs and set them on his scent." Not that it would do any good. Ranton had eluded dogs before.

"He won't stick around," Byerly predicted. "He'll go somewhere else and start over like he always does."

"God help the poor people who live there, wherever it is," the sheriff said.

# Chapter Two

The mountain man was being followed.

Nate King woke at dawn, as was his habit. He kindled the embers of his fire and put the coffeepot on. He could go without food in the morning, but he refused to go without coffee. His wife liked to tease that he wouldn't need to make as many long rides to Bent's Fort if his will wasn't mush.

Nate had two addictions in life, coffee and books. He was an avid reader, everything from James Fenimore Cooper to Mary Shelley to Plato. As he waited for the coffee to perk, he opened the beaded parfleche his wife had made for him and took out his copy of Thomas Paine's *The Rights of Man*. He was about to open it to where he had left off when his bay raised its head, stared off to the west, and whinnied.

Nate looked up. He was well out on the prairie, amid rolling swells of grass pockmarked by wallows and split by gullies. The rising sun cast a golden glow that caused the morning dew to sparkle. He saw neither man nor animal. The bay was still staring, though, so he shoved the book back into the parfleche, picked up his Hawken, and strode a few yards from the fire.

The prairie spread to the horizon. He had the illusion he and his horse were the only living things in all that vastness. But that's all it was, an illusion. The prairie teemed with life, and not all of it was friendly. There were grizzlies and wolves and cougars. There were hostiles who would like nothing better than to count coup on a white. Sometimes there were white men who preyed on other white men for no other reason than the coins in their poke.

Nate had lived in the wilderness a good many years. He'd lasted as long as he had because he never let down his guard. So it was that when he sat back down and resumed sipping his coffee, he kept an eye on his back trail and caught the glint of the sun on metal. He didn't let on that he had seen. He finished his coffee, saddled his bay, and got under way.

Buckskins clung to Nate's big frame. His broad chest was crisscrossed by a possibles bag, an ammo pouch, and a powder horn. Around his waist was a brace of flintlocks, a bowie knife, and a tomahawk. A walking armory, some would call him.

Nate held the bay to a walk, acting as if he didn't have a care in the world. Now and again he casually looked over his shoulder. Twice more he saw the gleam. It was closer each time.

Nate came to a hillock and went around. As soon as he was on the other side, he drew rein and dismounted. Bent low, he climbed to the top. Just below the crest, he flattened so he wouldn't be silhouetted against the bright sky. He crawled until he could see over.

There were four of them, plus a packhorse. Warriors armed with bows and lances, riding in single file, smack on his back trail.

Nate tucked the Hawken's stock to his shoulder. He put his thumb to the hammer and fixed a bead on the first warrior. The man's hair hung long and loose and hid part of his face.

As they neared the hillock, Nate saw that they were Crows. Usually, the Crows were friendly. He

waited until they were right below him, then stood
with the Hawken leveled. In their tongue he said,
"*Ka-hay. Sho'o daa' chi.*"

The first warrior drew rein and glanced up. "Grizzly Killer!" he exclaimed in English.

"Chases Rabbits," Nate said in some surprise. It
had been more than a year since he last saw the
young warrior, and Chases Rabbits had done a lot
of growing.

Slapping his legs against his pinto, Chases Rabbits trotted up the slope. He vaulted down, clasped
Nate's arms, and cheerfully declared, "Me great
happy at see you again."

"I'm glad to see you, too," Nate said, although the
news he had to impart might break the younger
man's heart.

"How be Evelyn?"

"She's fine," Nate said. He hesitated, then decided
to get it over with. "She has a beau now."

"She have ribbon in hair?" Chases Rabbit said. "It
pretty one?"

"Not that kind of bow. She's seeing someone."

"Evelyn have good eyes," Chases Rabbits declared.
"She see like hawk."

Nate reminded himself that he must speak simply
and plainly. "Let me put it another way. My daughter is being courted."

"Eh? She tied up? Why you do that?"

"What?" Nate laughed. "No, not *cord*. Not rope.
She is being courted as in she is smitten with a
young man and he is smitten with her."

Chases Rabbits appeared even more puzzled. He
wriggled his fingers and said, "She wear fur on
hands in summer?"

Now it was Nate who was confused. He held out

his own hands, and it hit him. "No. Not mittens. *Smitten*. It means she's in love."

"Me too!"

Nate had expected the young Crow to be greatly upset. A while back Chases Rabbits had wooed Evelyn. Nothing had ever come of it, though. Evelyn liked him as a friend and nothing more.

"You're not still in love with her?"

"Her who?"

"My daughter," Nate said in mild exasperation. "Who have we been talking about?"

"Oh. No. Me in love with Raven On The Ground." Chases Rabbits beamed. "She beautiful. She nice. She sweet. She all goodness."

"Well now," Nate said, pleasantly surprised.

"Well what?"

Nate sighed. He had almost forgotten how Chases Rabbits used to make him want to pull out his hair. "I'm glad that you have someone of your own."

"She not mine yet. First me must show me brave warrior." Chases Rabbits gave a start as if an idea had occurred to him. "You help me, Grizzly Killer? You my good friend."

"Help you how?"

"Help me kill heap plenty Blackfeet."

# Chapter Three

Bent's Fort had been the hub of white commerce for over a decade. Situated on the Arkansas River, it was the sole outpost between the States and Santa Fe. Freighters always stopped to rest their teams and stock up on provisions, which was why over thirty wagons were in a circle outside the walls.

Indians came often, too, to trade. Originally, the Bent brothers and their partner, Ceran St. Vrain, established the post to trade with the Arapaho and the Cheyenne. As word spread, other tribes traveled to the fort, tribes from far and wide, the Crows among them.

"There it be!" Chases Rabbits declared as they came within sight of the high adobe walls.

Nate didn't say anything. He was pondering what his young friend had told him earlier.

"Now me get rifle," Chases Rabbits said, with a nod at the packhorse he was leading. Tied to it were prime pelts, beaver and buffalo and others. "Then me go count coup on Blackfeet."

"About that," Nate said.

"Yes?"

"There's always a chance they might count coup on you."

"Me warrior!" Chases Rabbits said, and thumped his chest. "Me not afraid."

"You should be," Nate told him. The Blackfeet had long held sway over much of the northern plains.

They were fierce and proud and not ever to be taken lightly.

"Why you talk like that? Me no coward."

"I never said you were. But a smart man doesn't poke a hornet's nest."

"What stinging bugs have to do with it?"

Nate chose his words carefully. The Crows, as did so many tribes, placed a premium on courage. Warriors who performed daring deeds were the most esteemed and sat high in their councils. "Did Raven On The Ground say she wants you to go kill Blackfeet?"

"It my idea so she want me for husband. Women like great men."

"Says the sprout who has barely lived eighteen winters."

"Sorry?" Chases Rabbits said.

Nate remembered a time when his own son thought the same. Counting coup was all many a young warrior lived for. It was their stepping-stone to prominence. As a result, they took risks wiser heads avoided. "Can't you impress your beauty some other way?"

"Me can steal many horses, but it quicker to kill a lot of enemy."

About a score of Nez Perce were camped near the high walls. Not far off were Pawnees. To the south were some Arapahos and a few Cheyenne.

The freighters, Nate noticed, had posted guards. They didn't trust the Indians any more than the Indians trusted them.

Nate and his Crow friend were almost to the gate when it opened and out filed five riders. All were white. In the lead was a tall man with a face like a shrew. He wore a blue cap and cradled a long Kentucky rifle. Instead of veering aside, he drew rein.

"You're in my way, lunkhead."

Nate had no objection to moving, but he didn't like the insult. "And you're in mine."

"Suppose you move before you make me mad."

"Suppose you go suck on a cow buff's teat."

The man tilted his head as if he couldn't believe what he was hearing. "You should learn to watch that tongue of yours, mountain man." Over his shoulder he said to the others, "Did you hear this idiot?"

"I heard him, Petrie," growled a scraggly oldster with stringy gray hair that hung limp under a floppy hat.

Petrie brought his mount up close to Nate's bay. "You ever talk to me like that again, you stupid son of a bitch, and you'll be sorry."

Nate almost hit him. He was cocking his arm to swing when a third man jabbed his heels and barreled his buttermilk between them.

"That's enough, Petrie. You and that damn temper of yours. Leave him be and keep going."

Nate would have thought that a testy character like Petrie would object to being bossed around, but Petrie rode on without another word. "I'm obliged," Nate said.

"Think nothing of it, friend," said the peacemaker. It was hard to tell his age. He was lean and sinewy, with a sharp, angular face and a jaw like an anvil. Blond curls spilled over his small ears. "Our boss wouldn't like it, him causing trouble." The man thrust out a bony hand. "Geist is the name, by the way."

"Nate King."

"That's a strong shake you've got there," Geist said. "No hard feelings, I hope." He motioned to the others and rode off after Petrie.

"Who them whites be?" Chases Rabbits asked.

"I have no idea." Nate turned to the still-open gate, and smiled at the man he saw walking through.

Ceran St. Vrain had an aristocratic bearing. Always the best-dressed man at the fort, he was known for his keen mind and his fairness. "As I live and breathe," he said with a grin. "You're back already? You were just here last month."

"Out of you know what." Nate climbed down and warmly shook St. Vrain's hand.

"You have an entire lake to drink," St. Vrain said, "yet that's not good enough."

"As I recollect, you have no room to talk. Who is it orders brandy by the case?"

St. Vrain grinned, then fixed his attention on the Crows. "Friends of yours?"

Nate introduced Chases Rabbits. "He's here to trade for a rifle."

"How much furs you want for long gun?" the young warrior asked.

"The going rate is ten buffalo robes," St. Vrain informed him. "I give you my word it will be a quality piece and not blow up in your face like some of Hudson Bay's trade rifles did. You can hunt with confidence."

"He wants the rifle to kill Blackfeet," Nate said.

"You don't say."

"You don't say what?" Chases Rabbits asked.

"We don't sell rifles for tribes to make war," St. Vrain informed him. "We sell them to use to hunt and so you can protect yourself."

"Me not make war. Me count coup."

"There's a woman," Nate said.

St. Vrain arched an eyebrow. "You live a complicated life, young sir."

"Me do?" Chases Rabbits scratched his chin. "How I live it and not know it?"

St. Vrain motioned. "Let's not block the gate. You and your friends are welcome so long as you obey the rules. Come on in."

"Rules?" Chases Rabbits said.

"No hard spirits are allowed inside the walls. No discharging of firearms. No fighting. No quarreling. Any disputes, you come to me or Bill or Charles Bent, and we'll resolve the issue. One of us is always on the premises. Do you understand all I've told you?"

"What be spirits?"

"Liquor. Whiskey. Scotch. Rum. You name it. That includes ale and beer. We are most strict about alcohol."

"White man's drink," Chases Rabbits said. "Smell like horse piss. Me never drink. Crow who drink not be Crow anymore."

"Good for you, young sirrah."

"What that mean?"

"Your English has gaps, doesn't it?"

"Many," Nate said.

"Come on in," St. Vrain repeated, and after Nate and the Crows had ridden through, he nodded at two guards, who promptly closed the gate.

The central square bustled with freighters and other visitors. At the northwest and southeast corners were towers with field pieces. A blacksmith shop was near the gate. Nate made for the hitch rail in front of it.

"Have supper with me and invite your amusing friend," St. Vrain suggested, falling into step. "Perhaps we can dissuade him from getting himself killed."

"I've been trying."

"But he refuses to listen because he's young and stubborn and in love."

"Weren't we all once?"

"What else do you need besides coffee? Or did you come all this way just for that?"

"Don't start. I get ribbed enough by Winona and Shakespeare. I don't need to hear it from you."

"I'm just surprised you came all this way when you have somewhere so much closer to get your supplies."

Nate stopped. "What are you talking about?"

"You don't know?" St. Vrain smoothed his fine coat and clasped his hands behind his back. "I would have thought word had spread all over the Rockies by now."

"Keep me in suspense, why don't you?"

St. Vrain smiled. "How many settlers would you say there are in the foothills and deeper in? Besides the five families in King Valley, that is."

Nate shrugged. "About fifteen to eighteen, I reckon."

"Oh, it's more than that. The Wards, the Kendals, and there are many others. It's closer to two dozen, I would say. Enough, I imagine, to support the new general store that has opened for business."

Genuine shock gripped Nate. Stores and taverns were cornerstones of civilization, and until this moment he had cherished the reality that civilization, with all its many ills, was a thousand miles away, far across the prairie and the wide Mississippi. "Please tell me you're jesting."

"Would that I were. I don't appreciate having competition, but it's competition on a small scale. They don't sell nearly as much as we do. Mainly the basics, and drink and food."

"You've been there?"

"A social call, to be polite. And to gauge how they'll cut into our profits." St. Vrain grinned. "They sell coffee."

"Where is this place?"

"About four miles northeast of your old cabin, along the foothills. They built it in a basin they call Mud Hollow. There's a creek but no one has given it a name yet. The man who runs the store calls himself Toad," St. Vrain chuckled. "I kid you not."

"What is he like?"

"The name fits. But do you want to hear something even more interesting? This Toad has five helpers. His clerks, he calls them. You met the gentlemen a few minutes ago. They were here to buy flour and sugar from us. Seems their own shipment was short."

"You mean . . . ?"

"Yes. Those men you encountered on your way in. Mr. Petrie and Mr. Geist and the others."

"Petrie doesn't strike me as the store clerk type."

"Me, neither," St. Vrain said.

Nate gazed out over the west wall toward the distant mountains. "So what you're saying is that there is more to this than meets the eye?"

"I suspect so, yes. And I thought you would like to know."

"Damn," Nate King said.

# Chapter Four

The foothills rose in serial ranks. Those covered with more grass than trees were light green; those covered with more trees than grass were dark green. Interspersed here and there was the brown of barren hills, the ground too rocky to support plant life.

The new trading post was easy enough to find.

Rutted tracks left by the wagons that hauled the trade goods wound among the hills to a broad hollow. A meandering creek had formed a pond so shallow it looked to be more mud than water. Thus, evidently, the name the owner of the store had chosen—Mud Hollow.

The store was well constructed. It was two stories, the bottom built from pine logs, the top from boards. There were windows with glass. There were also gun ports, a lot of gun ports, on all four sides. A corral was at the rear, a long hitch rail in front. A large sign proclaimed to the world that it was TOAD'S MERCANTILE.

"I'll be damned," Nate said.

"Why?" Chases Rabbits asked.

The young warrior and his companions had accompanied Nate from Bent's Fort. Cradled in Chases Rabbits' arm was his new rifle, a smoothbore with a thirty-inch barrel, manufactured in London.

Nate didn't mind the company. In fact, he'd taken advantage and tried to talk his young friend out of venturing into Blackfoot territory. So far he hadn't been successful.

"Big lodge," Chases Rabbits said with a nod at the mercantile. "Heap important man live here."

"He'd sure like you to think so."

Several horses with saddles were at the hitch rail. In the corral were more without, milling or dozing. A short way past the mercantile, the three men Nate had seen with Geist and Petrie were erecting what appeared to be a stable or barn. All three, he noticed, kept pistols under their belts and knives in their sheaths as they went about their work.

"Me like this place," Chases Rabbits said.

"We haven't been inside yet." Nate dismounted and tied the reins to the hitch rail.

The door was open. From inside came voices and laugher. A wide window revealed a counter that ran the length of the room and rows of shelves piled with goods. To one side were several tables with linen and silverware.

A man was staring back through the window at Nate. He smiled, then came outside, his hand outstretched as he had offered it at Bent's Fort. "Mr. King. Fancy seeing you again so soon."

"Mr. Geist," Nate said.

"You must have heard about us at the fort and come for a look-see."

"Something like that."

"Allow me to show you around." Geist smiled at the Crows. "You and your friends. Indians are always welcome. They'll be a large part of our trade."

"You're in business with this Toad, then?"

"Oh, no," Geist quickly answered. "Toad is the boss. I'm just another of the hired help."

The inside smelled of tobacco smoke and food. In a corner sat a stove. By the counter was a pickle barrel.

Nate couldn't get over it: a mercantile in the Rockies. "I never thought I'd live to see the day."

"I beg your pardon?"

"Nothing."

"Come on over and I'll introduce you." Geist ushered them to the counter.

Behind it stood a remarkably grotesque individual. The man stood a few inches over five feet in height and was almost as wide as he was tall. His shoulders slumped, his body thickened at the middle, his legs were short and bowed, his feet wide and splayed. Then there was his face. It was broad across the chin but narrow at the brow. His brown eyes bulged as if seeking to burst from their sockets. His wide nose was flat, his mouth a slit. The total effect brought to mind the animal he was named after.

"Toad, I'd like you to meet Nate King," Geist said.

"Pleased to meet you," Nate replied.

Toad's bulging eyes fixed on him and he briefly touched a clammy palm to Nate's. "Heard about you."

Nate was dumfounded. The man's voice sounded just like the croak of a real toad. His reaction must have shown, because the other frowned.

"You're not one of those, are you?"

"Those?"

"The ones who look at me like I'm some kind of freak. I've had to put up with it all my life and I don't like it one bit."

"Now, Toad," Geist said.

Toad colored and balled his thick fingers. "Well, I don't," he said sullenly. He shifted his bulging eyes back to Nate. "I've done a lot of asking around. They told me at Bent's that you're well thought of. One of the most respected men in the Rockies, St. Vrain said."

"News to me," Nate replied.

"Don't be modest. Word is that you were a trapper once. You stayed on after the fur brigades disbanded and now you live deep in the mountains with a Shoshone wife and your family. The Shoshones even adopted you into their tribe, I understand. Grizzly Killer, the Indians call you."

"You have been asking around."

"I'm a businessman, King. And a businessman needs to know about those he might do business with. I came out to Bent's a year ago and nosed around to see if I could make a go of it with my mercantile, and here I am."

"I wouldn't think there are enough settlers for you to make a go of it."

"There aren't. But I'm close enough to the Oregon Trail that wagon trains will stop. And then there are the Indians. I hope to trade with all the tribes."

"Really?" Nate said.

Toad's eyes grew defensive. "Is it me, or do you not sound too happy about my being here?"

Nate decided to be honest with him. "Some years back another man opened a trading post. He said the same thing you have, that he was only interested in trade. But he stirred up trouble between two of the tribes so he could sell them a lot of rifles."

"I'm not him," Toad declared. "Making money is in my blood, you might say. But stirring up a war is a damn stupid way to do business. I aim to be here a good long while, and to do that I have to stay friendly with everyone, white and red alike."

"I'm happy to hear that."

"What happened to that other meshuggener?"

"The what?"

"The putz who tried to stir up the war."

"Someone shot him."

"You?"

Nate hesitated. "My son."

Geist had been listening with great interest. "We heard about him, too, at Bent's. The notorious Zach King. A natural-born killer, they call him. Someone told us it's because he's a half-breed."

Had it not been for Geist's perpetually friendly smile, Nate would have slugged him. "Who told you that?"

"We forget," Toad said with a pointed look of his bulging eyes at Geist.

"Not that I believe that nonsense about breeds," Geist added quickly. "Just because a person has mixed blood doesn't mean he's bad."

"No," Nate gratefully replied. "It doesn't."

"As for my mercantile," Toad said, "you have my word that we'll cause no trouble whatsoever."

"I hope to God that's true," Nate King said.

# Chapter Five

Nestled in the heart of the Rockies lay a valley ringed by towering mountains over three miles high. Several were capped with the white of snow. Other peaks were the brown of upthrust rock or the red of bare earth.

King Valley, it was called, and at its center was the great blue eye known as King Lake. Lush grass spread south of the lake. To the west, north, and east grew forest as dense and untamed as the day the first man set foot on the North American continent.

Wildlife thrived. Mountain sheep roamed the high crags. Elk bugled in the upper meadows. Deer were everywhere. Mountain lions and wolves helped keep the population in check. Coyotes and bobcats fed on the small game.

Birds were as numerous as the leaves on the trees. Robins, sparrows, jays, and ravens constantly flew about. Out on the lake, ducks, geese, and terns swam and quacked and honked. High above soared the predators of the air, eagles and hawks, and the woods harbored owls.

"It sure is beautiful here, Pa," Evelyn King said as she stood on the shore and skimmed stones on the lake's surface. "There are days when I want to pinch myself to be sure I'm not dreaming."

Nate cared for his daughter deeply. She was headstrong at times, but she had a good heart and a peaceful temperament. She was also very much in love—although she wouldn't come right out and admit it—with a young Nansusequa. "How is Dega doing these days?"

"Fine, I suppose."

Nate had been home less than an hour. He had hugged and kissed his wife and talked with their daughter-in-law, who was visiting. Then he had come out to stretch his legs and caught sight of his daughter on her way back from the Nansusequa lodge at the other end of the lake.

"The two of you have been awfully close since that day you went off together."

"We're friends, is all."

"Hard to find diapers for a man my age," Nate said.

"What would you need a diaper for?"

"I must have been born yesterday."

Evelyn laughed. About to throw another flat stone, she glanced to the north and said, "Uh-oh. What has him in such a dither?"

Nate heard the thud of hooves and guessed what he would see before he turned, and he was right. Riding hard toward them was his son, Zach. They looked somewhat alike, in that Zach had his father's green eyes and build, but Zach mostly took after his mother and the Shoshone side of the family. "You might want to go inside."

"Are you two going to argue again?" Evelyn threw the stone, which skipped several times before sinking. "I might just do that, then. When he's mad he's not fun to be around."

Nate walked to the water, hunkered down, and dipped his hand in. He sipped from his cupped palm and wet his neck. As he was rising, his son arrived in a loud clatter and a flurry of dust.

"It is true what Louisa just told me?" Zach demanded without dismounting.

"Unless she's taken to lying to you, I would say it was," Nate replied.

"She said she was visiting Ma when you got home. She said there's a new trading post in the foothills."

"They're calling it a mercantile."

"I don't like it, Pa," Zach said.

"I'm not fond of the idea, either, but it's there and there's nothing we can do about it."

Zach patted one of the pistols tucked under his leather belt. "Yes, there is."

"Climb down, son," Nate suggested, and when Zach alighted, Nate draped an arm over his son's shoulders. "Listen to me. We don't own these mountains. We can't go around running people off because we don't like them or because we object to what they do for a living."

"We can if what they do causes trouble. The last time we nearly had a war on our hands."

"Trust me. It's all I've thought about since St. Vrain told me about the new trader." Nate chose his next words carefully. His son had a tendency to let his feelings get the better of his judgment and was much too quick to resort to violence. "I've met the man. He's given me his word he'll be fair and decent and won't ply the Indians with liquor. So long as he abides by his word, we have no right to interfere with his livelihood."

"Which is a fancy way of saying we twiddle our thumbs and hope for the best."

Nate lowered his arm and gazed out across the beautiful blue of the lake. Patience was another trait his son had not yet fully mastered. But Nate couldn't blame him. He, too, felt a special bond with the mountains and the people who lived there. Many of the tribes were their friends. He felt especially protective toward the Shoshones, who had accepted him as one of their own. "We have to give the new trader the benefit of the doubt."

"You do, maybe," Zach said.

"The last time you took the law into your own hands, you ended up on trial for your life."

Zach's dark features clouded. "I did what was right and you know it. And aren't you forgetting something?"

"What?"

Zach gestured, encompassing their valley and the ring of mountains with a sweep of his arm. "There *is* no law out here. There is no government. There are no army posts."

"Yet," Nate interrupted, and was ignored.

"There are no politicians and lawyers to tell us how to live. We're free to do as we please. Truly and really free, as you've impressed on me since I was old enough to understand what being free means."

Nate didn't comment. The boy had him there.

"Out here, we live by what *we* think is right. We have to stand up for ourselves, for what we believe in, and for those we care for."

"I agree, wholeheartedly," Nate said. "But you're forgetting something, too."

"Which is?"

"That this new trader hasn't done anything wrong yet. He hasn't caused any trouble. We can't close him down and drive him off without a reason."

Zach put a hand on the hilt of his bowie. "All right, Pa. I won't do anything, for now. But I'll keep an eye on things, and my ears open, and if I find out this new trader is as bad as the last, there will be blood."

# Chapter Six

Chases Rabbits was surprised when Long Hair sent for him. He was in his father's lodge, letting his father admire his new rifle, when a runner came and said that whites had come to the village, and Long Hair needed Chases Rabbits to translate.

Chases Rabbits hurried back with the runner. Two horses with saddles were outside the chief's lodge, along with a string of four more. So was a gathering crowd of his people. He held his head high and made sure to hold his new rifle across his chest where all could see it. Then he bent and was in the chief's lodge.

Other warriors were already there, prominent men, the most important in their tribe.

Long Hair beckoned. He had seen over eighty winters and was one of the most revered leaders of the tribe. His name came from the fact that his hair, once black but now as white as snow, had never been cut. He wore it in a single braid drawn up at the back. When he let it down, as he sometimes did at celebrations, it was as long as two tall men lying down head to toe.

Chases Rabbits was deeply honored, and greatly proud, to be called upon. Because of their many dealings with whites, quite a few of his people spoke a little of the white tongue, but he spoke it best. He had his mother to thank for that. She had lived with a white trapper when he was a boy.

Long Hair indicated that Chases Rabbits should sit on his left, between him and the white men.

Not until Chases Rabbits sank down did he look at them and realize who they were. He had to think to remember their names. Then he turned his attention to the great chief.

"You will speak to these whites for us. Find out why they have come. They do not know our tongue and do not know sign. But they smile and are friendly and seem to have something important to say."

"I have met them," Chases Rabbits revealed. "They are with the man who has the new trading post."

"Then perhaps they have come to ask us to trade with them," Long Hair said. "Question them for us."

Chases Rabbits turned to their visitors and switched to English. "My heart be happy at seeing you again, Mr. Geist." He was not so happy to see the other one, Petrie. He had not liked how Petrie treated his friend Nate King.

"Well, this is a stroke of luck," the blond man said cheerfully. "Chases Rabbits, isn't it? I'll be grateful if you can help us."

"What it be you want?"

Geist was seated cross-legged, his elbows on his knees. He made a tepee of his fingers and tapped them to his square chin. "I have heard about Long Hair. They say he is a great and wise chief. Tell him for me that I am honored to be in his presence."

Chases Rabbits did as the white man wanted.

"I am here on behalf of Mr. Levi—"

"Me sorry," Chases Rabbit broke in. "Who?"

"On behalf of Toad," Geist clarified. "He has left it to me to drum up business for the trading post. I figure the best way to do that is to hook up with one of the tribes and have them spread word among the other tribes about how friendly we are."

"Me sorry again," Chases Rabbits said. "What mean hook up? Like hook Nate King use to catch fish?"

Petrie laughed.

"No, not like a fishhook," Geist said, glaring at Petrie. "Hook up means to be a special friend. We would like to be special friends with the Crows. As a token of our friendship, I brought four horses for . . ." He seemed to catch himself. "I brought three horses as gifts for Long Hair and one horse as a gift for you."

"Me?" Chases Rabbits said in great surprise.

"I would like you to be our interpreter. In exchange, you'll get free gifts. The horse is just the first of many."

The prospect of a flood of wealth dazzled Chases Rabbits to such an extent that he nearly missed what Geist said next.

"The rest of your people will get special treatment, too. We'll give you discounts on the trade goods that we won't give others."

"Discounts?"

"A blanket that might cost someone from another tribe four buffalo robes will only cost your tribe three. That sort of thing."

"It be nice of you."

Geist reached over and patted Chases Rabbits on the arm. "Like I said, we want to be special friends with the Crows."

"Why us?" Chases Rabbits thought to ask. "There be many tribes. The Shoshones, the Arapahos, the Nez Perce—" He would have gone on, but Geist had an answer.

"The Shoshones already have a special white friend in Nate King. As for the others, they're too far away. You Crows are the closest."

Long Hair impatiently asked what the white man was talking about.

Chases Rabbits explained. He made it a point to end with "They want me to talk for them in council because I speak the white tongue so well."

The burly warrior on Long Hair's right raised his head. "This is a good thing for the Apsaalooke," he said, using their name for themselves. "The Shoshones have done well by their friendship with Grizzly Killer. Why should we not benefit by having this white man for our friend?"

Another warrior spoke. "Think of what it will mean. More horses. More guns. More knives."

"More pots for the women," a warrior at the end said, and they all grinned.

"It is a good thing," Long Hair agreed, and turned to Chases Rabbit. "Tell the white man we accept. Thank him for me for the horses. Say that from this day on, we will regard him and the other whites at the trading post as our brothers. They are always welcome at our fire."

Chases Rabbits translated Long Hair's acceptance to the whites. Geist was pleased. "I can't tell you how much this means to us. You won't regret it."

A pipe was produced and passed around.

Chases Rabbits sat straight and tall. His status in the tribe had changed; he was now a man of importance. He thought of Raven On The Ground and how impressed she would be. He couldn't wait to tell the Kings. He was sure they would be happy for him.

# Chapter Seven

The pair was barely out of sight of the Crow village when Geist shifted in his saddle and snapped, "You almost gave us away back there when you laughed, damn you."

"Don't talk to me like that," Petrie said.

Geist drew rein. "I'll talk to you any damn way I please. There is too much at stake for you to act the fool."

"Now, hold on," Petrie said. "They have no idea what this is about. That boy and his fishhook was close to the truth, but he doesn't know it. That's why I laughed."

Leveling his rifle, Geist asked in a tone pregnant with menace, "Are you talking back to me?"

"Never," Petrie said, staring calmly at the rifle's muzzle. "How long have we been together? I've never had cause to complain. You outthink everybody. All I do is kill."

Geist lowered his long gun and flicked his reins. "I'm irritable, I suppose, because there's so much at stake. We can't have them suspect."

"They have no more brains than cows."

"And like cows we'll use them to our own ends. Six months from now we'll be back where we were before that sheriff and his posse closed in. Only better, because out here there's no law."

"It was the best idea we ever had, coming west of the Mississippi."

"We?" Geist said.

"Well, you know."

"I should have thought of it years ago. We can do whatever we please out here. Think about that. Whatever we damn well please." Geist's face practically glowed with fierce delight. "There's no one to stop us."

"What about St. Vrain and his partners, and that busybody King?"

"All St. Vrain cares about is his precious fort. The Bent brothers have ties to the Cheyenne and the Arapaho, not to mention the Crows. They won't give a lick what we do."

"That still leaves Nate King."

"Yes, it does. But if we do this right, if we do it smart, we'll have everything in place before he can lift a finger against us. By then, it will be too late."

"I can shoot him so it never comes to that."

"Use your damn head. If we kill him, we'll make the Shoshones mad, and we want their trade as much as the others."

"They'll never know it was me," Petrie said.

"Maybe not. But there's that son of his to consider. I had a long talk with St. Vrain about this Zachary King. He's our main worry. He wiped out an entire trading post for stirring up trouble with the redskins."

"What do you mean, wiped out?"

"What the hell do you think I mean? He and some Shoshones killed every last man. Killed some Crows who were involved, too, which didn't sit well with the Crows. Yet another reason for us to choose them and not another tribe." Geist shook his head. "No, this Zach King is a he-bear. The genuine article. We'll tread light so as not to involve him."

"A lot of trouble to go to," Petrie said. "I could kill him as well as his pa."

Geist rode for a while in silence, then said, "If it comes to that. In the meantime, do as I say."

"Don't you mean as Toad says?"

"Isn't he something?" Geist said.

The river they were following flowed through gorgeous country lush with vegetation and teeming with game. They spooked a female elk that barreled away through the undergrowth with her calf at her tail.

"That reminds me," Petrie said. "Why didn't you ask them about the women?"

"One step at a time," Geist replied. "First we win their confidence, and then we set it up."

"I can't wait," Petrie said.

"Me neither."

# Chapter Eight

The temperature was pushing one hundred the day that Zach King and two Shoshones came down out of the mountains to Mud Hollow. They drew rein on a hill that overlooked the new mercantile. Zach took in the horses that lined the hitch rail and the bustle of activity. "What we heard is true."

His uncle, Touch The Clouds, grunted. "If the rest is true, you can stop worrying."

"I have to see for myself."

The other Shoshone said, "Your father is satisfied, but you are still suspicious."

"I'm not my father, Drags The Rope."

The warrior smiled. "No, Stalking Coyote, you are not Grizzly Killer."

"The whites have a saying," Zach said. "Better safe than sorry. It's better if these traders prove to us we can trust them than if we take it for granted and end up like before." He kneed his dun.

The slope was broken by a new trail, courtesy of the many who had already paid the trading post a visit. Below, Crows, Nez Perce, and several Flatheads were moving about or talking.

"I do not see any Blackfeet," Drags The Rope said, and grinned.

"If they find out about this place, they might burn it to the ground," Zach predicted.

"It is too far south for the Blackfeet," Touch The Clouds said.

"Then the Sioux, maybe."

"Why do you resent these traders so much? It could be they have good hearts."

Zach didn't have a ready answer. His sister liked to poke fun at him by saying he was suspicious of all whites. But that wasn't entirely true. He trusted his father, and his father's dearest friend and mentor, Shakespeare McNair. Besides, he was part white himself.

A wagon was parked by the corral. A grizzled white man with gray hair and a floppy hat came out of what Zach took to be a small stable and stretched. He spied them and immediately hurried into the trading post.

Their arrival sparked considerable interest. Zach knew a number of the warriors and acknowledged the few who acknowledged him. More were interested in greeting Touch The Clouds. The giant Shoshone leader was famed not only among his own kind, but also among many other tribes—including their enemies—for his bravery and devotion to the welfare of his people.

Drags The Rope remarked with another of his wry grins, "I am happy to be ignored."

They dismounted and went into the mercantile. Zach recognized the man called Toad behind the long counter from his father's description. On the near side of the counter stood a man with blond curls. His father had called that one Geist. A small man with ratlike eyes was at the far end, a rifle on the counter next to him. That would be Petrie, Zach decided. The man with the gray hair and floppy hat and two others were leaning against the opposite wall. All of them were armed, but that was nothing new on the frontier; Zach was heavily armed himself. He walked to the counter with his Shoshone friends on either side.

"How do you do?" Toad said. "I understand that you're Nate King's son, Zach." He held out his hand.

Zach shook hands, but he didn't like doing so. The man's hand was clammy.

"I'm Geist," the blond man said, and he shook, too.

Zach introduced Touch The Clouds and Drags The Rope.

"I'm right pleased to make your acquaintance," Geist said. He offered his hand, but Touch The Clouds didn't take it. Instead, Touch The Clouds grunted.

"He's not insulting you," Toad said. "Shaking hands is a white custom." To the Shoshone chief he said, "I'm pleased to meet you as well. I hope your people will feel free to visit often."

In Shoshone, Touch The Clouds said to Zach, "You talk for us. I do not want them to know I know a little of their tongue."

Zach nodded at the three men against the wall. "Who are they?"

"They work for me," Toad said.

"Their names."

Toad seemed surprised. He pointed at the one in the floppy hat. "That's Dryfus. Next to him is Gratt. The tall one is Berber."

"Why do you want to know their names?" Geist asked.

"It is good to know who your enemies might be," Zach told him.

"Enemies?" Toad said. "Didn't your father tell you? I run an honest store. Anyone comes in here, white or red, they're treated the same."

"If that's true, it would make you . . ." Zach pretended to grope for a word. "What is it the whites say? Oh, yes. It would make you a saint."

Toad snorted. "I'm not any such thing. I'm a businessman. But an honest businessman."

"Is that possible?"

"Your friend St. Vrain is one. The Bent brothers, too, from what I'm told."

"Yes," Zach admitted. "They are."

"I am just like them."

Zach stared down the counter at Petrie. "That remains to be seen."

Geist stood outside the trading post and watched the younger King and the two Shoshones ascend the trail up the hill to the west.

Petrie came out and stood watching, too. "What do you think?"

"I think Toad was pretty convincing. They acted like they almost believed him."

"The half-breed didn't."

"Now that I've met him, I'm not so concerned."

"You're not?"

Geist shook his head. "He didn't seem nearly as dangerous as everyone makes him out to be. He was curious, mostly. And testy. But that comes from being a half blood." He thoughtfully rubbed his chin. "No, sir. I think we can get on with our plans and won't have to worry about Zach King one bit."

"About damn time," Petrie said.

"But we still have to be careful. That Touch The Clouds could bring his entire tribe down on us, so you make sure the others understand. No Shoshone women. Not one. You hear me?"

"We didn't aim to use any anyway."

"We'll start with the Crows," Geist said. "They're practically used to it. Anyone who stops in a Crow village for the night is allowed to help himself."

"Filthy heathens."

"Now, now. I sort of admire their honesty. But they're awful dumb, giving it away for free."

"What about the other tribes?" Petrie asked.

"One at a time, remember? Once we have a thriving trade with Crow females, we'll see about adding others. From what I hear, some tribes will sell their women outright if the price is right. A couple of horses and a few blankets could get us one who brings in three to four hundred a year."

"But will the whores be enough?"

Geist looked at him. "It never has been, has it? We'll run the liquor on the side. And if all goes well, we'll sell some guns to tribes we're not supposed to."

"Like the Blackfeet and maybe the Sioux?"

"For a start." Geist smiled. "These wilds are everything I'd hoped they'd be. There are opportunities galore for men with no scruples."

"That would be us," Petrie said.

"Yes, it would," Geist said, and they both laughed.

# Chapter Nine

Life was glorious.

Chases Rabbits came down out of Crow country to pay another visit to his new white friends. He was winding along a serrated ridge with patches of thick woods broken by small meadows. He sat straight and tall on his new sorrel, thinking of how magnificent his reflection had looked in the stream. The next patch of woods ended and he emerged into another sunny meadow.

Chases Rabbits drew rein in alarm. There was a grizzly in the center of the meadow. It had been so long since he saw one of the silver-tip bears that he had forgotten how enormous they were: as huge as a buffalo. Even worse, each of their giant paws was rimmed with long claws that could flay flesh like sharp knives, and their maws were rimmed with sharp pointed teeth powerful enough to crunch through bone.

The bear was rooting at what appeared to be a badger burrow, and had not seen him yet.

Chases Rabbits debated what to do. He could rein around and ride like the wind, but the grizzly might hear him and give chase. Or he could sit quietly and hope the beast went on its way without noticing him.

Grunting and snorting, the grizzly dislodged large clumps of dirt. Evidently it was intent on digging the badger out.

Chases Rabbits sat quietly. The sorrel raised its

head and pricked its ears, quivering. To keep it from bolting, Chases Rabbits bent and patted its neck, whispering, "Be brave, horse. I am here." He looked up.

The grizzly was staring right at him.

Chases Rabbits's mouth went dry. He had his new rifle, but it only had one shot. Grizzly Killer had once told him that it could take seven or eight to bring a silver-tip down. Their skulls were so thick, they were impervious to bullets. As for a heart or a lung shot, their massive bodies were so padded with muscle and fat that the lead couldn't penetrate.

Chases Rabbits also remembered Grizzly Killer saying that sometimes a loud voice would scare a bear off. So he shouted, "I am Chases Rabbits of the Apsaalooke! I am a mighty warrior and a fierce fighter! Go away, bear, and do not arouse my wrath or you will be sorry!"

The grizzly roared and charged.

Chases Rabbits didn't have to rein the sorrel around. It wheeled on its own and raced into the trees with a recklessness he found as frightening as the bear. Branches whipped at his face and tore at his buckskins, threatening to dump him to the ground.

A glance back showed the bear in swift pursuit.

"Faster, horse!" Chases Rabbits cried, and slapped his legs.

A thicket loomed and instead of going around, the panicked sorrel plunged in. Chases Rabbits was aghast. It slowed them and they needed all the speed the horse possessed.

The grizzly hurtled in after them.

Chases Rabbits twisted, intending to shoot it. He raised his rifle and tried to aim, but he couldn't hold the gun steady no matter how hard he tried.

The bear was gaining.

Facing front, Chases Rabbits stiffened. They had burst out of the thicket and a low tree branch flashed at his face. He ducked just in time and felt it brush his hair.

A loud wheezing filled his ears. The bear was breathing so hard, it sounded like a stampeding bull buffalo.

Chases Rabbits reined right and then left. Thankfully, the sorrel responded. But the bear was still gaining. Its ears were back and its teeth gleamed, and as Chases Rabbits swept around a pine the bear swung a front paw and nearly caught the sorrel's leg.

Chases Rabbits had never been so scared. He recalled the time another warrior was killed and eaten, and how the man's stomach had been torn open and the intestines left hanging out like so much pale rope, and the terrible stench.

The sorrel squealed. The bear's claws had torn its flank.

Chases Rabbits sensed his doom. It wasn't right for him to die now, of all times. A lovely woman was interested in him. His people looked up to him as their important link to the whites. And best of all, he got to sit in council with Long Hair and the other leaders.

Suddenly he realized that he didn't hear the wheezing anymore. He glanced over his shoulder and whooped in joy. The bear had stopped. Grizzlies could run fast, but only for short distances. They tired much sooner than a horse.

When he was an arrow's flight away, Chases Rabbits brought the sorrel to a stop, and turned.

The bear was lumbering off in search of easier prey.

"I told you I am a mighty warrior!" Chases Rabbits

yelled, and shook his rifle and yipped. He would have a great story to tell when he got back to the village, and the claw marks on the sorrel to prove it was true.

He waited a good long while to be sure the bear was gone, then smacked his heels and resumed his journey. He rode warily in case the grizzly circled to come at him again. It was not unheard of.

The sun was high in the sky when Chases Rabbits reached Mud Hollow. A silly name, but then the whites gave many names to things that made no sense.

The mercantile was busy, as usual. Chases Rabbits squared his shoulders. He smiled at Crows he knew and nodded at several Nez Perce he had met as he drew rein at the hitch rail. He tied the sorrel off as the whites liked to do, cradled his rifle, and strode in.

Geist, over at a table with Petrie and Dryfus, spotted him right away and waved.

Chases Rabbits went over. "It be good to see you again, my friend."

Petrie looked him up and down. "Ain't you the dandy? Where'd you get white buckskins?"

"Mother make," Chases Rabbits said. "From white buck father kill."

"An albino? You don't say." Petrie fingered Chases Rabbits's sleeve. "I'd like to get me a set just like yours one day."

"Me handsome, yes?"

"Oh, very," Geist said. He bobbed his chin at the other two. "Leave us alone, boys. Our partner and me have something to talk about."

Chases Rabbits sank carefully into a vacated chair. He had never understood why whites insisted on sitting in these uncomfortable things when there was always the perfectly flat ground or a floor to sit on. "I be partner?" He was trying to remember what the word meant.

"You bet," Geist said. "We couldn't do any of this without you."

Chases Rabbits was flattered. He was important to his people *and* to the whites.

"What would you like to drink?"

"Water."

"Oh. That's right. You don't drink liquor. Too bad. You don't know what you're missing." Geist chuckled. "What's that saying you're so fond of?"

"Not just me. My people." Chases Rabbits recited, "The Crow who drinks white whiskey is no longer Crow."

"Haven't your people ever heard of moderation?"

"What that?"

"You only drink enough to wet your whistle, not enough to drown." Geist raised an arm and extended two fingers.

Toad promptly came around the counter with a bottle and two glasses and set them down without comment. Toad stared at Chases Rabbits, then went back.

"Him strange man."

"All his people are."

"His people? Him white like you."

"All whites aren't the same," Geist said. "I come from good European stock. He's a dreg."

"What that?" Chases Rabbits asked.

"Forget him." Geist opened the bottle and filled both glasses halfway. "We need to talk, you and me, about how we can help each other even more." He pushed one of the glasses across the table.

"No, thank you," Chases Rabbits said politely.

"Come on. Just a sip. It's considered rude to refuse a drink from a friend." Geist raised his glass. "Let's toast our friendship."

Chases Rabbits reluctantly picked up the glass. He didn't want to insult anyone. Geist touched glasses and drained his in a gulp. Chases Rabbits took a sip and grimaced at how terrible it tasted.

"That's a start," Geist said. "Now then, let's talk about your women."

Not that many winters ago, Chases Rabbits had thought that Evelyn King was the most beautiful girl alive. Now he knew better. Raven On The Ground was all the beauty in the world in one body. When he looked at her, his mind stopped working and his whole body went numb.

Now, standing in the shade of an oak, Chases Rabbit watched the woman of his dreams wash clothes in the stream. She was on her knees at the water's edge, dipping a doeskin dress in a pool. Her lustrous hair, her curves, her face, her lively eyes—she was perfection.

Chases Rabbits stepped out from under the tree and coughed to get her attention. She looked up and smiled, and his brain refused to work.

"Chases Rabbits! You are back from the new trading post."

"Yes," Chases Rabbits forced his mouth to say. None of his people called it a mercantile as the whites did. He walked over, his new rifle in the crook of his elbow.

"What is that around your waist?"

Chases Rabbits looked down at himself as if he didn't know what she meant. "This?" He touched his new leather belt, which he wore over his buckskins as Grizzly Killer did. "The whites gave it to me."

Raven On The Ground stood and ran her hand from the buckle to his hip. "It is very smooth."

A sudden constriction in Chases Rabbits's throat prevented him from replying.

"I am proud of you. Everyone is talking about how you have helped our people."

"It is nothing," Chases Rabbits said, his voice strangely strained.

"You are too modest." Raven On The Ground touched his cheek. "And so handsome."

A hot feeling spread from Chases Rabbits's neck to his hair.

"Will you come visit me tonight?"

Chases Rabbits grew hotter. "Does this mean I can court you?"

"Silly man. What else have you been doing all this time?"

Her laughter was the music of a flute and the beauty of a rainbow all in one.

At that moment Chases Rabbits would have done anything for her—scaled the highest cliff, caught a wild horse, slain the grizzly he had encountered. Well, maybe not the grizzly, he reflected.

"So tell me what happened with the whites," Raven On The Ground urged. She drew him to a log and perched with his hand in hers.

"They want me to make a request before the council," Chases Rabbits related. "I will do so tonight."

"What do they want of us?"

Chases Rabbits explained how the whites were interested in hiring women to do work at the mercantile. "They will give blankets and beads and whatever else the women might like."

Raven On The Ground's lovely eyes lit up. "That is something I would be interested in."

"I know. That is why I came straight to you before I told anyone else."

"Maybe I could get a hand mirror like Yellow Butterfly has. I have always wanted one." She bubbled with excitement. "Oh, this is grand. What kind of work would I have to do?"

"The whites want women to cook and clean and do other things."

"What other things?"

"The man called Geist didn't say."

Raven On The Ground stood. "Come. I will ask my mother and father right away. And when you bring it before the council tonight, I will be the first to step forward and say I am interested." She tenderly placed her palm on his face. "You have done me a great favor. I am grateful."

"I would do anything for you," Chases Rabbits said.

# Chapter Ten

Well after night had settled in, and long after the last of the Indians had left, Geist and Petrie walked from the mercantile to the new building that from the outside resembled a stable. It didn't have double doors, as a barn or stable would, but only a single door that Geist opened and strode through.

Dryfus, Gratt, and Berber were already there. Dryfus pushed his floppy hat back on his head and said, "What do you think?"

Instead of stalls for horses, there were four rooms just big enough for a bed and a stand for a lamp. They had made the beds from planks and used blankets for a mattress.

Geist went from room to room and nodded in satisfaction. "It's not much, but it will serve our needs."

"Are four beds enough?" Berber asked.

"We could put two beds to a room," Gratt suggested. "Do twice the business."

"All you think of is filling your poke," Geist said. His face hardened. "Or is it you'd rather run things?"

Gratt thrust out both hands and vigorously shook his head. "Hold on. I never said any such thing. I just remember how it was in Missouri when you crammed them in like apples in a barrel."

"We start slow and build," Geist said. "A year from now we could have three beds to a room. It all depends."

The door opened and Toad filled the doorway. He came in and looked at each of the rooms, then came back again to stand in front of Geist. "I am against this."

"I don't give a damn what you are against," Geist said, and the others laughed and sneered.

"This wasn't what I thought you meant when you approached me in St. Louis."

"If I'd told you I was coming west to set up the first Indian whorehouse, would you have taken us on?" Geist scornfully asked.

"Of course not."

"There you go." Geist indicated the door. "Go back to your precious mercantile and don't butt in again."

"This is wrong," Toad said.

"Oh, hell," Geist said.

"You'll ruin everything! I'm trying my best to earn their trust, and you'll bring it all crashing down."

Petrie leveled his rifle. "Want me to take him back and see that he stays there?"

"No need." Geist glared at Toad and poked him in the chest. "You listen to me, you dumb bastard. All you are to me is a means to an end. I'll make more money in one month from my whores than you'll make in six months from your store."

"The Crows won't like it. They'll massacre us."

Geist was growing angry. He put a hand on his pistol. "Shows how much you know, Levi. When a stranger visits a Crow village, guess what he's allowed to have for the night if he wants one?"

"You're not implying . . ." Toad began.

"I sure as hell am. They let the stranger have a female for the night. Now think about that. If they let a man have a woman for free, why in hell would they raise a ruckus over their women parting their legs for money?"

"Maybe because the women would be doing it for you and you're white."

"So? The Crows are almost as friendly to whites as the Shoshones. And besides, we'll be greasing the wheel with gifts to that idiot Chases Rabbits and to their chiefs." Geist tapped his temple. "I have it all figured out."

"I still don't like it, Ranton."

"The name is Geist now. And if you ever talk to me like this again, I'll have Petrie blow out your wick."

"With pleasure," Petrie said.

Louisa King came out of their cabin and saw her husband by the lake with a storm cloud on his brow. She went past the chicken coop and their cow. "What are you doing out here, as if I can't guess?"

"I should go back," Zach said.

Lou fluffed her sandy hair and put her hand on his arm. "You brood better than anyone I know."

"Thanks."

"Don't get prickly on me. You've been there once with Touch The Clouds and Drags The Rope and you all agreed those traders are treating the Indians properly. But you're still not happy."

"I can't shake the feeling that something isn't right."

"What's not right," Lou said, "is you getting worked up when there's nothing to get worked up about. And you have something more important to focus on." She took one of his hands and placed it on the swell of her belly.

Zach smiled and squatted and put his ear to her. "Can you feel it move?"

"It?" Louisa said. "You're calling our son or daughter an *it*?"

"We haven't picked names yet."

"It's still not an *it*."

Lou then realized what she had said, and laughed. Zach chuckled and caressed her stomach.

"Our first child. I can't wait."

"Well, it'll be months yet, so don't hold your breath." Lou embraced him as he straightened and hugged him with all her strength. "I'm so happy and I'm so scared."

"Scared?"

"What if something goes wrong? We're in the middle of the mountains. There's no sawbones for a thousand miles."

"Now who's brooding?" Zach teased. "You have my mother and Blue Water Woman to help. Everything will be fine." He kissed her.

"A woman can't help worrying. To have a new life come out of me . . ." Lou looked down at herself. "It's a miracle."

"Pa says they were some of the greatest moments of his life, when my sister and I popped out."

"You did not just say popped."

"Slid, then? Or is it squeezed out? Or maybe pushed? Whatever it is you women do."

"You'll see for yourself."

"What?"

Louisa raised his hand and pecked his palm. "I want you there with me."

"You want me in the room with you when the baby is born?"

"You're the father, aren't you? What a ridiculous

question." Lou grinned. "You'll be there holding me and comforting me."

"But you'll be . . ." Zach stopped.

"I'll be what?"

"You know. On your back with your legs, well . . ."

Lou giggled. "You've seen me that way plenty of times. It's how I got this way to begin with."

"That's not what I meant. The baby will be coming out, and all that other stuff."

"Stuff?"

"I've seen horses give birth and other animals. All that wet and the smell."

Lou put her hands on her hips. "Zachary King, how dare you? You are my husband and you will be there for me, smell or no smell."

"Now who's being prickly?"

"What I am is eating for two and we are out of fresh meat. So why don't you take your rifle and go off hunting and think about how it makes me feel when you talk about me as if I'm a horse."

"I never said that."

Lou wheeled around and stalked toward the cabin, muttering, "Men are the most aggravating creatures on God's green earth."

Louder, Zach repeated, "I never said that!" But she paid him no mind. "Women!" He kicked a rock and it clattered a few feet.

The dun was in the corral attached to their cabin. Zach threw on a saddle blanket and saddle, fitted the bridle, and mounted up. He rode north into the dense woods. At this time of day, the deer were lying up in the brush. He knew just where to find some.

As Zach rode, he pondered. He supposed he was being unduly suspicious about the trading post or mercantile or whatever Toad wanted to call it. But he couldn't shake a feeling deep in his gut that those men were more than they seemed. Call it a hunch. Call it instinct. Something was bothering him.

The sharp call of a grosbeak brought Zach out of his brooding thoughts. A little farther on, a gray squirrel chittered at him from a high branch.

Zach stayed alert for deer. There was plenty of sign. A jumble of prints showed where the deer went regularly to the lake to drink. He also came across old beds, some with the strong reek of urine.

A magpie flew overhead, distinctive with its white underparts and uncommonly long tail. Where there was one, there were usually more, although they made solitary domes high in the trees when they nested.

Zach breathed deep, savoring the rarefied air, and grinned. He did so love the mountains, or any wilds, for that matter. He had been born and bred in the wilderness, as the whites would say, and he was supremely glad. He had been to towns and cities and couldn't stand them. Not that he had anything against people. He didn't like how city life hemmed a man in, how stone and brick replaced the trees and grass, how a man could hardly go anywhere without being under the watchful scrutiny of others. There was barely any privacy, and what little there was came only when a person locked himself in a room.

That wasn't for Zach. Give him the wide-open spaces where a man could ride for hours or days or even weeks, if he was of a mind, and not see another living soul.

Ahead the forest thinned. Zach rode out of the shadows into the bright sunlight of a meadow—and drew rein.

Not fifty feet away was a wolf.

# Chapter Eleven

In his room at the back of the mercantile, Toad paced. He kept glancing at a sheet of paper on the table. Finally he sat and hastily penned a note. He folded the paper in half, then folded it again and slipped it into his pocket. "It is the best I can do," he said out loud.

Toad stood and went to the window. It faced the foothills to the west. To his left was the building that looked like a stable but wasn't. Gratt was just going in. "May you all rot in hell," Toad said.

Toad stepped to the door. He smoothed his shirt and patted the pocket. His palms were sweaty and he wiped them on his pants. He jerked the door open and was startled to see Petrie leaning against the wall. "You!"

Petrie unfolded. "Had a nice nap, did you?" he asked sarcastically.

"Yes," Toad lied. He made it a habit to rest for half an hour after his midday meal. It helped with his digestion. "What are you doing here? Keeping an eye on me?"

"Neil wants to see you."

"Shouldn't you call him Geist?" Toad said.

"I can call him any damn thing I want, you sack of pus."

Toad had been wondering about something and now he came right out and asked. "Why do you hate me so much? I've never done anything to you. I resent that Geist deceived me, but I've gone along with what you've demanded of me, haven't I?"

"You don't have a choice. You go along or you die."

"There's that," Toad admitted. "So why do you hate me?"

"Three reasons," Petrie said. "First, you're about the ugliest son of a bitch I've ever set eyes on. Looking at you, I want to puke."

Toad winced. "I was born this way. You can't blame a man for that."

"Care to bet?" Petrie rejoined, and then said, "Second, your last name is *Levi*."

"So you're one of those."

"Third," Petrie said, ignoring the interruption, "and this is the most important, I hate most everybody. People are worthless and stupid and good for nothing and better off dead. Except Neil."

"You go around killing people just for that?"

"I do it all the time. Back in the States, I'm wanted for more murders than you have fingers. Neil too."

"Good God."

"There ain't one, you simpleton. There's just us."

"Wait. Geist is like you? He kills people just because he despises them?"

"No. He always has a reason." Petrie's mouth curled in a vicious smirk. "Sometimes it's because they're no longer of any use to us." He gestured. "Now move your fat ass. He's waiting."

Several Crows were examining the knife display. A Nez Perce was fingering blankets.

Geist was behind the counter, a glass of whiskey at his elbow. "About damn time."

"You said I could rest," Toad reminded him.

"I aim to please," Geist said, his tone suggesting the opposite.

"What is it you wanted to see me about?"

"I've decided to change our business arrangement."

"Is that what you call it when you hold a gun to a man's head and demand he take you in as a partner, or else?"

Geist emptied his glass and turned to the shelf for a bottle. "I haven't pulled the trigger yet, have I?"

Petrie chuckled.

Geist refilled his glass and leaned on the counter. He cast an eye at the Crows, who were several shelves away, then fixed his gazed on Toad. "I didn't like your little flare-up in the whorehouse. It hit me that you still don't understand. So I'll make it as plain as plain can be." He paused to take another sip. "When I saw your advertisement in the St. Louis newspaper, I knew you were just the cover I needed. The law was hot on my trail and I had to get out of the States. So me and my men signed on to help you get your goods across the prairie and start up this mercantile. Halfway here I took over and now you work for me. I can get rid of you any time I want."

"Why don't you, then?" Toad asked sullenly. "Why do you toy with me like a cat with a mouse?"

"You don't know anything, do you?"

"I know I hate being forced to do your bidding. I hate living in constant fear."

Petrie said to Geist, "At least he has the brains to be scared."

"So long as you serve a purpose, you get to go on living," Geist said.

"What purpose is that, might I ask?"

"Weren't you listening? You're my cover, Levi. I

wouldn't put it past the law to send someone this far. So I pretend to work for you, while the whole time I really run things. But if you become too much of a nuisance, you'll disappear."

"By disappear, you mean die."

"Everything has to be spelled out for you, doesn't it? Petrie here will take you off into the hills and dispose of you. Anyone asks, we'll say you got attacked by a bear or bit by a rattler."

"One less *Levi* in the world," Petrie said.

"Now are we clear?" Geist said. "No more talking back. Do exactly as I say when I say it." He reached across the counter and gripped the front of Toad's shirt. "Let me hear the words."

Toad flushed, and swallowed. "From here on out you won't hear a peep of protest out of me."

"Good." Geist let go and smoothed the man's shirt. "Now go make yourself useful and sell something to those Crows."

"Whatever you say."

"I like the sound of that," Geist said, and chuckled.

Toad went down the third aisle to the Crows.

They turned and smiled and one said something in their tongue.

"I'm sorry, I don't speak your language," Toad said. "Do any of you speak English?" When all they did was stare blankly, he lowered his voice and said, "Chases Rabbits? Do you understand that at least? I have something for you to give him." He started to reach into his pocket but stopped when it was obvious they didn't comprehend. He let out a sigh. His luck of late was all bad.

There had to be a way to turn the tables on Geist,

Toad told himself. There had to be someone who could do what he wasn't capable of.

Zach King snapped his Hawken to his shoulder. Wolves this close to the cabin were a danger to the livestock. He had seen wolf tracks around his cabin off and on for some months now, but could never catch the wolf. At first he'd been concerned that it was after the chickens, but it never tried to get into the coop or attack the rooster and hens when they were roaming about during the day.

Zach took aim, then noticed that the wolf was just standing there, staring. It showed no fear or alarm. He noticed, too, that it was uncommonly old; it was mostly hide and bones, its muzzle almost entirely light gray while the rest was darker. It had a white mark that reminded him of the wolf cub he'd raised when he was young. Curious, he said out loud, "Blaze?"

The wolf pricked its ears and whined. It took a few steps in his direction, limping.

Zach lowered the Hawken a little. "It can't be," he said. Years ago his wolf had gone off to answer the call of the wild. He'd always reckoned that it was long since dead. "Blaze?"

The wolf whined again and came haltingly forward, its limp more pronounced.

The dun snorted and pranced. Zach spoke to it and patted its neck, then climbed down, keeping a firm grip on the reins. He held the Hawken ready to shoot as the wolf came to within a few yards and stared at him as he was staring at it. "Blaze? Is that you, boy?" He couldn't be sure. "After all these years?"

Zach held out a hand as he used to do, his fingers extended.

The wolf slowly came up and sniffed. It whined and licked his fingertips.

Zach carefully touched the white mark. He was coiled to defend himself should the wolf attack, but all it did was lick him some more. "Well, what do you know?" He decided to put it to another test. Sinking onto his knee, he said, "Do you remember what you used to do?"

The wolf's jaw was so close that with a lightning snap it could rend Zach's throat. Instead, it dipped its muzzle and pressed its forehead to his chest as Blaze used to do when he wanted to be petted. Zach rubbed its head and its neck and ran a hand over its side; he could feel every rib.

"Blaze, is it really you?"

The wolf raised its head and licked him.

Zach scratched and petted its chin. "Has to be you. No wild wolf would let me do this." It licked him again and he beamed. "I can't wait for my wife to see you."

# Chapter Twelve

The four young women wore their best dresses, their lustrous hair freshly washed and braided.

As they wound down the last stretch of trail to the mercantile, Chases Rabbits glanced back, his gaze lingering on Raven On The Ground. To his mind, she was the most beautiful, but he had to admit they were all lovely. He hoped the whites would be pleased.

Chases Rabbits was resplendent himself. He wore his new white buckskins and the new moccasins his mother had made. His rifle gleamed in the sun. He imagined that he was as handsome as a man could be.

The trail widened and Raven On The Ground brought her mare up next to him. Her eyes were lively and excited, her full lips spread in a smile. "I am proud of you."

Chases Rabbits's cheeks burned. "What have I done?" he asked.

"You know very well. You are doing more to help our people than any warrior since Long Hair. You are to the Apsaalooke as Grizzly Killer is to the Shoshones."

Chases Rabbits thought it should be as Grizzly Killer's wife, Winona, was to her people, but he let it pass and gloried in the compliment. "I do what I can."

"You will be one of the great ones. Everyone says so."

It had long been Chases Rabbits's secret dream to be just that, but he didn't reply.

"The woman who takes you for her husband will be envied above all others."

Among the Crows, it was the custom for a man who married to move into the lodge of his wife's mother. Chases Rabbits was not overly fond of Raven On The Ground's mother; she complained too much, about everything. But he would not have to talk to her. Another Crow custom was that once a man married into a family, he never spoke to his mother-in-law again, and she was never to speak to him.

"I would not say no were you to ask me," Raven On The Ground said.

Chases Rabbits felt a flutter in his chest. There it was, out in the open. "You could not be a wife and be away working for the whites."

"No," Raven On The Ground conceded. "My place would be in my lodge with my husband. But I will not work for the whites long. Only enough time for a new blanket and a few other things I want."

"We will talk of marriage more then," Chases Rabbits said, hardly able to believe his wonderful fortune.

"I see a happy life for us. You will be high in the council and we will have many horses and dogs."

Chases Rabbits almost bit his tongue to keep from responding. The Crows had more dogs than any other tribe. It wasn't unusual for a warrior to have several. He didn't own a single one. He would never say so, but he didn't like them. He didn't like how they smelled, didn't like how they panted and barked and sniffed and scratched themselves. And he really didn't like it when a dog licked him. Dog slobber made his stomach churn. Suddenly he was aware that the love of his life was still talking to him.

". . . saw great promise in you that the others did not. You are a friend of Grizzly Killer, and he is thought highly of by all the tribes."

"Not all." Chases Rabbits could think of a few who would like nothing better than to count coup on Nate.

Ahead, the mercantile and the outbuildings rose out of the basin like squat fingers thrust at the sky.

Chases Rabbits sat straighter. He was conscious of the gazes of Crows already there, and of men and women from other tribes who had likewise come to trade. All were from friendly tribes, so there was no danger. He rode to the hitch rail, but it was full, so he reined to the side and slid down. No sooner had his feet touched the ground than Geist was there, pumping his hand. Behind him were Petrie and the man with the gray hair and floppy hat.

"Chases Rabbits! You came just like you said you would. And you've brought four beauties with you."

Chases Rabbits introduced the women. He didn't mention that Raven On The Ground was his sweetheart. These were whites, after all, and while he liked them, his personal life was none of their affair.

"Ladies, I am right pleased to meet you," Geist said. "Tell them for me, will you?"

Chases Rabbits complied.

"Say that we will make their stay here well worth their while. Tomorrow I will explain exactly what it is they're to do, and until then they're free to roam around and look at all the merchandise."

"You need me stay to speak your words?" Chases Rabbits asked.

"That's not necessary," Geist said. He indicated

the gray-haired man with the floppy hat. "Dryfus here knows sign language."

This was news to Chases Rabbits. He had the impression they did not know much about Indian ways. "Where him learn?"

"He was a trapper once," Geist explained. "I take it your squaws can use sign?"

"Raven On The Ground good at finger talk," Chases Rabbits proudly revealed. They often signed affection to each other.

"Good. Then we'll communicate through her. You can go back to your village and leave the rest to us."

Chases Rabbits was surprised that they wanted him to go so soon. "I stay. Make sure all go well."

"There's no need," Geist said, and clapped him on the back. "I've imposed on your goodwill enough as it is." He crooked a finger at Petrie. "My pard here will take you inside and let you pick whatever you would like for bringing the women. Within reason, of course."

"Of course," Chases Rabbits echoed as he had heard whites do, although he was not quite sure what he was agreeing too. Reluctantly, he followed Petrie into the mercantile while Geist and Dryfus escorted the women toward the new structure.

"What is it you'd like?" Petrie asked. "A knife? Ammunition? What?"

"I have new knife," Chases Rabbits said, and patted it. "I not sure."

"Then look around. There's no rush. I'll be having a drink. Give a holler if you need me."

"I give." Chases Rabbits moved down an aisle, absently fingering clothes and blankets and tools. He was thinking of Raven On The Ground. He would rather be with her.

Someone nudged him, and Chases Rabbits turned. "Toad," he said, and the stout man put a finger to his lips.

"Not so loud or they'll hear you and wonder what I'm up to."

"Sorry?"

Toad glanced around as if he was afraid. In a whisper he said, "If I give you something, will you get it to Nate King?"

"Give me what?" Chases Rabbits asked.

Toad reached into a pocket and pulled out a folded sheet. "This."

"It called paper." Chases Rabbits had seen paper before, at the King cabin.

"It's a message for him and him alone. No one else is to read it. Can you do that?"

"I can do, yes."

Toad gripped Chases Rabbits's wrist so hard it hurt. "You don't realize how important this is. Important for your people and important for you."

"I can do," Chases Rabbits repeated, disturbed at how upset the man was.

"Take it," Toad said, and started to put the paper in Chases Rabbits' hand.

"What's going on here?"

Toad gave a start.

Chases Rabbits saw him quickly lower the paper behind his leg, adopt a broad smile, and turn. He did the same, bewildered as to what was going on.

"I asked you a question," Petrie said to Toad. "What are you two up to?"

"Nothing much," Toad responded.

Petrie came down the aisle and looked from one of them to the other. "Suppose you tell me, Crow."

"My name Chases Rabbits."

"I know what the hell it is. What I don't know is what he was whispering to you about."

Toad said, "He asked if I had any spyglasses to sell and I told him I didn't."

"Is that true?" Petrie asked.

Chases Rabbits tried to recall if he knew what a spyglass was. Then he remembered the fabulous brass tube Nate King owned that could bring far objects up close. "I want spyglass many winters." Which was true; he'd desired one ever since Nate let him look through his.

Petrie sniffed and wheeled, making for the entrance.

"That was close," Toad said. "If they catch me with this, my goose is cooked."

Chases Rabbits's mother had plucked and roasted geese a few times. Grouse, too. And quail. Even an owl once. "Better cooked than raw."

Toad didn't seem to hear him. He glanced down at the folded paper. "Perhaps I should rethink this. Breathing is better than not breathing."

"Breathing good," Chases Rabbits agreed.

"I have a better idea. Bring Nate King here. Will you do that for me? I'll give you a pistol for your very own if you do."

Chases Rabbits tingled with excitement. Few Crow warriors owned rifles; fewer still owned a rifle *and* a pistol. "Me happy bring him."

"If he wants to know what it's about," Toad said, "tell him there are foxes in the chicken coop."

"You have chickens?" Chases Rabbits would like a few. Their eggs were delicious.

Toad gripped the front of his shirt. "Swear to me by all you hold holy that you'll bring him. Bring him just as fast as you can."

"I do for you," Chases Rabbits promised, wondering why it was so urgent.

"Good." Toad shoved the paper into his pocket. "Because if you don't, you'll be sorry." He lumbered away.

His mind in a jumble, Chases Rabbits went out. He stared at the new lodge the women were in and wished he could talk to Raven On The Ground before he left. But Toad had been clear he must hurry. So he climbed on his horse and rode west, hoping Raven On The Ground would forgive him for leaving without saying good-bye and that she would be all right until he got back.

Louisa King loved her husband dearly. She loved him passionately. She loved him with all that she was—yet there were times when he did things that drove her to distraction. Little things, like always expecting her to clean up after they ate. His pa, Nate, helped Winona, but Zach wouldn't wash a pan or a plate unless she practically begged him. And there were the big things, like the time she had to endure the terror of Zach being put on trial for murder.

She never knew what to expect next. He was forever doing things that surprised her, such as taking her to Bent's Fort for a new shawl on the spur of the moment after she casually mentioned she would like one, or going off after a cow that time she'd mentioned how much she missed drinking milk.

But she never, ever expected him to do what he had done now.

"Let me get this straight. I'm in the family way, and you bring home a wolf?"

"I think it's my old pet Blaze," Zach said, rubbing the animal's neck.

"I'm going to have a *baby* and you bring home a *wolf*?"

"Why are you making such a fuss? I thought you liked animals."

"I do," Lou said. "I like cats some. I like dogs more. I think puppies are adorable."

"Look at him. He's adorable, too."

Lou looked. She had never seen such a scruffy, emaciated animal in her life. It was a wonder it was still breathing. Its bones about popped from its body, its face was sunken, and its legs were sticks. "I don't reckon it has long to live."

"What a terrible thing to say." Zach scratched under the wolf's chin, and it licked him.

"He's skin and bones," Lou said. "And he was limping when you rode in."

"Yet he kept up with me." Zach patted the wolf on its front shoulders. "I honest to God think it's Blaze."

Lou gazed at the dun and then at the ground around them and then back at the wolf. "And you were so excited at finding him that you forgot to bring home the fresh meat I asked for."

"What?"

"Unless it's invisible, I don't see a deer anywhere."

"Oh."

"Sometimes, Zachary King, you are a vexation."

"I know I'm in trouble when you get all formal." Zach turned and swung onto the dun. "Blaze and me will go hunt. We shouldn't be gone long."

"You don't know for sure it's him."

"What other wolf would be half as friendly?" Zach reined around. "Come on, Blaze. We'll leave her to her mood." He jabbed his heels and rode into the woods. The wolf stayed at his side, just as Blaze used to do. Zach grinned. He had loved that wolf.

They had been inseparable. If this truly was Blaze, it would be like old times.

Zach thought of another test, a trick he had taught Blaze when Blaze was small. "I'm after a deer," he said, and then repeated with emphasis, "Deer. Deer. Deer."

The wolf looked up at him with a quizzical expression.

"Don't you remember?" Zach asked. "Deer meat."

They had gone barely a dozen yards when the wolf abruptly stopped. Zach drew rein. The wolf raised its muzzle and sniffed, turning its head from side to side as it tested the wind. Then it turned to the northeast. Zach followed. Thick brush appeared, and the wolf peered into it with an intensity that made Zach smile.

"You do remember."

Zach dismounted. He wedged the Hawken to his shoulder and thumbed back the hammer. At the *click* the wolf glanced up sharply and took a step back. Zach moved toward the brush. Crouching, he scoured the shadows and nooks. He began to think the wolf was mistaken. Then he registered movement; a doe was rising from her bed, looking straight at them. He didn't have a clear shot. Sidling to his right, he saw her plainly.

A stroke of the trigger, and the heavy ball cored her skull, splattering brains and hair.

Zach laughed happily. "Lou will get her fresh meat now." He started to go in after it, then stopped. He mustn't violate the cardinal rule of survival in the wilds: always reload after he shot. His pa had ingrained that into him from the day he was old enough to hold a gun. Methodically, he opened his powder horn and poured the proper amount down the barrel. From his ammo pouch he took a bullet and wrapped it in a patch, then slid the ramrod from its housing and tamped the ball and patch down the barrel.

The wolf sat and watched.

"You remember me doing this all the time, don't you?" Zach had never been much of a talker; Lou was always saying how he never gabbed enough. But he'd always talked to Blaze. "Why did you shy like that when I was getting set to shoot?" As he recalled, Blaze had gotten used to guns. Even the blast wouldn't spook him.

Zach took a stride to go in after the doe and the wolf took a limping step to follow. It was favoring its left front leg. On a sudden hunch, Zach stopped and hunkered. "Let me have a gander at that, boy." The wolf didn't snarl or bare its teeth as he gently moved his hand up and down. Where the leg widened into the body he found thick scar tissue. He moved the hair, and frowned. The scar was perfectly round.

"Now I savvy. You were shot."

There was more scar tissue under the wolf's belly. An inch or so higher, and the wolf's guts would have come spilling out.

"You were lucky."

The wolf whined and licked him.

Zach gazed into its eyes and felt his throat tighten and his eyes begin to mist. "It is you, Blaze." He hugged the wolf close, and it didn't resist. "Why don't you stick around awhile this time?"

They were so near the cabin that Zach dragged the doe out, threw it over the dun, and walked back leading the horse by the reins with Blaze at his side. He kept glancing at him. He couldn't believe Blaze was really there.

"You've missed a lot, old fella. My pa and ma have a cabin across the lake, and my nuisance of a sister is a lot older and has a beau, if you can believe it."

The wolf padded along quietly. "Shakespeare McNair is still around. He's as old as you, only in people years, but he's held up better. I bet he'll remember you. The two of you always got along pretty well."

The wolf's shoulder brushed Zach's leg.

"Do you remember when I found you? In the snow and the cold? You were all alone in the world. We were friends for a good long while, until you ran off to find a mate." Zach stopped and looked down and the wolf stopped and looked up. "I never did understand why you had to go. Pa explained, but I was young." He smiled. "I understand now, though. I have a mate of my own."

Lou was waiting by the corner of the cabin, her arms folded across her bosom. "You didn't have to go far," she said as they emerged from the greenery. "I heard the shot."

Zach motioned at the doe. "All the fresh meat your little heart can desire."

"That animal is still with you, I see."

"He's my friend and you should make friends with him, too. He might be here awhile."

"Men," Lou said.

# Chapter Thirteen

Raven On The Ground and the other three Crow maidens followed the white man known as Geist into the wooden lodge. She smiled to be polite and to hide how nervous she was. She had never been in the company of white men before, save for the few times whites had visited her village and once when Chases Rabbits brought Grizzly Killer to meet her. She liked Grizzly Killer. He was an adopted Shoshone and much like an Indian. He wasn't strange, like other whites.

The man called Geist was smiling and being friendly, but he was strange, too. He talked too fast and he had an odd smell, and his smile didn't touch his eyes.

Raven On The Ground definitely didn't like the white called Dryfus. The very first time he looked at her, he ran his gaze down her body in a manner any woman would recognize. It was rude of him, and she did not like rude people. Unfortunately, Dryfus was the only white who knew sign, so she had to put up with him for the time being.

Geist had just finished showing them four small spaces enclosed in wooden walls. In each, blankets had been spread on upraised legs. Their purpose eluded her until Dryfus pointed at one of the areas and raised his hands.

*Where you sit*, he signed.

Raven On The Ground was appalled.

Dryfus pointed at each of the other enclosed spaces in turn, and at each of the other women, signing the same thing.

"Can this be?" Spotted Fawn said. "This is where they want us to live?"

"So it seems," Raven On The Ground said. To make sure, she signed, *Question. We sit long time?*

*Yes*, Dryfus signed.

Lavender frowned. "I do not like this. Why have they covered the ground with wood? Where do we build a fire? And there is no hole above us for the smoke to go out."

Flute Girl made it unanimous. "These whites do not know how to treat guests."

Geist barked words at Dryfus and the latter signed, *Question. Why you no happy?*

Raven On The Ground signed that they would rather live in the kind of lodge they were accustomed to.

Through Dryfus, Geist responded that they would like it here after a while, that sleeping on the blankets on the raised legs was better than sleeping on the ground, and that they didn't need a fire since the walls would keep them warm.

"The man is touched in the head," Lavender said. "How will we cook if we cannot make a fire?"

Raven On The Ground put the question to the whites and was amazed when Dryfus signed that the whites would do the cooking for them.

"But I thought they brought us here to cook for them?" Spotted Fawn said.

So did Raven On The Ground. She put the question to Dryfus. He and Geist talked, and Dryfus signed that they could build a fire outside the wooden lodge.

"Only whites would have such empty heads," Flute Girl said.

"What work do they expect of us?" Lavender wanted to know.

Raven On The Ground signed the query. The answer puzzled her. Dryfus signed that Geist would explain soon, and they both grinned as if it were some sort of joke. Until then, Dryfus signed, they were free to walk about as they pleased. He warned them not to stray too far from the lodge, for their own safety.

"Do they think we cannot take care of ourselves?" Flute Girl asked.

Geist and Dryfus left.

The four women looked at one another, at the wood walls, and at the wood over their heads.

"I am sorry I came," Lavender said.

"We should not judge them too quickly," Raven On The Ground advised. "The whites made this place for us thinking we would like it."

"They should know better," Spotted Fawn said. "It is like being in a cave made of wood."

"We know how strange they are, so we should not be surprised," Raven On The Ground said. "They have befriended our people and put their trust in us, so we should put our trust in them."

"I cannot sleep in here," Flute Girl declared. "When it grows dark I will go outside and sleep on the ground."

"Me, too," Lavender said.

Raven On The Ground was tempted to do the same. To take their mind off the shock of their dwelling, she proposed that they go to the trading post and see all the wonderful goods the whites had brought.

"That is one thing the whites know how to do," Flute Girl said. "They know how to make the money they love so much."

"Yes," Raven On The Ground agreed. "They do."

Chases Rabbits was having a bad moon. First it was the bear that tried to eat him. Now he had a worse problem. He was two days out from the mercantile and had at least three more of hard riding before he would reach King Valley. Suddenly he came to a crest dotted with firs and spotted a line of riders below. They were too far off for him to tell more than that they were warriors. He hoped they were Crows or maybe Shoshones, who were on good terms with his people. He hoped they weren't Blackfeet or Piegans or Bloods, who would count coup on any Crow they came across.

As it turned out, they were something else. He was in the cover of the firs, watching the nine riders ascend, when the style of their hair and their faces sent a tingle of worry down his spine. They were Utes. They were far from their own land, and they were painted for war.

The Crows and the Utes weren't at war with each other at the moment, but they weren't friends, either. Chases Rabbits was glad they hadn't spotted him. They would reach the crest a good arrow's flight from where he was and go on their way none the wiser.

Then his pinto whinnied.

Immediately, several of the foremost Utes looked up, and one of them pointed at the shadows that concealed Chases Rabbits, yipping in the Ute tongue.

Chases Rabbits wheeled his pinto and fled. Should they catch him, there was no doubt what they would do: the same as Crows would do to captured Utes. He would be mutilated to test his manhood and then slain.

Whoops rose in a chorus and hooves pounded hard. The war party was after him.

Chases Rabbits fought down panic. His pinto was fast, but their horses could be faster. His capture seemed inevitable.

He flew down the other side, reining right and left to avoid trees and boulders and vaulting logs. He tried to calm himself so he could think clearly, but his heart hammered in his chest and his blood pulsed madly in his veins.

Chases Rabbits glanced over his shoulder. The Utes hadn't appeared yet. He swept around a spruce and into a stand of alder. To his left down a short slope grew a dense thicket of chokecherries. The instant he spotted it, he reined down and in, his pinto crashing through the tangle with ease. When he had gone as far as he could throw a rock, he came upon a clear spot, drew rein, and jumped down. He could hear the Utes, but he couldn't see them yet.

Quickly, Chases Rabbits grabbed the rope bridle and pulled while putting his foot against the pinto's front leg and pushing. Quite a few moons ago, he had witnessed Nate King use the trick with his horse, and he had been trying to teach the pinto. Sometimes it cooperated. Sometimes it didn't.

Right now it didn't.

"Down!" Chases Rabbits urged, and pulled and pushed harder. The pinto balked.

Above them, the forest crashed with the sound of the onrush of warriors out for his blood.

"Down!" Chases Rabbits pleaded, and practically hung from the bridle by both hands. The pinto tucked at the knees. He pulled with all his might, and to his elation, the pinto lowered onto its side. He flung himself on top of it, his shoulders and head on its neck, and wrapped his fingers around its muzzle to keep it from whinnying.

Yipping and screeching, the Utes swept out of the trees and hurtled down the mountain. They passed so close that Chases Rabbits could have brought one down with his bow. Any moment he expected to be spotted. Then they were past and the forest swallowed them, and he released the breath he hadn't realized he was holding.

Not until the hoofbeats faded to welcome silence did Chases Rabbits rise and pull the pinto erect. Swiftly mounting, he resumed his ride, only with more care. It wasn't unheard of for war parties to split up when in enemy territory to be less conspicuous.

Where there were nine Utes, there might be more.

# Chapter Fourteen

Raven On The Ground was confused and more than a little worried.

Chases Rabbits had told her that the whites wanted women to cook and sew and mend for them. In return, they would be allowed to have things from the trading post. She and her companions had been at the post living in the awful wood lodge for several days now and they'd hardly had to do anything. She kept asking Dryfus what they were to do. He would go to Geist, then come back and say that they should be patient and enjoy themselves, and all would be made clear soon. But there was nothing to do but talk and walk. They were tired of talking and had walked all over Mud Hollow without seeing anything worth their interest.

That evening the women held a council.

"I am for going back to our village," Flute Girl announced.

"I as well," Lavender said. "We waste our time here. The whites sent for us but they don't need us."

"They are puzzling people," Spotted Fawn remarked.

"They are as different from the Apsaalooke as dirt is from water," Flute Girl said.

"In the morning I will ask Dryfus one more time what it is the whites wish us to do," Raven On The Ground said. "If they do not have work for us, we will leave."

"Maybe you should not go to him," Lavender said.

"He is the only one who knows sign."

"But he will just go to the one they call Geist, and Geist will say what he always says. Relax and enjoy ourselves."

"What else, then?" Raven On The Ground asked.

"Go to the one they call Toad," Lavender suggested. "He is their leader, is he not?"

"Chases Rabbits did say that Toad is their chief, yes," Raven On The Ground confirmed.

"Yet not once has he to come to talk to us," Spotted Fawn said. "He is not a polite host."

"He is white," Flute Girl said.

"Maybe he will give us work if we ask him face-to-face," Lavender said.

It was worth a try, they all decided. Raven On The Ground would speak for them, as she had been doing.

So the next morning, shortly after the trading post opened and while there were yet few people, Raven On The Ground made sure her dress was clean and her hair was perfectly done in two braids. Then she went into the post to present herself to the white chief. Two of the others—Gratt and Berber, she believed their names to be—noticed her but went on about their business.

Raven On The Ground looked for Geist and Dryfus but didn't see them, which was good, as she had grown concerned about them. It was their eyes. Something she saw in them, something she could not quite define, bothered her. She did not see it all the time. Usually when they thought she wasn't looking at them, she'd catch an unguarded expression, the kind of expression that hinted at a hunger which had nothing to do with food.

Toad was behind the counter, as he nearly always was. She rarely saw him come out from behind it. The first day she had gone up to it to thank him for inviting them, and he had moved to the other end without saying a word to her. She had thought it terribly rude. But then she had reminded herself that he was a chief and she had not approached him through one of the whites under him, as she should.

This time she would do it directly. She marched up to the counter and calmly stood with her hands folded, waiting.

Toad had a fabulous stick in his hand that left black squiggly lines on flat white squares of paper bound together somehow. He glanced up and blinked as if he were surprised. "Good morning."

Raven On The Ground had heard those words before, from Grizzly Killer. She did not know what they meant, but she repeated them and went on smiling.

Toad put down the fabulous stick. "I didn't know any of you spoke English."

His sounds were alien to Raven On The Ground except for the last sound, "English." She knew that it referred to the white tongue. She repeated it. "English."

"My God." Toad looked apprehensively around. He motioned, beckoning for her to follow, and moved around the end of the counter and into a narrow space with doors on both sides. He looked around again, opened one of the doors, and gestured for her to go in ahead of him.

Raven On The Ground hesitated. She did not know what kind of man he was; she did not know if being alone with him was safe. But then, he was the white chief, and he had invited them, so she smiled and went through into a small room lined with shelves and stacked with trade goods.

Toad entered and quickly lit a lantern on a peg, then quietly closed the door. "We don't have much time, so I will make this short."

Again his tongue was alien. Raven On The Ground said in hers, "I do not understand."

Toad suddenly seized her forearm. She tried to pull back, but he held her fast and stared into her eyes with an intensity that was frightening. "Please listen and heed me. You are not safe here, do you understand? You must take your friends and go. Slip away tonight after Geist and his gang have gone to sleep."

The only sound that Raven On The Ground grasped was "Geist." She said the name to show as much.

"He is evil. I didn't realize it when I hired him. Not until he turned on me and took over and told me who he really is. He's wanted for murder and some other things, and it's those other things that you have to worry about."

Raven On The Ground didn't understand a single thing the white chief said. She responded as she had been doing. "Geist."

"Yes, Geist. His real name is Ranton. But that's unimportant. What matters are his plans for you and the other women. You must . . ." Toad stopped.

Raven On The Ground heard them, too: voices outside the door.

Toad's face was a mask of fright. Suddenly he took a step forward and enfolded her in his arms, pressing his thick lips to her cheek.

Raven On The Ground was so startled that she

hadn't yet collected her wits to resist when the door opened, revealing Geist, Petrie, and Dryfus.

"What the hell do we have here?"

Chases Rabbits needed a new charm. He had one, but it had apparently lost its power. First there had been the bear, then the Ute war party, and now a new calamity.

Nearly all Crows, men and women, had charms. Objects of power or influence or protection, often purchased at great price. Once a famous warrior, when he was young, gave five horses for a piece of wood said to come from far away. The wood was as hard as the white man's metal, and was purported to imbue in its owner invincibility in battle. The young man went on to count many coup and distinguish himself on the field of conflict. Another time, a man obtained a special seed that was said would keep its owner free of sickness and pain, and his whole life he was never ill or wounded. Other men had charms for other purposes. Women were fond of charms that would cause men to fall in love with them.

Chases Rabbits had an uncle to thank for his. Around his neck in a small pouch was a lump of yellow rock that gleamed brightly in the sun and was supposed to impart good luck. He had paid two horses for it several winters ago, and so far it had served him well. But now his luck had changed, and it had to be that his special charm had lost its power. Charms did that sometimes.

At the moment, he sat astride his pinto with the pouch in one hand and his rifle in the other, staring in dismay at the creature perched on a high boulder directly in his path. He had drawn rein in alarm when he saw it. "Go away!" he shouted. "Go away or I will shoot you!" It was doubly frustrating because he was close to King Valley. Another sleep, he figured, and he would be there.

The wolf stared back.

Chases Rabbits did not want to shoot if he could help it. He was not a good shot. He needed a lot more practice. And if he wounded the wolf, it was bound to attack. "Didn't you hear me? I said to go away!"

"Bellow a little louder, why don't you? They'll hear you in Apache country."

Around the boulder rode Zach King. He grinned and stopped below the wolf and nodded up at it. "Meet an old friend of mine."

Dumfounded, Chases Rabbits saw the wolf descend and stand at the dun's side. He switched to English. "You be brother to a wolf? How you do that?"

"I had him when he was a pup," Zach said. "Raised him for years until he went off one day." He nodded at it. "Blaze, this is Chases Rabbits, a friend of my sister."

Chases Rabbits's feelings were hurt. "Me not your friend, too?"

"Friends enough." Zach brought his dun over to the pinto. "To what do we owe the honor of your visit? Have you come to see my knot-head sis?"

"What be knot-head?"

"Someone whose brain is all in a knot as hers always is."

Chases Rabbits was confused. Zach seemed to be saying that Evelyn's brain didn't work right. "Me not savvy. Her brain be fine when me visit before."

"You didn't have to live with her. You didn't have to put up with all her teasing. Or her knack for getting herself into trouble. She was kidnapped once, for crying out loud."

"She sleep a lot as kid?"

"What?" Zach snorted and then laughed. "Oh, I get it. No, she was taken once. But let's forget about her and talk about you. This is the trail into our valley, so I reckon you're on your way to pay us a visit, and if not to her, then who?"

"Me need speak your father," Chases Rabbits said, annoyed that he got the white tongue wrong but doing his best.

"I don't know if he's back yet."

"Sorry?"

"Pa and Shakespeare McNair went off hunting this morning. I don't know if they'll be back tonight or tomorrow."

"Oh." Chases Rabbits was crestfallen. He had ridden so far, endured so much.

"What's wrong?" Zack asked.

"Ugly man at trading post want me bring him quick."

"Toad?"

"That the one, yes." Chases Rabbits related what Toad had said to him. He also told about his encounter with the bear.

"Sounds like you had a close shave."

Chases Rabbits vaguely remembered what that meant, and rubbed his smooth chin. "Me not need shave. Crows not have hair on face like whites." Except for one warrior named Hairy Face.

Zach chuckled, then sobered. "Why do you suppose Toad needs to see my pa so bad?"

"Him have problem with foxes."

"What?"

"That what him say. Him have foxes in chicken

coop. Which strange because he not have chicken coop like you and your father do."

"It could be he wasn't talking about real foxes and chickens."

"Then why him say that?"

"Maybe it was his way of saying there's trouble brewing." Zach grew thoughtful. "You say that you took women there to work for them?"

"Me do, yes. Why?"

"Because chickens is another word for hens and hens is another word for women."

The white tongue was so bewildering, Chases Rabbits despaired of ever learning it well. But he didn't miss the most important part. "Trouble for women? What kind of trouble?"

"How about I go back with you in Pa's stead and we find out?"

"Toad want Grizzly Killer, but maybe him make do with you." Chases Rabbits pursed his lips. "You not be like last time and kill everybody?"

"That depends," Zach King said.

# Chapter Fifteen

"I will not put up with much more," Flute Girl declared.

"Why have they done this?" Spotted Fawn wondered.

Raven On The Ground didn't have an answer. She went over what had happened in the hope it would make sense. Toad had taken her into the small room. He was trying to tell her something when the door opened and in came Geist. Geist had been mad, and walked up to Toad and hit him. Incredibly, Toad hadn't done anything. An Apsaalooke warrior would have pulled a knife and killed Geist; no man of their tribe ever let himself be struck with impunity.

Geist and Toad had argued. The whole time, Petrie pointed a rifle at Toad. The insult to Toad was monumental. He was their leader, their chief, yet they treated him as if he were an enemy.

Geist had Dryfus ask her in sign what she and Toad had been doing. She answered honestly that she thought Toad had brought her in to talk until he hugged and kissed her. Dryfus asked what they talked about. She answered that she hardly understood a word Toad said.

For some reason, Geist became amused. He pointed at her and clapped Toad on the shoulder, and called him a "horny bastard." Whatever that was.

Toad acted sheepish, like a child caught taking food when he shouldn't.

Petrie had lowered his rifle and looked at her, smirking.

Then Geist had Dryfus bring her to the lodge she shared with the other women. She did not want to be inside and had tried to go back out, but Dryfus closed the door and was still out there, refusing to let any of them leave.

"I will stab him and we will take our horses and go," Lavender proposed. She alone among them wore a knife on her hip.

"That is too drastic," Raven On The Ground said. She clung to the belief that there must be some sense to it all.

Just then the door opened and in strode Geist, followed by Petrie and Dryfus. Geist smiled and had Dryfus sign that if there was anything they needed, they had only to ask.

Raven On The Ground decided to get right to the heart of the matter. *Question*, she signed. *You chief?*

Geist and Dryfus talked, and Dryfus signed that Geist was.

Raven On The Ground asked why no one had told them.

Dryfus answered that the whites thought the women knew. He also signed that Geist was sorry about how Toad had acted toward her.

Flute Girl raised her hands and her fingers flowed. She told the whites that the women were tired of doing nothing. That if the whites wanted them to work, they should have them start. Otherwise, the women were leaving.

Geist bid them all sit in a half circle on the floor. Then he sank down with Dryfus on his left and gave a long speech, which Dryfus translated in sign.

Geist was happy the four of them had come. He

was especially pleased at how lovely they were. Crow women, in his estimation, were some of the most beautiful he had ever seen. He went on for so long about their faces and their hair and how they wore their dresses that Spotted Fawn turned to Raven On The Ground and grinned and whispered, "Maybe he is in love with one of us."

Through Dryfus, Geist explained that he was a businessman, like Toad, but not in the same business. The trading post was not his main interest. His real business, Dryfus signed, was women.

"Women?" Lavender repeated out loud. "What can he mean by that?"

Geist launched into a long speech about how he had heard a lot about the Crows before he came west to the mountains. How he had been informed they were a handsome people, and how he had first listened with great interest to an old trapper who related a custom of theirs. Was it true, he had Dryfus ask, that visitors who spent the night at a Crow village were allowed to have a woman?

Raven On The Ground answered with her fingers, *Yes.*

Did the visitors have to pay for the women?

Raven On The Ground signed that they did not.

Geist told them that the whites did not have such a custom. That so far as he knew, neither did any other tribe. Only the Crows. He thought it wonderful, and had Dryfus sign as how he had been doing the same thing for a long time.

By the looks on their faces, Raven On The Ground could see that her friends were as puzzled as she was. *Question. You have many wives?*

*Not any,* Geist replied. The women he gave to other men were not his, but women who wanted to give themselves on their own, as the Crows did. And here came the best part, he excitedly had Dryfus relay—the women were paid for being with a man. Some of the money was then theirs to keep and spend as they chose.

Flute Girl signed the thought that was uppermost in Raven On The Ground's mind—what did any of this have to do with them?

Geist smiled broadly and had Dryfus sign that he had invited them to the trading post not to sew and cook, as he had told Chases Rabbits, but to sleep with men and be paid for it.

Raven On The Ground began to suspect the white man wasn't in his right mind. *We would never do that*, she indignantly signed on behalf of all four of them.

*Why not?* Geist had Dryfus sign. They had already admitted that Crow women slept with other men, so why not be rewarded for it with trade goods or money?

To begin with, Raven On The Ground explained, the white men needed to understand a few things. Once, her people had been as numerous as the blades of grass on the prairie, many thousands of them, a strong and prosperous tribe able to hold their own against any enemy. But war and disease took a heavy toll so that now there were only about two thousand Apsaalooke, only eight hundred of which were men. Because of the disparity, most warriors had two or three wives. When a stranger visited their village, it was considered nothing at all for a wife to spend the night with him. But unmarried maidens were never offered, and Raven On The Ground, Spotted Fawn, Lavender, and Flute Girl were maidens.

Geist scowled. *So you wouldn't sleep with men for money?*

*To think we would is an insult*, Raven On The Ground responded.

"We were lured here falsely," Flute Girl said in anger. "This white man tricked Chases Rabbits."

"We should leave this moment," Spotted Fawn said.

Raven On The Ground agreed. She informed the whites that they were departing.

*No*, Dryfus signed at Geist's command. *You are not.*

*We are free to do as we please*, Raven On The Ground told them. She was angry now, too.

Geist stood. *No, you are not*, he had Dryfus sign. He nodded at Petrie, who pointed his rifle at them.

"This can't be happening," Spotted Fawn said.

*I need women, and you're it whether you want to be or not*, Geist made it clear through Dryfus.

*Our people will learn what you have done*, Raven On The Ground warned. *Our warriors will wipe you out.*

*They won't ever know*, was Geist's reply.

*You cannot make us do what we do not want to do*, Raven On The Ground insisted.

*Watch me*, Geist rebutted. He went to the door. *We will talk more of this later*, Dryfus signed.

The three whites went out. The instant the door closed, Flute Girl grabbed hold of the latch and lifted and pushed, but the door wouldn't open. It was locked or barred.

"We're trapped," Lavender said.

"What do we do now?" Spotted Fawn asked anxiously.

Raven On The Ground had no idea.


Toad was measuring a bolt of cloth when Geist stormed into the mercantile, Petrie in his wake. Geist was so mad that he slammed the door. The half dozen Indian customers turned and regarded him quizzically.

Geist didn't seem to care. He and Petrie came to the counter and Geist glared at Toad. "You lied to me, you son of a bitch."

"About?"

"Don't play innocent," Geist snapped. "When I caught you and that squaw in the storage room, you claimed it was her idea as much as yours."

"It was," Toad said.

"Like hell. She just told me that she and her friends are as pure as the driven snow, which means you're a goddamned liar." Geist reached across and grabbed Toad's shirt and balled his other fist.

"I wouldn't, if I were you," Toad said.

"Give me one good reason."

Toad swept an arm at the Indians. "You want to stay on their good side, don't you? They see you beating on me, they'll wonder why. Word will get around."

"So?" Petrie said.

Geist relaxed his fist and let go. "No, Levi's right. If the redskins think we don't get along, they won't trust us as fully as we need them to."

"Let me take him into the storeroom and give him a bloody mouth," Petrie said. "That'll teach him not to lie to us again."

"Time enough for that later." To Toad, Geist growled, "I warned you there would be consequences if you didn't behave. You should have listened."

Toad wisely kept silent. It wouldn't take much to trigger Geist's temper.

"But first, I've got the squaws to deal with. I was hoping it would be easy, but they've made it hard. Now I'll have to force them."

"To be whores?" Toad was horrified.

"You make it sound like I'm out to slit their throats."

"Ours will be slit if their people find out. The Crows won't stand for having their women abused."

"Abused?" Geist snorted. "All I want is for them to spread their legs and get paid for it."

"It's wrong," Toad said flatly.

"It's what I do, and neither you nor a bunch of stinking redskins will stop me."

"You can't fight an entire tribe."

"No," Petrie said, to Toad's surprise. "We can't."

Geist turned to him. "You too? Damn it, there has to be a way. I'll figure it out."

"We can't keep those girls locked in forever," Petrie said.

"Why not?"

Toad spread his hands on the counter. "I don't believe what I'm hearing."

"Shut the hell up." Geist pressed a hand to his forehead. "I need time to think. I didn't count on the Crows being so damn finicky about being paid to have sex. The jackasses would rather give it away free." He moved toward the back hall and Petrie went with him. "Levi, not one word to anyone about this, or I'll have you snuffed like a candle."

Toad shook his head, and sighed. He walked to the front window and saw Dryfus standing guard at the women's quarters. He swore and returned to the counter. "Geist isn't the only one who has to think," he said to himself, bowing his head. Almost under his breath he summed up the state of affairs with "This is bad. This is very bad."

# Chapter Sixteen

Zach and Chases Rabbits were making good time. They pushed the dun and the pinto hard, but not so hard as to wear the horses out. At the dun's side loped the wolf. Whenever they stopped to rest their mounts, the wolf was at Zach's side.

Chases Rabbits was wary. Whenever the wolf came near him, he'd tense. That evening, after they made camp and had a small fire going, the wolf lay at Zach's side, staring inscrutably across the flames at Chases Rabbits.

"Me think maybe your wolf not like me."

"His name is Blaze. He won't harm you."

"How you know?"

"He listens well." Zach ran a hand along Blaze's throat. "He's not much different than a dog."

"Bear is bear and bird is bird," Chases Rabbits said. "Dog is dog and wolf is wolf."

"You're a worrywart."

Chases Rabbits remembered that warts were bumps people got on their skin. "Me not have any warts."

"You still worry too much."

"How you know this wolf you have as boy?" Chases Rabbits asked. "Him gone many winters."

"It has to be. No wild wolf would let me do this." Zach put his head to the wolf's and rubbed his hair back and forth. "See how tame he is?"

"Wolf never tame. Only pretend."

"Have you ever had one as a pet?"

"Me know animals," Chases Rabbits stubbornly persisted. "Not trust rattlesnake in blankets not to bite. Not trust bears any time. Not trust wolf not to be wolf."

Zach sighed. "There's no convincing you, is there?"

"Not about wolf . . ." Chases Rabbits would have said more, but Zach looked past him and jumped to his feet.

"Another fire." Zach moved to where he could see it better. "About half a mile off, I'd say."

"Must be Ute war party," Chases Rabbits guessed.

"You've seen them?"

"They try catch me but me too smart."

"A Ute war party this close to King Valley." Zach placed his hands on his pistols. "Something has to be done."

"Utes not know you live there," Chases Rabbits said. "Valley hard to find."

"I want to keep it that way."

Chases Rabbits didn't like the sound of that. "What you do?"

"I'll keep an eye on them and make sure they don't go anywhere near the pass."

"What about Toad?"

"He'll have to wait. Whatever is going on, the women should be fine. The whites won't dare harm a hair on their heads."

Chases Rabbits hoped his friend was right.

The maidens were mad.

They had a long talk. It was unanimous. They would leave and have nothing more to do with the whites at the trading post. But there was only the one way in or out, and it was blocked.

"I have wondered why the other lodge has a front door and a back door and many windows but this lodge has none," Flute Girl said. "Now we know."

"You think they planned all along to keep us here against our will?" Spotted Fawn asked.

"We are their prisoners, aren't we?"

"Not for long," Raven On The Ground said. She had been thinking hard. "We must escape and get to our village. We will tell Long Hair what the whites have done and he will send warriors to punish them."

"It will not go well for Chases Rabbits," Lavender said.

"He was deceived as we were," Raven On The Ground said.

"He speaks the white tongue. He should have suspected the whites lied."

"We did not suspect."

"You are fond of him. If you were not, you would be as upset as we are that he got us into this."

Raven On The Ground looked at the others.

"I understand that he was tricked," Flute Girl said. "But I agree with Lavender. This is partly his fault."

Spotted Fawn said, "I should not hold it against him, but I do."

Raven On The Ground withdrew into herself. She cared about Chases Rabbits, cared about him a great deal. He was awkward and unsure of himself at times, but some men matured faster than others. As one of the few Apsaalooke who knew the white language, he stood to rise in prominence, and as much as she liked him, she liked even more the thought of being the wife of a prominent warrior. She became aware that Flute Girl was speaking to her.

". . . to escape? If we break down the door they will hear us."

"We have lamps," Raven On The Ground said. "We will light one and throw it against the door. It will set the door on fire and burn a hole big enough for us to get away."

"But the whites will see the flames and the smoke and be waiting to stop us," Lavender said.

"Then we will throw it against the back wall," Raven On The Ground proposed. "They will not notice the flames until it is too late."

"But the smoke," Flute Girl said. "We won't be able to breathe."

"We will if we lie on the wood under our feet. The smoke will rise and we will be able to breathe. As soon as enough of the wall has burned, we will run off into the hills."

"Without our horses?" Spotted Fawn said.

"We will come back for them with our warriors. I want to see the whites punished for their insult."

"It is too dangerous," Flute Girl said. "The fire might spread too fast and we will be burned."

"I would rather be dead than let a man I do not know or like take me," Raven On The Ground said.

"As would I," Lavender concurred.

"We are agreed, then?" Raven On The Ground said. "We might as well do it right away. By now the sun has gone down and we can lose ourselves in the dark."

"If you say so," Spotted Fawn said dubiously.

Raven On The Ground rose and went into the cramped space the whites insisted she sleep in and brought out the lamp. The whites had shown them how to light it. They used little sticks called lucifers that came in a small box. She didn't like them. They made a loud noise when they were struck and gave off an unpleasant odor.

Raven On The Ground squatted at the back wall. She raised the glass, swiped the lucifer, and held her breath at the stink. Quickly, she held the lucifer to the wick until it caught. She let go of the lucifer and took a few steps back.

"I hope this works," Flute Girl said.

Raising the lamp over her head, Raven On The Ground hurled it at the wall. It hit with a loud crash and there was a sizzle of spreading flames as the bowl broke and the liquid in the bowl splashed across the wall. Whale oil, the whites called it. Shattered pieces of glass fell to the floor.

Raven On The Ground retreated. The flames spread rapidly. Already thick coils of smoke writhed toward her.

"This was a mistake," Spotted Fawn said.

"Stay calm."

"I do not want to be burned alive."

"We won't be," Raven On The Ground assured her. "Just do as I do." She tried to sound confident, but she was having doubts. The flames leaped and grew at an alarming rate, licking at the ceiling and the floor. The wood, mostly pine, caught remarkably fast.

Coughing from the smoke, Raven On The Ground backed up farther. The others clustered close to her, their worry apparent.

"If I die today, tell my mother and father I loved them," Spotted Fawn said.

The ceiling was on fire. The writhing coils had become a cloud, and the crackling and hissing of the flames was ominous.

"What if the back wall doesn't burn through before the fire reaches us?" Flute Girl brought up.

Raven On The Ground refused to consider the possibility. "It will." She realized an oversight on her part. "Quick. We need blankets." She ran into her living space and yanked the top blanket off the frame. Wrapping it around her shoulders, she came back out and was instantly engulfed in smoke.

The crackling was a roar.

"Raven On The Ground? Where are you?" Spotted Fawn called out.

A groping hand found Raven On The Ground's arm. "I am here!" she shouted so all of them could come to the sound of her voice. "Be ready." The smoke was so thick that she could hardly see the flames. The heat was unbearable. She backed farther away and bumped into someone.

"I told you this was a mistake," Spotted Fawn said.

All of them were coughing. Raven On The Ground covered her mouth and nose with the blanket. She peered into the smoke, trying to tell if the back wall had burned enough for them to get through.

Suddenly there was a rush of air and harsh bellows. She recognized the voice of Dryfus. She turned. The air had moved the smoke enough so that she could see the open front door and Dryfus standing in the doorway, astounded. His yells were bound to bring the others.

Geist would be furious. She glanced at the back wall again and shouted to her friends, "Out the front instead. Lavender, it will be up to you."

"I understand."

Bundled in their blankets, they dashed out. Dryfus stepped aside and made threatening gestures, as if he would strike them.

Raven On The Ground breathed the precious, clear air deeply and shouted, "Do it!"

Lavender swept her knife out from under her blanket and stabbed Dryfus. He clutched at himself and staggered. His rifle clattered to the ground and he dropped to his knees.

Raven On The Ground snatched up the rifle. Lavender raised her knife to stab Dryfus again, but a yell from the trading post gave her pause.

Gratt and Berber were coming.

"Run!" Raven On The Ground cast off her blanket and bolted around the corner. She took for granted that the others would follow. "Hurry!" she cried, and flew into the night.

Behind them the flames roared.

# Chapter Seventeen

Nate King was adrift in dreamless sleep when the pounding woke him. He sat up with a start. Years ago hostiles had attacked his uncle's cabin and slain his uncle, and it was a secret fear of his that one day hostiles might try to do the same to him and his loved ones. His hand went to the small table beside the bed, groping for his pistols.

The pounding continued.

"Go see who is at our door, husband," Winona said sleepily, her body a vague outline in the dark of their bedroom.

"Better not be hostiles," Nate muttered.

"I doubt they would knock."

Nate got up and tugged on his buckskin britches. In his bare feet he padded out into the front room and over to the door.

"Who's out there?"

"It's me."

"Louisa?" Nate quickly threw the bolt and opened the door. She was in a dress and shawl. "What are you doing here at this time of night?"

"May I come in?"

"Of course." Nate sheepishly moved aside, then peered out. There was just her horse, a few yards away. He thought maybe his son's cabin had been attacked. "Where's Zach?"

"That's what I came to talk to you about." Louisa bit her lower lip. "I'm a little worried."

Light flared. Winona, in the blue cotton robe Nate had ordered for her at Bent's Fort, was lighting a lamp. "Have a seat," she said in her calm manner, "and tell us what is the matter."

Nate never ceased to marvel at how well she spoke English. Far better than he spoke Shoshone. She had a knack for languages. He had to struggle.

Louisa lowered the shawl from her head and wearily sank into a chair. "Thank you. I'm sorry to bother you so late."

"Nonsense," Winona said. "You're family. Come to us any time you feel the need."

"What she said," Nate said.

"Would you like tea or coffee?" Winona asked.

"Tea would be nice."

Winona turned toward the counter and glanced at Nate. "You can close the door now, husband, unless you would like the coyotes to join us."

Nate shut it and threw the bolt. He tucked the pistol into his pants and moved to a chair. Since Lou wasn't crying or acting upset, he figured the emergency wasn't life-threatening, which was a relief. "What's wrong?"

"Zach didn't come home tonight."

"Did he go off hunting?" Nate would go on overnight hunts sometimes, but he hated to be away from Winona. He hadn't liked it any better when he was younger and gone for days at a time working his trap line. Shakespeare McNair always teased him about it, saying he was too sentimental.

"No," Lou was saying. "He just went for a ride. I took it for granted that he'd be home for supper since he didn't say he wouldn't. He's usually so considerate."

"He gets that from his father," Winona said.

Nate was flattered. "I didn't think you noticed all the nice things I do."

"How could I not when you always remind me?"

"I guess it's silly of me to worry," Louisa said. "But with the baby on the way, and all . . ."

"It's perfectly understandable," Winona said.

"And then there's that stupid wolf."

Both Nate and Winona said at the same time, "What?"

"He hasn't brought the wolf over to show you? He thinks it's the one he had as a pet years ago, Blaze."

"I'll be darned," Nate said.

"Everywhere he goes, everything he does, that wolf is at his side. He'd even bring it into the bedroom at night, but I put my foot down."

"Good for you," Winona said. "Men must be reminded how to behave."

"Hmmmmph," Nate said.

"What does that mean?" Winona said.

"Just hmmmmph."

Lou went on. "The wolf was with him when he rode off, and they never returned."

"You don't think this wolf would harm him?" Winona asked.

"It's a wolf."

"Wolves don't attack people that often," Nate said. He could recall only a few instances. In one, it had been the icy dead of winter and the wolves were starving. In another, a trapper had tried to catch a pair of wolf cubs and the mother had defended her young.

"All it would take is a bite to the neck," Lou said. "And Zach is always hugging the thing and treating it like a lost friend."

"If it's Blaze, it is," Nate said.

Winona finished filling the teapot with water from a bucket and moved to the stone fireplace. "Blaze and Stalking Coyote were fond of one another." She often used Zach's Shoshone name. "I doubt Blaze would harm him."

"Even so," Lou said, "I can't help but worry. Zach would have told me if he aimed to stay out the whole night."

Nate shrugged. "Maybe his horse went lame. Maybe he shot a big buck and couldn't finish butchering it before dark. Maybe the wolf ran off and he's looking for it."

"I suppose it could be any of those things," Lou said. "And if the wolf did run off, I hope he doesn't find it. I don't want a wolf in our cabin after the baby is born."

"I never heard of a wolf eating a baby."

Lou stared at him.

"Well, I haven't."

Winona was rekindling the fire. "If Stalking Coyote isn't back by an hour after sunrise, we'll go search for him."

"*I* will search for him," Nate said.

"Why just you?"

Louisa said, "I want to go, too."

"That's why," Nate addressed his wife. "In her condition she shouldn't do a lot of riding."

"I am right here," Lou said. "A few hours in the saddle won't bother me."

"No, my husband is right," Winona said. "Zach might show up while we are gone. You should stay in case he does and I should stay in case you need me."

"I'm perfectly fine, I tell you."

"Zach isn't the only hardhead," Nate said.

"I just hope he's all right," Lou said. "There are so

many things that can happen to a person in the wilderness."

"Yes," Nate had to admit. "There are."

The women thought they would be pursued, so they kept running, even when they were well out of sight of the trading post. Raven On The Ground in the lead, they went up the first hill and down the other side. They paused to look back and listen, each of them a shadowy shape in the darkness.

"Are they after us?" Lavender asked.

"Not yet," Flute Girl said.

"But they will be," Raven On The Ground declared, and ran on, her dress swishing against her legs.

"I wish we had our horses," Lavender puffed.

So did Raven On The Ground. On horses they were safer from the beasts that prowled at night, the bears and mountain lions and others. The shriek of a big cat lent substance to her fear. Still, she ran.

When Raven On The Ground finally stopped, she had an ache in her side. Bending over, she gulped for breath. They had put three hills between them and the trading post, but it was nowhere near enough.

Lavender dropped to her knees. "I can't run another step. I'm sorry."

"We must," Flute Girl said. She was breathing hard, her body stooped over. "I think the whites are waiting for daylight, and then they will give chase." Looking around, she asked, "Where is Spotted Fawn?"

Only then did Raven On The Ground realize that she had not seen the youngest of them since they left the burning lodge. "She has to be here," she said, and called Spotted Fawn's name.

There was no answer.

"We left her?" Lavender said in shock.

"Everything was happening so fast," Flute Girl said.

"That is no excuse."

Raven On The Ground blamed herself for not noticing when Spotted Fawn let go of her. "The two of you keep going. I will find her."

"Be sensible," Flute Girl said. "If you go back, they will catch you."

"I'll be careful."

"It will be better if we get away and get word to Long Hair," Flute Girl said. "Let our warriors deal with the whites and bring Spotted Fawn back."

Raven On The Ground started back, but Lavender grabbed her wrist.

"Please don't."

"She is my friend."

"She is a friend to all of us," Flute Girl said.

"Please," Lavender pleaded.

With great reluctance, Raven On The Ground gave in. To keep from thinking about Spotted Fawn, she said, "We have rested long enough."

On through the night they jogged while around them the wilds were alive with the roars and snarls of predators and the bleats and cries of prey.

Gnawing apprehension ate at Raven On The Ground. Not for herself, but for Spotted Fawn. There was no predicting what the whites would do to her in their anger. They had to know that if they harmed her, Crow warriors would swoop down on the trading post in overwhelming force. That would be the end of the whites. They would get what they deserved.

Geist and his bunch were not like Grizzly Killer,

Raven On the Ground reflected. They were vile men with no regard for anyone else. They were worse than the beasts that filled the night around her with so much noise. The beasts were only being true to their natures.

It occurred to Raven On The Ground that Geist and those with him were being true to theirs—and she was more worried than ever.

# Chapter Eighteen

Toad's father had been a doctor. He personally had never had any great love for the profession, although his father had always hoped that he would follow in his footsteps. Blood made Toad squeamish and he couldn't stand even to chop the head off a chicken. Forget cutting into a human being. But he'd learned how to stitch people up, and Dryfus needed stitching, so he volunteered.

Berber brought Dryfus in and laid him on his back on the floor.

Toad carefully pulled at Dryfus's shirt. Soaked with blood, the shirt had started to dry, and it clung to Dryfus like a second skin. Toad had Berber fetch hot water while he chose a small knife from the collection in a glass case and tested it by running the edge across his thumb. A thin red line welled. He found thread and a big sewing needle, the kind used to stitch canvas, and proceeded to stick the end of the thread through the eye of the needle and tie it.

Dryfus had his hand over the wound and was grimacing in pain. "The damn bitch!"

"You were lucky," Toad said. The blade had glanced off a rib, sparing Dryfus from a fatal wound. The cut was deep, but he would live.

"I don't feel lucky," Dryfus rasped. "It hurts like hell."

"You wouldn't feel anything if you were dead."

"Quit jabbering and stitch me up."

The front door opened, and in strode Geist. Petrie was behind him. Geist went to the counter and pounded the top. "The building is a loss. By morning it will be cinders."

"That's too bad," Toad said, although secretly he was delighted.

"Where is she?" Geist snapped at Berber.

"We put her in the storeroom. Gratt is keeping watch. She won't get away like the others did."

"No, she sure as hell won't," Geist declared. "Burning our building. Trying to kill Dryfus. Who do they think they are?"

"You were holding them against their will," Toad said. "It's stupid to blame them for trying to get away."

Geist wheeled and came over. His face had an icy cast and his fists were balled. "Stupid, am I?"

"I didn't mean you personally," Toad said. "I meant stupid in general."

Geist turned to Petrie. "Ever notice how their kind twists words to suit them?"

"They do it all the time."

"My kind?" Toad asked.

"One of us is stupid and it's not me." In a blur Geist drew a pistol, gripped it by the barrel, and savagely clubbed Toad. Once, twice, a third time, and Toad buckled and would have fallen, except that he thrust an arm against a shelf for support.

"No more," Toad said.

Geist raised the pistol to hit him again. "I've had my fill of you."

Succor came from an unexpected source—Dryfus. "Kill him if you have to, but he was fixing to stitch me up and I sorely need to be stitched."

Geist glanced down and then slowly let his arm

drop, his whole body shaking from the violence of his rage. "For you I'll stop. But the next time he insults me we bury him and I run the mercantile myself."

"Too bad," Petrie said. "I'd have liked to see you bash his brains out."

Toad fought off nausea and dizziness. "I rue the day we met," he said.

Still glaring, Geist shoved the pistol under his belt. "I'd shut my mouth, if I were you. You're this close to buying the farm." He held a thumb and a finger a fraction apart. "Now then." He turned to the others. "We have a bigger problem than Levi. The three who got away will make for their village. We have to stop them. They're on foot, so they can't move fast. I figure if we head out at first light, we can have them back here by the end of the day."

"Are all of us going?" Berber asked.

"Use your damn head. Gratt will stay to make sure Levi behaves himself. In the meantime . . ." Geist hitched at his belt. "I'll go have a talk with that little red fluff in the storeroom."

"You won't hurt her?" Toad said.

Geist put his hand on his pistol and made as if to jerk it. "Want a second helping?"

Toad shook his head and was racked by another wave of nausea. His stomach flip-flopped and he swallowed bile.

"I didn't think so. Get to work on Dryfus and do a good job." Geist turned toward the hall. Grinning, he made a smacking sound with his lips. "You know, boys, all this excitement has made me randy."

Spotted Fawn had never been so afraid. She stood in a corner of the small room the whites had thrown her in and fearfully watched the white man by the door. He was leaning back, his arms folded, and didn't seem the least bit interested in her.

She should have run, Spotted Fawn told herself. When she lost hold of Raven On The Ground, she shouldn't have stood there in the smoke wondering which way to go. She should have just run.

There was a thump on the door. The man leaning against it straightened and opened the door. Geist stormed in. He said something, and the other white man grinned and went out, closing the door behind him. Smiling, Geist came toward her.

Spotted Fawn backed up as far as she could go. She glanced left and right, but there was nothing but shelves piled with goods.

Geist began talking and gesturing.

It was the chattering of a squirrel to Spotted Fawn; she didn't understand any of it. "Stay back," she warned. "I will not let you hurt me."

Geist's eyes roved from her hair to her moccasins and back again.

Spotted Fawn's breath caught in her throat. She had seen that kind of look before. Geist wasn't there to hurt her. He had something else in mind. "Do not come near me. I do not want you."

Geist reached out.

"No!" Spotted Fawn smacked his hand away. It seemed to amuse him. He reached out again and she smacked him harder. He was staring at her breasts. "You cannot do this," she said, knowing full well he was going to, that there was no appeal she could make that would dissuade him.

Suddenly lunging, Geist wrapped his arms around her waist. He laughed and nuzzled her neck and stuck his wet tongue in her ear.

Spotted Fawn kneed him. He grunted and his grip slackened, but he didn't let go. She kneed him again, but he shifted and caught the blow on his thigh. His eyes acquired a glitter that had nothing to do with his hunger for her. He growled some words and tried to press his mouth to hers.

Spotted Fawn fought. She pushed and kicked and struggled to break free, but he was much too strong. In desperation, she butted his face with her forehead. Wet drops spattered her face, and he stepped back, blood streaming from his nose. He bunched his fists.

Spotted Fawn tried to dart past him to the door. A punch to her belly sent her reeling. She slammed against a shelf but managed to stay on her feet.

Outside, there were yells. The door started to open, but Geist barked and it slammed shut again. He sneered at her, said something, then touched himself and advanced.

Spotted Fawn yearned for a knife. She grabbed a folded blanket and threw it at him, and he laughed. Backpedaling, she picked up a metal tin and threw that at him, too. He easily dodged. She retreated and bumped into more shelves. On one was an object with a wood handle and a head made of metal. She had no idea what it was. Standing so Geist couldn't see, she grabbed the long handle in both hands.

"Stay away from me."

Geist sneered and came on, blood on his mouth and chin. He spoke in a harsh tone.

Spotted Fawn pretended to cower, and just as his fingers touched her, she swung with all her might. He tried to duck, but he wasn't quite quick enough and she clipped him across the top of his head. He fell at her feet. She raised her weapon to strike him again, but he wasn't moving.

Dropping to a knee, Spotted Fawn put down the thing with the long handle and helped herself to Geist's knife. She hefted it, uncertain. It would do her little good against the other whites. There were too many. They would overpower her. She put the knife down and pulled his pistol. It was heavier than she had expected. She had never held one, but she had seen whites use them and knew that one of the secrets to firing it was to pull back the metal spike on top. She applied both her thumbs and the spike clicked.

Swallowing her fear, Spotted Fawn went to the door. She pressed her ear to it, but heard nothing. Cautiously, she worked the latch as she had seen the whites do. There was another click and it opened. She quickly stepped out.

Gratt and Berber were talking. Berber froze in astonishment, but Gratt started to take a step toward her.

Spotted Fawn pointed the pistol at him and he froze, too. "Stay where you are," she commanded. They might not understand the exact words, but the tone was clear. Keeping her eyes on them, she backed down the hall. When she and her friends were exploring, they had discovered a back door into the trading post. She would use it and flee into the welcome sanctuary of the night.

Gratt yelled.

Probably telling her to stop, Spotted Fawn thought. She continued to retreat until her back bumped the door. Reaching behind her, she fumbled at the latch. Finally it moved and she pushed on the door and was outside.

Flooded with relief, Spotted Fawn whirled around and ran to the west. Although the flames had dwindled some, the other lodge still burned. She raced toward it, eager to reach the dark beyond.

The pounding of running feet behind her filled her ears.

Spotted Fawn glanced behind her. It was Petrie. She sought to raise the pistol, but he was so very, very quick. The stock of his rifle filled her vision and then she was on her back on the ground, in great pain. He raised his rifle to hit her again, but a shout stopped him. Petrie lowered it and stepped back.

Spotted Fawn tried to rise onto her elbows, but a boot caught her. The breath left her lungs, and she was nearly paralyzed by agony. Blinking, she stared up into the fiercely contorted features of the man known as Geist. He was holding his knife.

Geist bent and spit in her face.

Spotted Fawn wanted to defend herself, but her arms wouldn't move as they should. His did, though. She saw his knife gleam in the light from the fire, gleam in an arc again and again and again, and she felt wet and warmth and an emptiness that knew no end.

# Chapter Nineteen

The three women had run all night and were on the verge of exhaustion.

Raven On The Ground gasped for breath. She came to the bottom of yet another slope and into the shadow of the hill they had crossed, and stopped. "This should be far enough. We will rest."

No one objected. They had put a lot of distance between them and the trading post.

To the east, the black sky was lightening to gray. Dawn was breaking. The birds were astir, and in a nearby copse of woodland, sparrows chirped.

Lavender wearily sat. "I haven't run this much since I was a girl."

"I have lost feeling in my legs," Flute Girl said.

"It was worth our effort," Raven On The Ground said. "They won't catch us now."

"Unless they have a tracker," Flute Girl said.

"I can't stop thinking about Spotted Fawn," Lavender said. "Do you think she is all right?"

"They wouldn't be foolish enough to harm her," Raven On The Ground replied.

Flute Girl disagreed. "They are white. They do not think like we do. What is foolish to us might not be foolish to them."

"Don't say that."

"Poor Spotted Fawn," Lavender said.

"Let's not talk about her," Raven On The Ground

said. She eased to the ground and wearily scanned the crown of the last hill they had crossed.

Flute Girl was bent over with her hands on her knees. "If your lover was here, I would tell him what I think of his precious whites."

"Don't call him that."

"Why not? You have made no secret of your desire to have him be yours."

"You blame Chases Rabbits for our plight when it is the fault of the whites?"

"Who convinced us that working for the whites was a good thing to do?"

"You forget. The whites held council with Long Hair. They fooled him, too. They pretended to be our friends when they were not."

Lavender raised her head. "Enough, both of you. There is no question who is to blame. The whites schemed to use us to fill their pokes with money. That is what brought us to this."

That ended the argument. Raven On The Ground eased onto her back. Streaks of gold lit the eastern sky. The sun was rising. She closed her eyes. Fatigue overwhelmed her. Almost instantly she fell asleep.

Although it felt as though she had slept for only a few minutes, when she opened her eyes the sun was directly above them. She had slept half the day away.

Feeling sluggish and sore, Raven On The Ground sat up. Her friends were sound asleep, Flute Girl snoring. She stood, wincing at the discomfort in her legs.

To the west, mountains reared. Timber covered most of the slopes. Here and there were high cliffs with specks moving on the sheer heights. Mountain sheep, their meat so succulent—it was one of her favorites.

Raven On The Ground stretched. Her body demanded more rest, but they had slept long enough. She went to Lavender and shook her. Lavender mumbled and moved an arm as if to push her away.

"Wake up. We must keep going." Raven On The Ground shook her harder.

Lavender stirred and blinked, squinting in the bright glare of the sun. "I was having the most pleasant dream."

"I am sorry."

"We were in our village. It was night and we were celebrating. Our warriors had killed many buffalo. We had butchered them and there was meat for everyone. We were dancing and singing."

"We will dance and sing again."

Raven On The Ground moved to Flute Girl. She placed her hand on the bigger woman's shoulder and Flute Girl came awake with a start. She sat up and glanced about in alarm.

"What is wrong?"

"We are fine. We must move on."

For a while they hiked slowly, their leg muscles stiff. The farther they went, the less it hurt. They were walking briskly when Lavender looked over her shoulder and blurted, "No!"

In the distance three riders came on at a trot. There was a fourth, but he was leading extra horses and lagged behind.

Raven On The Ground shielded her eyes with her hand. "It is them. Dryfus is tracking us. They are on our trail, but haven't seen us yet."

"We must hide," Flute Girl said, and took the lead.

Ahead grew cottonwoods, usually a sign of water. They burst in among the trees and found a small spring.

"I am so thirsty." Flute Girl threw herself down. She put her face in the water and greedily gulped.

"Not too much," Raven On The Ground cautioned. "It will make our bellies hurt." But it was hard to resist. They had been without anything to drink since before the fire. She tore herself away and nudged her companions to get them to do the same.

"I could drink it dry," Flute Girl said, her chin dripping wet.

"Listen," Lavender said.

The thud of hoofbeats warned them that they had squandered precious time.

"Keep up with me," Raven On The Ground said, and ran. Her people were fond of racing, both on foot and on horseback, and she loved to run.

The undergrowth was thick, but that was good, since it would slow the horses. Raven On the Ground vaulted logs and avoided boulders. She was pleased at how her legs were bearing up under the strain. Lavender was close behind her, mouth set in grim determination. Flute Girl had fallen behind, but Raven On The Ground glimpsed her, struggling hard to keep up.

The drum of hooves was louder.

Raven On The Ground was going as fast as she could, but she couldn't outrun horses. She and the others needed somewhere to hide. A thicket appeared, but the whites could surround it and they would be trapped. She raced on, and suddenly the woods thinned, revealing a slope littered with boulders before them. She barely slowed. Lavender was farther back, wheezing with every stride. There was no sign of Flute Girl.

Raven On The Ground stopped. She refused to leave her friends. Wheeling, she waited for Lavender to reach her. Lavender was flushed and swayed unsteadily.

"I can't go on."

"Rest a moment."

"I need more than that."

Raven On The Ground looked for Flute Girl, but she didn't appear.

Out of the woods exploded two riders.

Whirling, Raven On The Ground took flight, but she had only taken a few bounds when a blow to her shoulder slammed her to the earth. She heard Lavender cry out. Dust got into her eyes and nose as she rolled across the ground. Above her loomed Geist on a stallion. He pointed a rifle at her and said something. Although she didn't understand the words, his meaning was clear.

Sitting up, she saw Lavender on the ground in Petrie's grasp. She punched at his chest, but it had no effect.

Raven On The Ground bowed her head in sorrow. She had been so sure they would reach their village. Geist's saddle creaked and iron fingers seized her by the hair. She was thrown down again and kicked. The pain was terrible, but it hurt worse to be thwarted in their escape.

Petrie bound Lavender's wrists behind her back and then tied Raven On The Ground.

By then Dryfus had joined them, Flute Girl walking in front of his horse, a bloody smear on her forehead.

Last to arrive was Berber, leading the extra horses. One by one, the women were thrown roughly over a mount. Berber held onto the lead rope.

Geist growled at Dryfus, who listened and translated in sign.

*You make bad mistake. You make us mad. Now we hurt you. We hurt you much.*

# *Chapter Twenty*

Chases Rabbits never thought he would be grateful to Utes, but he was. The war party had gone off to the south and nowhere near the pass into King Valley. So now he and Zach were riding hard for the trading post, the wolf loping tirelessly beside Zach's horse.

Chases Rabbits couldn't wait to get there, couldn't wait to set his eyes on Raven On The Ground. He missed her with all that he was, although he would never tell Zach that.

Early on the morning of the third day, they wound down out of the foothills toward Mud Hollow. Chases Rabbits rose in his saddle to try and see the trading post, but they weren't close enough yet.

"We almost there."

"Toad gave you no notion why he needed to see my pa?" Zach asked.

"No. Him only say it urgent. Urgent mean hurry up quick, yes?"

"Pretty much," Zach confirmed. He stiffened suddenly and said, "What the hell?"

The hollow had come into sight.

Chases Rabbits felt his heart leap into his throat. Where the lodge for the women had been was a wide black spot and charred wood. "What that be?" he wondered without thinking.

"The building burned down," Zach said. He bent and motioned to the wolf. "Sit."

To Chases Rabbits's amazement, the wolf did.

"Stay," Zach commanded, and used his heels on the dun.

Chases Rabbits followed suit. Fear for Raven On The Ground filled him. He was close behind the dun when Zach drew rein in a flurry of dust next to the spot where the burned lodge had been.

A few Nez Perce were in front of the trading post. A couple of Pawnees were there. Two of the whites, Berber and Gratt, were lounging at the hitch rail, and when they saw Chases Rabbits and Zach ride up, they hurried inside.

Chases Rabbits swung down and stared at the pile in dismay. "Raven On The Ground," he said softly.

"I don't see any bones," Zach said.

"Sorry?" Chases Rabbits couldn't think of what bones had to do with it.

"Bones don't always burn up."

"Oh." Chases Rabbits didn't find that particularly encouraging.

"Come on," Zach said. He wheeled toward the mercantile, then stopped short.

Toad, Geist, and Petrie were walking toward them, Geist smiling, and Petrie with his rifle in the crook of his arm, the muzzle practically brushing Toad's shoulder.

"How do you do, gentlemen?" Toad said. "It's a pleasure to see you again."

"Forget that," Zach said, and pointed at the blackened circle. "What happened? Where are the women?"

"Where Raven On The Ground?" Chases Rabbits specifically demanded.

"We had a fire, obviously," Toad said. "A lamp was knocked over. We did what we could, but it wasn't enough to contain the flames."

"And the women?" Zach pressed him.

"Raven On The Ground?" Chases Rabbits said.

Geist stepped past Toad and good-naturedly clapped Chases Rabbits on the arm. "Don't fret, my friend. The women are fine. They got out in plenty of time and ran to us for help."

"Where they now?" Chases Rabbits anxiously asked.

"They've gone back to your village."

Chases Rabbits almost fainted with relief. But that wouldn't be becoming of a warrior, so he adopted a stony expression and said simply, "Good."

"We plan to rebuild," Geist said. "Then we'll send for the women again, provided they're still willing to work for us."

"Me bet they be," Chases Rabbits said, remembering how eager Raven On The Ground was to acquire some red cloth and beads.

"We're just glad they weren't hurt," Geist said.

Toad cleared his throat. "Mr. King, how about a drink on the house?"

"I don't drink," Zach said flatly.

"Not ever?"

"No."

"How about a meal, then?"

"I'm not all that hungry."

"Some coffee and a biscuit, perhaps? You've ridden a long way."

Geist shifted toward Toad and lost some of his smile. "You heard him. He's not hungry and he's not thirsty."

"I just thought . . ." Toad said.

"Me thirsty," Chases Rabbits said. "Can me have water?"

"Of course you can," Toad answered. "Come inside."

"There's the stream right there," Geist said, and pointed.

"You make it difficult to be polite," Toad remarked.

Chases Rabbits was about to lead the pinto to the stream when he realized he was forgetting something. "Oh. Me sorry not bring Grizzly Killer. Stalking Coyote come instead."

Toad smiled an odd smile.

"What was that?" Geist asked.

"Grizzly Killer," Chases Rabbits repeated, then realized the white man might not know whom he was referring to. "Nate King. Mr. Toad ask me fetch him urgent."

"He did, did he?"

"Yes."

"Did he say why?"

"I was wondering that myself," Zach said.

Toad opened his mouth to say something, glanced at Petrie, and hesitated. "I merely wanted to have your father invite the Shoshones to pay us a visit. None have been here yet, and I'm counting on doing business with them."

"I'll have my mother ask them for you," Zach said.

"I would be very grateful. Thank you."

Geist rubbed his hands together. "Well, then. We have work to do. If you'll excuse us . . ." He nodded at Petrie and Toad, and Toad walked off with Petrie behind him. Geist smiled and trailed after them.

"Him nice man," Chases Rabbits said.

# Chapter Twenty-one

Elihu Levi was his birth name. When he was little, his family took to calling him "Pudgy" and he hated it. By his tenth year, his bulging eyes and squat build sparked a cousin to one day laughingly call him a toad, and the nickname stuck. He hated that even more, and had disliked his cousin ever since.

His schoolmates teased him mercilessly. His relatives weren't much better. Small wonder he felt like an outcast, even among his own kind. He shunned people and devoted himself to his passion—business. For a few years he worked with his family in dry goods, but his dream was to own his own store. Thanks to his grandfather, who had left him a few thousand dollars in his will, he moved from Indiana to St. Louis and set up a mercantile.

His family was against it. Why St. Louis? they asked. Toad explained that it was the gateway to the frontier, that it was the supply point for freight trains and wagon trains streaming to Santa Fe and to Oregon Country, and there were riches to be made. His mercantile flourished and he was content, or he would have been, if not for the tales.

From the freighters and frontiersmen, Toad heard endless stories about the mysterious lands to the west, about nigh-endless prairie, majestic mountains, and a host of wonders to dazzle the eyes; about friendly Indians, hostiles, and beasts galore. The tales took root. He began to want to see some of the wonders for himself. The desire built and built until it couldn't be denied.

So it was that one day, Toad promoted one of his assistants and left the man to oversee his St. Louis store while he ventured off into the great unknown. He was determined to have the first-ever mercantile west of the Mississippi River. He advertised for adventurous men willing to brave the dangers of his employ, and Geist was one of the first to respond. It turned out that Geist knew of four others, and before Toad knew it, he had the helpers he needed.

Now, standing alone behind the counter late in the afternoon, his insides in turmoil, Toad berated himself for being so gullible. He'd hired a viper and not realized it. A pack of vipers who'd taken over his store, murdered a Crow maiden, and imprisoned her friends in the storeroom.

Toad had no illusions about the outcome if the Crows found out. The mercantile would become a smoldering ruin. Worse, the Crows might vent their wrath on him. He'd heard that some tribes were fond of torture, and he could do without being staked out and having his skin flayed.

Toad came to a decision. He was going to rescue the maidens. He would sneak into the storeroom, free them, and help them slip away before Geist or any of his men caught on. But no sooner had he come around the end of the counter than Geist and Petrie stepped from the hall, barring his way.

"Where the hell do you think you're going?"

"Out back," Toad said.

"No, you're not." Geist pushed him. "You're not going anywhere. We have some talking to do."

Toad had to swallow to say, "What about?"

"That urgent business you sent Chases Rabbits on. You sent for Nate King to warn him about me, didn't you?"

Toad glanced behind him to see if the aisle to the door was clear. It wasn't. Dryfus and Berber were behind him.

"Any redskins outside?" Geist asked them.

"A few Flatheads, is all," Dryfus said.

"You told them the rule that all Indians are to be gone by dark?"

"I did. They said they'd be back in the morning to trade."

Geist gave Toad a vicious smile. "We'll wait until they leave."

"I'm no threat to you," Toad said.

"The hell you're not." Geist shook his head. "No, you know too much." He drew a flintlock and said to Dryfus, "Tie him up and throw him in the storeroom with the bitches. We're getting the hell out of here at daybreak."

"We're tucking tail and running?" Petrie said.

"We're being smart. This hasn't gone anywhere near the way I planned. I should never have left the States. Out here there's too much I can't control."

"We could head down Santa Fe way or off to Oregon," Petrie said.

"And what? Rob people for a living? What kind of life is that? The pickings would be slim and we'd always be on the run." Geist shook his head. "The States is where we belong." He pointed the flintlock at Toad's face. "Now do as I told you with this fat slob and we'll get to packing."

Dryfus prodded Toad in the back with his rifle and Toad moved down the hall to the storage room. Gratt was standing guard over the women. Dryfus and Berber shoved Toad inside, but it was Petrie who tied him.

"Better say your prayers, *Levi*. You don't have long before you'll be burning in hell."

"If there's any justice in this world," Toad said, "you won't get away with this."

"There isn't," Petrie said, and laughed.

# Chapter Twenty-two

Not all warriors were good trackers. Bull Standing was the best of all the Crows; he could track a turtle across hard earth. Chases Rabbits was fair at it. He could track a buffalo if the ground was soft enough.

Zach King was as good as Bull Standing. And it was Zach who abruptly drew rein and announced, "There's tracks here that shouldn't be."

When Zach stopped, so did the wolf.

"What kind?" Chases Rabbits asked. He had been thinking of how much he missed Raven On The Ground and had not been paying much attention.

Sliding down, Zach squatted and pointed. "See for yourself."

"Moccasin tracks?" Chases Rabbits dismounted to study them better. Their size sent a jolt of consternation through him. "Those be women tracks."

"And they were running." Zach rose and led his dun, paralleling the prints. "Three of them." He hunkered and touched a particularly clear print. "Definitely Crow."

"Geist say Raven On The Ground and rest go to village. Why they use feet and not ride?"

Zach was bent over a series of large pockmarks. "Hoofprints," he said. "Made by shod horses going in the same direction."

"Shod means white men," Chases Rabbits said, and scratched his head. "Me very confused."

"Geist and his friends would be my guess," Zach

interpreted the tracks. "They were after the three women."

"Why?"

"That's what I'd like to know." Zach uncurled. "Are you up for some spying?"

Chases Rabbits stared at the sky and then at the ground and said, "Me little bit up."

"We're going back and keeping an eye on the mercantile. It'll be dark soon and I'll sneak down for a look-see."

"You think maybe something wrong?"

"That building burned down. And now we find these tracks. Then there was the way Toad was acting."

"Toad?"

"You didn't notice how nervous he was?"

"No," Chases Rabbits admitted.

"Yes, I'd say something is wrong."

The sun was roosting on the rim of the world when they came to just below the crest of the hill above the hollow. They crawled on their bellies to where they had an unobstructed view.

The wolf lay between them.

"Flatheads," Zach said, and nodded at a knot of warriors and horses.

"No whites outside," Chases Rabbits noted.

Soon the Flatheads departed. The mercantile's shadow lengthened and the bright of day gave way to the spreading gray of twilight. Windows lit with the glow of lamps.

By the stream a frog croaked, and crickets began to chirp.

Chases Rabbits saw shadows flit across the windows. Faint to his ears came gruff laughter and loud voices.

"Sounds like they're having a high old time," Zach said. "They must be drinking."

Something had been bothering Chases Rabbits since they found the moccasin tracks, and now he gave voice to it. "Why there only tracks of three women?"

"I don't know."

"You think they at village or down there?"

Zach nodded at the mercantile. "I'll find out when I go down."

"I go, too."

"One of us should stick close to the horses in case we need them in a hurry."

Chases Rabbits saw the logic, but he was troubled. "You did say we friends, yes?"

"I'm as good a friend with you as I am with any-one."

"Then me have favor must ask. You stay with horses. I go see what whites do."

"Why you?"

Chases Rabbits struggled with how to put into white words how much he cared for Raven On The Ground, and how if she was in trouble, it was partly his fault since he was the one who had suggested she come work for the whites, and how, as a Crow warrior, he had to protect the women. But that was a lot to express, so he simply said, "Raven On The Ground."

"I savvy," Zach said. "I have Lou. She's as impor-tant to me as your sweetheart is to you."

"Sweetheart?" This was new to Chases Rabbits.

"It stands for the woman you care for the most," Zach explained.

"Sweetheart." Chases Rabbits grinned. "That fit. Me like it."

"The whites have a saying," Zach said. "We can't live with them and we can't live without them. Or as Uncle Shakespeare puts it, we can't live without them and we can't chuck them off cliffs."

"Chuck?"

"Throw."

Chases Rabbits was lost. "Why we throw sweethearts off cliff? They maybe die."

"Doesn't Raven On The Ground ever get your dander up?"

"Dander?"

"Temper. Doesn't she ever make you angry?"

"She mostly make me happy and warm."

Zach suddenly switched his attention to the hollow. "One of the whites."

The twilight had darkened, but there was sufficient light to reveal Petrie walking in a wide circle around the trading post.

"What him do?"

"Maybe he's getting some fresh air," Zach speculated. "Or maybe he's making sure everyone has gone for the day."

"Him never talk much, that one."

"He strikes me as a sidewinder. The most dangerous of the bunch."

"How you know that? You see him shoot or use knife?"

"It's how he carries himself. It's his eyes. He's a killer. You stay shy of him, you hear?"

Chases Rabbits had learned to trust Zach's judgment. It compounded his worry: his sweetheart in the hands of a killer. "The other whites like him?"

"Could be, but he's the one I'd watch out for."

An inky mantle replaced the velvet blue of sky, and stars sparkled like so many diamonds. A coyote yipped, and as if that were a signal, the night pealed with a bestial chorus of roars and shrieks and bleats.

"Petrie's gone back in," Zach said. "Time for your look-see. Give a holler if you run into trouble and I'll come on the run."

"What I holler?"

" 'Help' is always good."

Careful not to bump the wolf, Chases Rabbits rose and crept down the slope. He excelled at stalking. Crow children played a game where they snuck up on one another, and he had always been good at it.

The smell of the burned wood got into his nose, and he felt the urge to sneeze. Quickly pinching it, he waited until the urge faded.

Moving slowly, Chases Rabbits came to the front corner of the mercantile and peered around it. The door was closed. Inside, the whites were still talking and laughing. A celebration of some kind, he concluded. Crouching, he sidled to the window and raised an eye to the bottom of the glass.

The mercantile was a mess. Goods had been thrown all over the floor and shelves had been upended. Geist was on the counter, drinking from a long-necked bottle. Petrie was watching Dryfus and Gratt, who also had bottles. They were pushing a woman back and forth, cuffing her and squeezing her bosom. The woman was horror-struck.

So was Chases Rabbits.

It was Raven On The Ground.

Chases Rabbits was at the front door before he realized his feet were moving. Jerking on the latch, he pushed the door open and rushed inside, his new rifle level at his hip. He was so mad, he wasn't thinking. "Stop!" he cried.

The whites turned to stone. Geist had the whiskey

bottle to his lips. Gratt was about to shove Raven On The Ground and had his hand on her shoulder. She turned, her face pale and sweaty, and said in Crow, "Chases Rabbits? Is that you?" Her speech was slurred and she couldn't seem to stand up straight.

Petrie started to raise his rifle.

"No!" Chases Rabbits yelled, and took aim. His brain began to work. He had blundered in charging inside. He was one against four; he couldn't possibly shoot them all before they shot him. In Crow he said, "Come to me, Raven On The Ground."

"I can't."

Chases Rabbits didn't take his eyes off Petrie, the one Zach had warned him about. "Why not?"

"I can hardly walk. They held me down and poured firewater down my throat."

Moving wide around Dryfus to reach her, Chases Rabbits said, "I will get you out of here."

"Lavender and Flute Girl are in a room in the back," Raven On The Ground said.

"Where is Spotted Fawn?"

"They killed her."

Shock gripped Chases Rabbits. He had feared something like this, but to have it happen, to have the whites prove to be so callous and cruel after they had sought to convince him they were friendly, tore at him like the claws of a grizzly. "How could you?" he said to the one who had done the most convincing.

"Stupid Injun," Geist muttered. Lowering the bottle, he wiped his mouth with his sleeve. "She got what all your kind deserve."

"All Crows?"

"No, you damned numbskull. Anyone with red skin."

Chases Rabbits almost shot him. He had been tricked, shamefully and terribly tricked, and now a Crow maiden was dead because of his mistake. He reached out to Raven On The Ground. "Take my hand."

She started to but put her hand to her head instead and groaned. "I think I am going to be sick."

"We must . . ." Chases Rabbits trailed off when a hard object was jammed low against his spine.

"Not a twitch, redskin, or I'll blow you in half," Berber said.

Chases Rabbits had made another mistake. He had failed to look behind him. He hesitated and was undone. Petrie was suddenly there, wrenching the rifle from his grasp and saying to the other whites, "Cover the windows and the doors."

"What for?" Gratt said.

"When he was here last he was with the breed."

"Zach King?"

Geist swung off the counter and drew a pistol. "Do as Petrie says. Gratt, you go watch the back door. Berber, keep your rifle on the simpleton." He ran to the front door and opened it but only a hand's width. "King!" he shouted. "Can you hear me out there?"

Silence reigned, save for the whisper of Petrie's boots as he glided to Geist's side.

"Zach King! I won't ask you again! And in case you're thinking you won't answer me, I have your Injun friend and all of the women."

More silence.

Chases Rabbits reached for Raven On The Ground, but Berber struck his arm with the rifle, sending pain and numbness from his elbow to his shoulder.

"Don't move."

Geist looked worried. "By God, I will shoot them

one by one! So help me, I will!" He pointed his pistol at Raven On The Ground. "Starting with the prettiest."

From out of the darkness came, "I'm here. What do you want?"

Geist smiled and winked at Petrie, but Petrie was grim. "Drop your weapons and walk in here with your hands in the air."

Zach laughed.

"I wasn't joshing about shooting her or any of the rest," Geist threatened. "I'm a man of my word."

"Like hell you are. But I am."

"Meaning what?"

When Zach answered, it was apparent he had changed position. "For every shot I hear, I'll shoot one of your horses."

"Hell!" Dryfus blurted. "He does that, we'll be sitting ducks for the Crows."

"Shut the hell up," Geist snapped. "I'm trying to think." He chewed on his lower lip, then yelled, "I'm not sending them out to you, if that's what you're expecting."

"All I care about is that they go on breathing." Zach had changed position yet again.

"Damn him," Geist hissed. "He has us over a barrel."

"Only until daylight," Petrie said.

Geist glanced sharply at him, and nodded. Then he raised his voice once more. "All right, King. I won't harm them so long as you don't try anything. But if you shoot any of our animals, if I hear so much as one shot, I start the killing. You hear me?"

"I hear you."

Geist shut the door, leaned against it, and smiled. "Listen up," he said to the others. "Tie up Chases

Rabbits and his girlfriend and put them in the store-room with the rest. We'll hunker down until first light."

"Then what?" Dryfus asked. "What can we do with him out there covering the place?"

"You sound scared."

"I've been with you long enough, you know better," Dryfus said.

"King is just one man. That's our edge. Come morning, I have a surprise in store for him. A surprise he's not going to like one little bit."

# Chapter Twenty-three

Zach King was on his knees where the bank of the stream curved, fifty yards from the mercantile, when dawn splashed the eastern sky with color. He had been there most of the night, Blaze beside him.

Zach smothered a yawn and ignored twinges of pain in his legs. Soon the sun would be up. With luck he would get a clear shot at Geist. Geist was their leader. Shoot him, and the rest might panic.

Barring that, Zach was counting on Indians to show up, as they customarily did. If the first to arrive were Crows, he would enlist their help. If they were from another tribe, he would ask them to get word to the Crows. Either way, once reinforcements got there, the whites were as good as worm food.

Zach saw movement inside. He took aim with the Hawken, but the window was too dark for him to make out targets. He raised his head from the rifle. He could be patient when he had to. He could be very patient.

A blazing arch peeked above the world.

Zach looked down and patted Blaze. When he looked up again, the front door was open. Instantly, he put his cheek to the Hawken.

"King! You hear me?" Geist shouted.

Zach didn't respond.

"King, damn it!"

Zach still didn't reply.

"Fine. Maybe this will loosen your tongue."

Suddenly Chases Rabbits was in the doorway, his wrists bound. He was pushed and stumbled, but someone jerked on him from behind. He regained his balance and stood still.

Geist's face appeared above Chases Rabbits's shoulder.

Zach fixed a swift bead. His thumb on the Hawken's hammer, he went to pull it back.

Geist was glancing every which way, trying to spot him. "Take a good look, King!"

Chases Rabbits turned sideways. Geist had a hand to the back of his neck. In his other hand, Geist held a cocked pistol to Chases Rabbits's head.

Zach uncurled his thumb.

"This is how it's going to go!" Geist hollered. "We're leaving, and we're taking your friends with us! We'll have guns to their heads, and if you shoot, if you so much as throw a damn rock at us, we'll blow their brains out!"

Zach frowned. Geist was clever; by getting out of there as early as possible, the whites would have a good lead should Zach and any Crows come after them.

"It's up to you, King! I'll kill every one of these red scum if you give me the slightest excuse! Don't think I won't."

Zach didn't harbor any doubts there. He yearned to squeeze off a shot, but he had to crouch and do nothing as, one by one, Petrie, Dryfus, and Gratt came out with guns to the heads of Raven On The Ground, Lavender, and Flute Girl.

Berber was last, his arms laden with rifles and supplies. They took turns boosting their captives onto horses and then climbed on their own mounts.

Geist was beaming. Not once had he lowered his

pistol from Chases Rabbits. He looked toward the hill and then around the hollow and shouted, "I know you can see me. So pay attention. We're taking your friends. I'll let them go as soon as I'm sure it's safe. Tell the Crows so they don't try anything."

Zach had never wanted to shoot someone so much.

Geist tugged on the reins of the horse Chases Rabbits was on, and the whole bunch rode off into the rising sun. "Damn it," Zach said, and stood. He had two choices. He could wait there for Crows to come, or he could follow them and attempt a rescue. Since Zach wasn't about to trust Geist's promise to release his captive friends, he hurried to his dun and mounted.

Zach was passing the mercantile when he remembered an item in a glass display that would be of considerable help. Drawing rein, he alighted and ran inside. A lamp still burned on the counter. He had to go behind the case to open it. As he was taking the item out, he heard a thump and then a peculiar sort of scraping from somewhere in the back.

Zach moved to the hall. At first the wriggling form on the floor blended into the shadows. Hurrying down, he squatted. "You."

Toad's ankles and wrists were bound, and he had a gag in his mouth. He made sounds of distress through the gag.

Zach removed it and threw it aside. "I thought you were one of them."

"I'm not an animal, thank you very much." Toad waggled his arms. "Untie me, if you would be so kind."

"You heard everything?" Zach said as he pried at a knot.

"Are you kidding? Geist gloated to me all night about how he was going to outwit you."

"I'm surprised they let you live."

"I have you to thank."

"What did I do?"

"They were worried that if you heard a shot, you'd start killing the horses."

"They could have slit your throat."

Toad said, "You almost sound disappointed they didn't."

"You brought them here."

"It was either that or be killed, and I'm enormously fond of breathing."

Zach loosened the last of the knots. Enough light had filtered down the hall to reveal that Toad's face was a bruised and bloody mess. "Geist do that?"

"He delights in the suffering of others. Make no mistake. He is unspeakably vicious. Your friends are as good as dead once they are of no further use to him."

"I know."

"What will you do?"

"What else?" Zach King said. "I'm going to kill every last one of those sons of bitches."

# Chapter Twenty-four

Chases Rabbits was in despair. He was a warrior. It was his duty to protect the women of his tribe. Yet here he was, bound and helpless, at the mercy of his enemies, unable to be of any help to the three women whose lives were in peril.

Geist rode hard and fast. Again and again he looked back.

After they had put a considerable distance between them and the mercantile, he slowed his horse to a walk and remarked, "I thought for sure he'd try to stop us."

"Stalking Coyote good friend," Chases Rabbits said. "Him not do anything get us hurt."

"Is that his redskin name?" Geist said. "Let me tell you something, boy. I hope to God he comes after us. I truly and sincerely do. I have you and the women and four extra rifles, besides."

"Zach have Zach."

"That makes no kind of sense," Geist said.

The sun was at its zenith when they finally stopped alongside a stream.

Chases Rabbits waited to be told whether he should slide off or not. The answer came in the form of Dryfus, who gripped him by the shirt and flung him roughly to the ground. His arm and ribs flared with pain, and he grunted.

"Did that hurt?" Dryfus mockingly asked, and kicked him in the ribs.

"Enough," Geist said. "We need him in one piece when King catches up."

"I'd as soon gut all four of the vermin," Dryfus said, but he lowered his foot.

Chases Rabbits's shame was compounded when the women were dumped next to him. It was almost more than he could bear to sit up and look into their haggard faces. "I am sorry for all you have endured."

"It is not your fault," Raven On The Ground said.

Flute Girl and Lavender appeared to disagree, but they said nothing.

"We are still alive," Raven On The Ground said. "So long as we breathe, there is hope."

Chases Rabbits' love for her filled his whole chest. She had an indomitable spirit, this woman he adored. "We must be ready when Zach King comes. We must do what we can to help him."

"Why should the half-breed risk his life for us?" Flute Girl asked. "He isn't Apsaalooke."

"He is my friend," Chases Rabbits said. He resented her calling Zach a half-breed, but he held his tongue.

"Quit your jabbering," Geist snapped. "You don't talk unless I say you can. Tell the females."

After that there was nothing for Chases Rabbits to do but sit and wait for the whites to move on. He had been up all night and was tired to his marrow, but he refused to show it. He sat with his back straight, his head high. He decided that, if he lived through this, he would formally ask Raven On The Ground to be his wife. He would be hurt if she refused, but he wouldn't blame her. She deserved a warrior of great influence, one who had counted many coup and owned many horses. His dream of being that warrior had been dashed by Geist's brutal nature; his people were bound to hold Spotted Fawn's death against him.

A shadow fell across them, and Chases Rabbits squinted up into the face of the man he most wished to count coup on. "What you want?"

"Ever been hog-tied?" Geist asked.

"Me not know what that is."

"You will soon enough," Geist said with a smirk. "I aim to use you as bait."

That the whites made no effort to hide their tracks didn't surprise Zach. It would be pointless with him so close on their heels.

They had made a beeline down the foothills to the prairie. Only twice had they stopped to rest, and each time briefly. Their mounts were still fresh enough, though, that on reaching the plain, they headed to the east at a trot.

Zach matched their pace. He was in no rush to overtake them. Not in broad daylight on open ground. Once the sun went down—that was when he would close in. With most of the afternoon before him yet, he was content to stay far enough back that they wouldn't spot him.

At this time of year, the prairie was green with grass that would turn to mostly brown once the summer heat hit in all its searing force. Wildflowers grew in profusion and butterflies were everywhere. Grouse took wing at Zach's approach, prairie dogs stood on top of their dens and whistled shrill alarms. Sparrows played and swallows swooped, and hawks and eagles ruled the higher sky.

When Zach first saw the dark spot in the grass, he

didn't think much of it. An animal, he reckoned, an antelope or a lone buffalo. Then he saw how low to the ground it was, and that it was the color of buckskin. Drawing rein, he reached into his parfleche for the item he had helped himself to back at the mercantile.

The brass tube glistened in the bright sun as Zach unfolded the spyglass. He put his eye to the small end and fixed the large end on the distant figure. He took a moment to bring it into focus, then swore.

It was Chases Rabbits. Securely bound, the young Crow was on his knees, his head practically brushing the grass, held there by a rope around his neck that was tied to a stake. Another stake was attached to a rope around his ankles.

Zach lowered the spyglass. There was only one reason for Geist to leave Chases Rabbits out there like that. The devil of it was, trap or no trap, Zach had no choice but to go to his friend's aid. He held on to the spyglass until he was several hundred feet out. Stopping again, he scanned the ground around Chases Rabbits, then shoved the telescope into the parfleche and rode on at a slow walk. He had the Hawken cocked, the stock on his thigh.

Chases Rabbits looked up. A gag prevented the young Crow from saying anything. Frantically bobbing his head, he uttered gurgling sounds.

Tense with the certainty of being ambushed, Zach gripped the Hawken in both hands and he slid down. "If they're here, bob your head once for yes."

Chases Rabbits's chin rose and fell.

"How many? Bob once for each one."

Chases Rabbits nodded—one time.

Zach was mystified. All he saw was flat ground.

There was nowhere for anyone to hide. He edged closer and Chases Rabbits made choking sounds and jerked his head in Zach's direction.

Blaze was sniffing at the ground.

Zach looked down and saw that the grass was speckled with brown spots. He bent, and realized the brown was dirt.

The earth heaved upward. A swatch of grass six feet long and three feet wide was flung aside and out of the ground sprang Dryfus. Clutched in his right hand was a long-bladed knife and on his face was an expression of pure hatred.

Zach aimed and fired, but Dryfus swatted the barrel and the heavy ball smacked into the hole he had been lying in. Dryfus held on to the rifle, and wrenched. Zach let it go flying. Backpedaling, he streaked his hand to his bowie and swept the big knife up and out. Steel clashed on steel as he saved his throat from a savage cut. Dryfus snarled and came in fast, his blade a whirlwind. Zach dodged, parried, countered. He had considerable experience in knife–fighting, but so did his adversary. Their blades wove a glittering web of death. A mistake in this fight could be fatal. Dryfus sidestepped and speared his knife at Zach's chest. Zach blocked, shifted, slashed, and scored, opening Dryfus's sleeve and the flesh under it. But the cut had no effect other than to incite Dryfus into redoubling his efforts.

Stabbing and cleaving, they circled in one direction and then the other, both so intent on their duel that when the two of them stumbled over Chases Rabbits, their surprise was mutual. Zach came down on his side, and rolled. Dryfus landed on his back but was up in a bound and lancing his knife at Zach's neck. A lightning dodge, a flick of Zach's wrist, and his bowie was buried to the hilt in Dryfus's throat.

Only after the convulsions ceased did Zach yank the bowie out and wipe the blade clean on the dead man's shirt. Quickly, he cut Chases Rabbits free from the stakes and removed the gag.

Spitting and coughing, Chases Rabbits slowly sat up. "Thank you. Me cannot move much. Arms, legs hurt."

"They had you tied tight," Zach said. "It cut off the circulation."

"The what?"

"The flow of blood." Zach slid the bowie into its sheath. He examined where the sod had been cut out and the hole dug to hide Dryfus. "I bet this was Geist's doing."

Chases Rabbits, rubbing his wrists and grimacing, nodded. "He much clever, that one."

"Only four of them now," Zach said.

"But they have women," Chases Rabbits reminded him. "They have Raven On The Ground."

"Don't worry. I won't do anything to get the love of your life killed."

"They blame me," Chases Rabbits said sadly.

"Who does?"

"Flute Girl and Lavender. Maybe more of my people when hear of this."

"Geist had most everyone fooled. He even had Toad hoodwinked. I'll speak to your people for you, make it clear how two-faced Geist was."

"Him have two faces?"

"It's a white expression. It means a person who smiles at you and acts all friendly while at the same time he's reaching behind you to stab you in the back."

"That Geist," Chases Rabbits agreed.

Zach stood and scanned the prairie. "Where did Dryfus leave his horse?"

"In old buffalo wallow, that way." Chases Rabbits pointed, his lips compressed against the pain. "We go after them right away?"

"We sure as hell do."

# Chapter Twenty-five

"Dryfus should have caught up with us by now." Geist paced and glowered, his hands clasped behind his back, his fingers constantly flexing and unflexing.

"He's damn good with that knife of his," Gratt said.

"From what I heard, so is Zach King." Geist stopped and stared to the west and swore. "Lesson learned. The next time it will be two."

"Why not all four of us?" Berber asked.

"Two will be enough."

"You said that about Dryfus," Berber said.

Geist stopped pacing and turned. "Something on your mind?"

"I'm just saying four is smarter than two."

"Are you saying I'm dumb?"

Gratt glanced at Berber and gave a barely noticeable shake of his head.

"Yes," Berber said. "I am."

"You don't say."

"Don't get me wrong. I'm not bucking to take your place. I'm only saying that if this Zach King is as tough as everyone says, it might take all four of us and not just two."

Geist walked up to Berber and placed a hand on his shoulder. "Maybe you have a point." With his other hand, Geist drew a pistol and slammed it against Berber's temple. Berber staggered, and Geist hit him again, and then a third time. With a groan, Berber collapsed to his knees.

"And maybe if you ever talk back to me again, you're dead as dead can be," Geist said.

"Please," Berber pleaded.

"Please what? Don't hit you again?" Geist hefted the pistol, then jammed it under his belt. "You're right. I need you in fighting shape for Zach King."

"Let me try next," Petrie said.

"Always save the best for last." Geist grinned. "Or next to last." He stepped to where the three Crow maidens lay on their sides, bound fast. "Ladies, I know you can't understand a goddamned word I say, but I want you to know that after we take care of the half-breed, we're going to celebrate by treating ourselves to you. Then we're going to cut your hamstrings so you can't walk and leave you for the wolves and the coyotes to finish off."

Gratt was giving a wobbly Berber a hand up. "What's the next trap going to be?"

"How would I know? I haven't thought it up yet. Depends on the lay of the land." Geist scratched his chin. "It has to be something the half-breed won't expect, like that trick with the sod."

Petrie had a hand to his brow to shield his eyes from the glare of the sun. "I see trees yonder. Could be a stream."

Geist smiled. "Ask and you shall receive."

Zach and Chases Rabbits drew rein well out of rifle range. Zach took the spyglass from his parfleche and swept the belt of vegetation for movement.

"Are them there?"

"I don't see anyone. But it's where I'd try next if I

was him." Zach replaced the telescope and gigged the dun.

"Me much want to kill them," Chases Rabbits said. He had Dryfus's rifle, pistols, and knife. He had also appropriated the man's ammo pouch and powder horn.

"Some folks deserve to die," Zach said.

"Them bad people."

"Whites would call it being our own judge and jury, but this isn't the States."

"Sorry?"

"Whites don't believe in killing bad people outright. They put a bad man on what they call a trial, where one side says how bad he is and another side says he's not as bad as everyone claims. Then a chief decides whether to throw him in an iron cage or hang him."

"Apsaalooke banish bad men."

Zach patted his rifle. "Quick and final is best. Then they can never cause you trouble again."

The trees were a mix of cottonwoods and oaks. In places the brush was thick. A blue ribbon of water flowed as slow as molasses.

Tracks revealed where Geist and the others had stopped to let their horses drink and ridden on.

Chases Rabbits started to climb down.

"Wait," Zach said.

"Something wrong?"

Zach raked his gaze over a patch of brambles. He had the sense that something was amiss, but he couldn't put his finger on it.

"We not take long," Chases Rabbits chafed. "Raven On The Ground need us."

"We won't be any help to her if we're dead." Zach

looked at the brambles again. Few would choose it as a spot to hide, what with all the thorns. The center of the patch was especially dense, which would also discourage anyone from crawling in. Almost too dense, he thought, at the same moment that Blaze growled.

Details came into focus with sharp clarity—a squat form that seemed to be part of the brambles, but wasn't; branches that were going every which way, when most grew straight up or at right angles to the main stems; and the dark eyes that were fixed on him with fierce intensity.

Zach snapped his Hawken up. In the brambles a gun boomed. He felt a searing shock to his shoulder, and then his right arm and fingers went numb. He lost his hold on the rifle. As it fell, he dove from the saddle and clawed at a pistol with his left hand. He heard another shot behind him, and Chases Rabbits cried out. The water rushed up to meet him. He came down hard, but the stream was a wet cushion. He managed to hold the pistol in the air so that it didn't get wet. As he heaved to a knee, he pointed it at the form in the brambles and fired.

A few yards away, Chases Rabbits was thrashing in the stream and turning the water red.

"I've got you now, you stinking half-breed."

Zach whirled.

Berber was on the bank, a smoking pistol in one hand, a cocked pistol in the other. He glanced at the brambles in fury. "You shot him, damn you." Berber took aim. "Now it's your turn." He smiled, and then the top of his forehead exploded in a shower of skin, bone, and flesh, spattering in the stream and on Zach like so much grisly rain.

Hooves pounded, and from behind Berber appeared a giant rider on a black bay, holding a smoking Hawken. He drew rein and stared down at Berber's body and said, "I don't much like it when someone tries to kill my son."

"Pa!" Zach blurted.

Nate King swung down. "Are you hit?"

Zach examined his right shoulder and his arm and shook his head. "I don't appear to be." He snatched his rifle from the stream. A gouge on the stock explained the jolt and the numbness. The ball had struck the rifle instead of him.

"Thank God," Nate said. "I've been riding like the devil to catch up to you."

"You've been following us?"

"Your ma and your wife were worried and sent me to find you," Nate explained. "I came on your trail and have been after you ever since." He paused. "I had a talk with Toad. He told me everything."

"There are only two left. If we ride hard, we can end this before the day is done."

"I should have listened to you. You were right about them. I'm sorry."

"Toad is decent enough." Zach tried to wiggle his fingers, and found that some of the numbness was gone. "I reckon I won't have a problem with him."

"Remember me?" Chases Rabbits asked.

Father and son turned. The young Crow was sitting in waist-deep water. Blood trickled from under his hand, which was pressed to a wound high on his left shoulder.

"Let's get you to dry land and I'll have a look at that," Nate said. He moved around behind Chases Rabbits and carefully helped him to his feet, then held him as they moved to the bank. He had the younger man sit and hunkered down beside him.

Chases Rabbits winced. "Berber shoot me in back."

"It went clean through," Nate said. "The bleeding has almost stopped. You were lucky."

"Me not feel lucky."

Blaze came up and sniffed Nate. The big man looked at him and said, "Will miracles never cease."

Zach went to the brambles. Squatting, he peered in at the man sprawled on his belly. As he'd suspected, it was Gratt. Brambles covered Gratt's clothes and were even in his hair. It must have hurt, all those thorns sticking in him, but it was good camouflage. "Geist's idea, I bet," Zach said to himself.

Chases Rabbits was pale and pasty. "Me not feel so good," he remarked.

"I'll bandage you," Nate said. "In a couple of weeks you'll be good as new."

"No," Chases Rabbits said. "Me never be new again."

# Chapter Twenty-six

From atop a grassy knoll, Geist stared back the way they had come and vented his temper in a fit of lurid swearing. "He can't have gotten them both. They weren't you, but they were capable."

"They should have caught up to us by now," Petrie said.

"I know, I know." Geist glared at the three Crow women on their mounts. Suddenly, without any hint of what he was about to do, he drew a flintlock and shot Lavender in the face. She toppled to the grass, twitched a few times, and went limp.

Raven On The Ground was horror-struck. Flute Girl was too stunned to react.

"That'll give the damn breed something to think about," Geist said.

"Might make him mad."

"Good. When a man's mad, he's more likely to make mistakes." Geist commenced to reload. "Now that it's just the two of us, we need every edge we can get."

Petrie cradled his rifle. "Leave me and go on. I'll pick them off and catch up."

"Them?" Geist said, and swore. "That's right. I forgot about Chases Rabbits. King probably freed him." He shook his head. "But no. I want you by my side. When it comes time, we'll do it together."

"I can hold them so you can get away."

"I said no. You've been with me from the beginning. The rest were hired help, but you're more."

"Together then," Petrie agreed.

Geist shoved the reloaded pistol into place on his hip. He snagged the lead rope to the women's horses and used his heels on his own.

Mile after endless mile of grass and occasional flowers unfolded before them. They passed buffalo wallows and prairie dog towns, and antelope that bounded off in incredible leaps.

Geist hardly noticed. He was thinking of one thing and one thing only—how to kill Zach King. His trick with the sod hadn't worked, and his trick with the brambles hadn't worked. Now he needed a new trick, the best yet, a trick to ensure that Zach King breathed his last.

The terrain changed. Low rolling hills, some eroded into bluffs, were crisscrossed by washes. Stands of trees were plentiful, the grass high and thick.

Geist studied his surroundings with interest. From the top of any of the bluffs, a man could see a good long way. "I'm getting an idea."

Petrie followed his gaze. "Put me up there?" Geist nodded. "Where would you be?"

"Down low with a distraction."

"And the women?"

"They're the distraction. I could shoot them like I did the other one, but once we've disposed of King, we'll want to celebrate."

"I don't do redskins."

"A female is a female."

"Not if she has red skin."

"Didn't you lose your grandfather to some Creeks? Is that why you hate them so much?"

"I hate them because they're different. They look different. They smell different. They think different. They act different. Andy Jackson had it right. Throw them on reservations or exterminate them. When the last red man is gone, I'll give a whoop and a holler."

"That's the most you've talked in a month of Sundays."

"I don't keep track." Petrie looked at him. "We can't let Zach King get the best of us."

"We won't."

Geist went on searching for the ideal spot. They came around a hill and before them was exactly what he was looking for—a bluff with clefts wide enough to hide a grown man. Thick woods fringed the sides, and trees grew in profusion at the top. "Do you see what I see?"

"It's perfect," Petrie agreed.

Geist rode to the base of the bluff and dismounted. The women stared at him apprehensively. It tickled him, having them at his mercy. He inspected the clefts. One had a lip wide enough for him to stand behind and not be seen. "God is on our side," he joked.

"Don't jinx it," Petrie said.

Geist stepped to the horses and grinned up at Raven On The Ground and Flute Girl. "Ladies—and I use the word loosely—it's time you did more than sit there like lumps. I need to distract Zach King and you are made to order." He reached up and hauled Raven On The Ground off and steadied her on her feet. She stood uncertainly, unsure what he wanted.

"I'm going to enjoy this part." Geist chuckled and reached for her dress. She panicked and tried to run, but he was on her before she took more than a couple of steps. She screamed as he hauled her down.

Chases Rabbits simmered with rage and liked it, which surprised him. All Crow children were taught that anger was wrong. For a Crow to give in to it and strike another Crow, or for a parent to strike a child, was considered the worst behavior. So it surprised him that he liked being mad so much. He savored it, as he might savor a kiss from Raven On The Ground. He yearned to count coup on the whites who had taken her, and to redeem himself in her eyes.

Then they came upon the unthinkable.

Nate King was in the lead, tracking. Drawing quick rein, he said, "Dear God, no."

Zach was next. His countenance conveyed what his silence did not.

Blaze stopped and sniffed.

Chases Rabbits was almost on top of the sprawled body before he saw it. That it was a woman was obvious. It wasn't big enough to be Flute Girl. It had to be one of the other two.

"No!" Chases Rabbits cried. Vaulting down, he rolled the body over. "Lavender," he said, relieved.

"They shot her in the face," Nate said. "Must have been near point-blank range. Look at the powder burns."

Chases Rabbits didn't care about that. All he cared about was that it wasn't Raven On The Ground. He felt guilty for being so glad. "Why they kill her?"

"Their kind don't need an excuse," Zach said. "Maybe it's to get back at us for Dryfus, Gratt, and Berber."

A new fear coursed through Chases Rabbits. "Maybe they kill Raven On The Ground, too."

"They haven't yet," Nate said, "or we'd have come across her body."

"We must hurry," Chases Rabbits urged, and was on his pinto and trotting to the east. The Kings came up on either side.

"Better slow down," Zach warned. "This could be just what they want."

"For us to rush after them into their gun sights," Nate added.

"Me not care," Chases Rabbits declared.

"You should if you love her. We're her only hope."

Every fiber of his being screamed for him to ride like the wind, but Chases Rabbits slowed the pinto to a walk. "There. Happy?"

"Don't take it out on us," Zach said. "We didn't steal your one and only."

Chases Rabbits had not sulked since he was small, but he sulked now. He couldn't bear the thought of losing her.

A series of hills appeared, broken by bluffs and patches of woods. They spooked a few deer, but Chases Rabbits hardly noticed. In his mind, he saw only Raven On The Ground's face, floating in the air and beckoning him to hurry. "Me kill Geist for this," he vowed.

"You'll have to get in line," Zach said.

Chases Rabbits refused to be denied his coup. "Him not take your woman. Him take mine."

"We all have a stake in this," Nate said. "The mountains are our home. Anyone who poses a danger to one of us is a threat to all."

Chases Rabbits had to think for the right word. "This personal."

"I get the chance, he's dead," Zach said.

A bluff reared ahead, its face split by cracks.

Nate reined up. "Do you see what I see?"

"What?" Chases Rabbits asked.

Zach produced his spyglass. He trained it on the bluff, and swore.

"What?" Chases Rabbits said a second time.

"Take a gander," Zach said, handing him the brass tube. "But keep hold of yourself."

"What you mean?" Chases Rabbits asked, and pressed the spyglass to his eye.

"Turn it a bit if you can't see clearly."

Chases Rabbits saw a blur. He fiddled with the end, and the bluff came into focus. So did the two figures wedged into cracks, their long hair loose and spilling over their shoulders. It was Raven On The Ground and Flute Girl. They were bound and naked.

# Chapter Twenty-seven

Zach was reaching for the spyglass when Chases Rabbit let out a war whoop and slapped it against the pinto. "Don't!" Zach cried.

Pumping his rifle in the air and yipping, Chases Rabbits charged toward the bluff.

"Consarn it. He'll get us all killed." Nate charged after him.

Zach slapped his legs and reined to the right, then to the left. High on the bluff, a rifle boomed and a leaden wasp buzzed his ear, missing by a whisker's width. Bending, he lashed the reins. Out of the corner of his eye, he glimpsed his father swing on the offside of the bay. He did likewise on the dun.

Chases Rabbits, though, continued to charge straight ahead and was almost to the bluff when a blast from a cleft sent him catapulting backward over the pinto's rump.

Zach let go of the reins and dropped. He was in waist-high grass and hidden from the shooter in the cleft, if not from the rifleman on the bluff. As if to confirm it, a shot cracked from up high and dirt kicked into the air a few inches from his face. He crabbed into thicker grass. The shooter in the cleft must have spotted him, because another shot clipped stems close to his head. He heard his pa's bay galloping around the bluff, and figured his pa was going after the rifleman.

A low groan fluttered on the breeze. It had to be

Chases Rabbits, but there was nothing Zach could do for him until he dealt with the killers. Wisps of gun smoke told him which cleft the shooter was in, and when a shadow moved, Zach reared up and fired. The shadow pulled back.

Zach reloaded. Whoever was on top of the bluff had stopped shooting at him, no doubt to deal with his pa. He fought down a bout of worry. His pa could take care of himself.

"You hear me out there, boy?" Geist yelled.

The man did love to talk, Zach thought, as he tamped the patch and ball down the barrel with the ramrod.

"No need to answer. The important thing is that you listen."

Zach wondered how Geist had lasted so long, with the mistakes he made.

"I want you to stand up where I can see you, with your hands in the air."

Zach almost laughed.

"If you don't, your friend's sweetheart dies. I planted a keg of black powder at her feet. All I have to do is light the fuse, and she's a goner."

Zach didn't recall seeing any kegs of black powder at the mercantile—but there could have been.

"I'll count to five, boy, and then it's all over for her," Geist hollered.

Zach slid the ramrod into its housing and took aim at the cleft Geist was in.

"One."

Both Raven On The Ground and Flute Girl appeared to be unconscious.

"Two."

Zach debated firing even though he couldn't see him. The slug might ricochet and score.

"Three."

Zach coiled his legs under him but didn't show himself.

"I thought you liked that simpleton," Geist said. "Or is it that the squaw means nothing to you?" He paused. "Four."

Zach's every instinct was to stay put. Instead, he laid the Hawken on the ground and rose with his arms overhead. "Don't kill her."

From the cleft came a cackle. Geist stepped out, a burning lucifer in one hand, a pistol in the other. "Well, now. I honestly thought you'd let me do it." He blew on the lucifer. "Tell me true. Dryfus, Gratt, and Berber, are they dead?"

"Dead as dead can be."

"Damn, you are a hellion. Any last words before I squeeze the trigger?"

"The war party will be here soon," Zach said, and took a step.

"What are you talking about?" Geist peered past Zach to the west. "What war party?"

"About a dozen Crows." Zach took another step. "They showed up at the mercantile as I was heading out. We split up to cover more ground, but they were bound to have heard the shots."

"You're lying."

"Suit yourself. But I sure wouldn't want to be in your boots when they get their hands on you." Again Zach edged forward.

"I have the squaws."

"You disgraced those girls. The warriors might figure they're better off dead." Zach advanced another stride. He was close enough; he might take a slug, but he mustn't let it stop him.

"I hate those damn Crows almost as much as I

hate you. Their women aren't the whores I thought they were."

"You made the same mistake a lot of whites do," Zach said, and took another step for good measure. "You think Indians are inferior. You think they're animals. That they're nothing but savages. But most of them are smart, and decent human beings."

"Don't lecture me, boy," Geist snapped. He was still scouring the terrain to the west for any sign of the war party.

"People are people. They might dress different, and talk different, and eat different, but that doesn't make them less than you."

"I said no lectures!"

"How about I just kill you," Zach said, and sprang. Geist thrust his flintlock out to shoot, but Zach swatted it. The gun went off, but the barrel was pointing down. Zach got hold of Geist's wrist. Geist cursed and punched Zach on the chin. It hurt, but Zach stayed on his feet and slugged back.

There was a flash and puff of smoke, followed by a loud hiss.

Zach glanced down. Geist hadn't been lying; there was a fuse, and it had somehow ignited. Sparks and smoke were rippling along it toward Raven On The Ground. At her feet was a small keg with the other end of the fuse attached. Zach let go and turned to try to stomp the fuse out, but Geist slammed the spent pistol against his temple while flinging out a leg and tripping him. Zach fell to his knees. Before he could rise, Geist was behind him, his boots on either side, the pistol against his throat. Zach's breath was choked off as Geist, holding the pistol in both hands, sought to throttle the life from him.

Zach pried at the flintlock. He tore at Geist's

hands, but they were vises. All the while, the fuse crackled and hissed, and the sparks were that much closer to Raven On The Ground.

Out of nowhere, a four-legged form appeared. Snarling and biting, Blaze tore at Geist's leg.

The pressure on Zach's throat eased as Geist twisted to confront the new threat.

Zach swooped his hand to his hip and drew his bowie. He cleared the sheath and drove the tip down into Geist's boot and was rewarded with a shriek. He streaked his other hand to his waist and jerked a pistol even as he twisted around. Geist's head was thrown back, his mouth wide open in a howl. Zach rammed the muzzle of the pistol between Geist's teeth and fired. The top of Geist's head spewed hair and brain matter.

Whirling, Zach scrambled toward the sputtering fuse. It was barely a foot from the keg. He slashed with his bowie, but cut the fuse behind the sparks, not in front of them. The fuse was still burning. He threw himself forward and arced the big knife down. The sparks finally fizzled, scarcely inches from disaster.

Winded, and every muscle aching, Zach leaned against the bluff. The wolf's nose touched his cheek, and it licked his neck. "Blaze," he said softly.

High above, someone screamed.

The horses were hidden on the far side of the bluff. Near them was a game trail to the top.

Nate King drew rein and was off his bay while it was still in motion. He raced up the slope, dreadfully aware that every second of delay increased the chances of his son being slain. He wasn't concerned for himself, only for Zach. He pumped his legs like steam engine pistons and flew over the top with his Hawken to his shoulder, but there was no one to shoot—he saw grass and brush and a few boulders, but that was all.

Nate took several more steps. Metal glinted beside a boulder, and he flattened as a rifle went off. He felt a tug on the whangs of his buckskins. Rolling, he came up next to the boulder, and next to Petrie, who had dropped his rifle and was grabbing for his pistols. Nate rammed the Hawken's stock into Petrie's gut. That would double most men over, but all Petrie did was grunt and take a step back. There wasn't space for Nate to level his rifle, so he swung it at Petrie's legs. With a nimble bound, Petrie leaped up and over while simultaneously unlimbering his flintlocks. Nate threw the Hawken at Petrie's face, but Petrie ducked under it. Nate lunged and tackled him. They grappled and rolled. Nate was a lot bigger, but Petrie was solid muscle. Suddenly Petrie had a hand free. He pointed a pistol at Nate's face and fired. Nate jerked his head aside, barely dodging the bullet. The blast sent pain up his ear, and his hearing dimmed. Petrie clubbed him and his vision swam. They rolled to a stop with Petrie on top.

Nate's head cleared. His right hand closed around the handle of his tomahawk. He jabbed a finger at Petrie's eye, but the man shifted and the finger missed. Petrie was focused on avoiding the jab, as he had intended, and Nate took advantage of Petrie's distraction to sweep the tomahawk up and around. The edge bit into Petrie's head behind the ear and cleaved skin and flesh and bone as a knife would cleave wax. Blood spurted. Petrie stiffened and screamed like a stricken bobcat, a high, piercing cry of denial and disbelief, and then his body collapsed atop Nate's.

Nate pushed the body off. He slowly rose, his side sore, his shoulder throbbing. He moved to the edge and gazed down at his son, who was gazing up. "Are you all right?"

"Fine, Pa. Blaze saved me. You?"

"As soon as I get my tomahawk out of his head, I'll be right down."

# Chapter Twenty-eight

Half a moon had passed.

Chases Rabbits lay on a buffalo robe, his head and shoulder bandaged, and gazed forlornly at the smoke rising through the hole at the top of the lodge. The flap was open so anyone could enter, and someone did.

Other than a few fading bruises on her face and neck, Raven On The Ground showed no sign of the ordeal they had been through. She came and knelt beside him, placing her hand on his arm. "How do you feel?"

"I heal slowly."

"Maybe because you think that you do not have a reason to heal fast."

"I have disgraced myself in the eyes of our people," Chases Rabbits said. "When I am up and about, they will shun me."

"You are mistaken."

"Two women died because of me."

"The whites with no hearts killed them, not you."

"They made a fool of me."

"They fooled Grizzly Killer and Stalking Coyote, too. But now they are dead, and the trading post is still there. The man they call Toad has sent word that he still wants to trade with us."

"Toad has a good heart."

"So do you." Raven On The Ground clasped his

hand. "The council has decided. They would like for you to be the mouth of the Apsaalooke."

"After the shame I have brought?"

"Grizzly Killer has talked to Long Hair and the others. He has told them how even though you had been shot, you tried to save Flute Girl and me. He says you have as much courage as anyone."

"Grizzly Killer is a good friend."

"Your shame is only in your own head. The rest of us forgive you. You must forgive yourself. You can start by taking a wife."

Chases Rabbits started to rise, and winced. "You would want a man like me?"

"I want no other." Raven On The Ground grasped both of his hands and held them to her bosom. "What do you say? Will you take me as your wife, or do I need to seek a husband elsewhere?"

"Here is good," Chases Rabbits said.

## EDEN'S PRISONER

"No!" Nate wanted to roar but couldn't. The thing's fingers were over his mouth.

Suddenly, he was moving. The creatures were carrying him as effortlessly as he might a rag doll. The feel of their skin on his was like dry leather, and hot breath fanned his throat. He made one more try to cast them off, a Herculean heave that would have thrown them from him if they were human. But they weren't, and it didn't.

He was captive of the Se-at-co.

# WILDERNESS #66:
## *GARDEN OF EDEN*

# David
# Thompson

Dorchester
Publishing

*Dedicated to Judy, Joshua and Shane.*

DORCHESTER PUBLISHING

Published by

Dorchester Publishing Co., Inc.
200 Madison Avenue
New York, NY 10016

ISBN 13: 978-1-4285-1153-8 (Trade Double Edition)
E-ISBN: 978-1-4285-0978-8

First Dorchester Publishing, Co., Inc. edition: September 2011

Visit us online at www.dorchesterpub.com.

# Chapter One

The old man came out of his cabin and squinted at the bright sun high in the afternoon sky. He sighed and turned to regard the cabin one last time. Then he stepped to the horses tied to the top rail of the small corral. His shoulders were hunched and he moved stooped over. The buckskins he wore were loose and baggy on his spare frame.

"I will miss this place," he said to his sorrel. Grunting, he climbed on and snagged the rope to his pack animal. Cradling his rifle, he headed down the valley, following the stream he knew so well.

Methuselah was his name. His mother picked it from the Bible. His eyes were a pale blue, his skin as tough as rawhide and almost the same color.

Reaching into his possibles bag, Methuselah pulled out a plug and bit off a chaw. Chomping methodically, he softened and loosened the tobacco to where he could spit.

The long, winding valley was so far from anywhere that Methuselah was the only white man who had ever set foot in it. To his knowledge, no red men had, either. Others were there when he had discovered the way in, but they weren't white and they weren't red. They weren't like any men anywhere.

Methuselah raised his face and let the sun warm

him. He was cold a lot these days, even in the heat of the summer. Yet another reason he was leaving. There was something he would like to do before an eternal cold claimed him.

The valley had been his home for so long, it was part of him. He had never loved any place so much. He regretted having to leave, but there it was.

Methuselah's gaze roved to the virgin forest and the towering peaks that seemed to reach to the moon. The highest peak, to the west, had always made him think of a bird's beak. He was almost to the east end of the valley when he became aware of movement in the trees. He showed no alarm. Instead, he drew rein and called out, "I have to do this."

The high grass rustled on all sides.

"I'm sorry," Methuselah said. "I would stay if I could. But none of us live forever."

Stems parted and eyes were fixed on him. Peculiar eyes, yellow-green and slanted, they possessed an almost inhuman intensity.

"That you?" Methuselah said, and added a name that no human ear other than his had heard and no white mouth other than his had ever uttered. "Show yourself."

The eyes stayed where they were.

"I thought we were past this."

The eyes blinked. It was a slow, almost languid blink, like what a big cat might do. But this was no cat.

"You can at least shake my hand," Methuselah said. "I've taught you that much."

The grass was motionless.

"I've explained why this has to be. Why act so contrary when we've been friends for so long?"

The grass rippled and one of them scuttled toward him, growling.

"Consarn it!" Methuselah cried. He slapped his heels against the sorrel and gave a sharp tug on the lead rope.

He tried not to dwell on the consequences if they caught him. He knew how they were. He used his heels again, with vigor.

All around him the grass moved. Methuselah glimpsed his pursuers. How they could run like that was beyond his fathoming. In so many ways, they were different from everyone and everything.

One of them lunged at the packhorse, but the horse was moving too fast.

Methuselah tucked low and rode for his life. The valley narrowed. Ahead was a cliff, a seemingly solid wall of rock too sheer to climb. He made straight for it.

From out of the grass in front of him rose another.

A sharp tug on the reins and Methuselah shot by. He braced for the impact of its body on his back, but it didn't pounce. Then he was at the cliff and to all appearances about to smash into it.

The cliff face swallowed him and the two horses, and the thunder of hooves faded. Behind him the grass stopped moving. The figure that had barred his path melted away.

Methuselah burst out the other side of the notch. He went a short distance and reined up and wheeled the sorrel. On this side was another cliff as sheer as the other. "Why?" he said to the unresponsive stone. "Why did you have to go and do that?"

A great sadness fell over Methuselah as he turned down the mountain. It was a mile before the sorrow left him and he smiled slightly and said, "Look out, world. Here I come."

# Chapter Two

King Valley lived up to its name. Sculpted as if by an artist, it had everything a frontiersman could ask for. A lake and the mountain streams that fed it provided plenty of water.

Grass for grazing covered much of the valley floor. A variety of thick timber grew on the facing slopes. Game was abundant—so much so, it was rare for any of the valley's inhabitants to spend more than a few hours hunting. Fish and water fowl thrived.

Shakespeare McNair had never beheld a valley so grand, and he was the oldest living white man in the Rocky Mountains. He had come West before the fur trappers, drawn by an indefinable urge to explore the vast unknown. Now, decades later, he had seen most everything the mountains had to offer, and he was as versed in the ways of the wilderness as any man alive.

On this particular sunny morning, Shakespeare was strolling along the lake with his Hawken in the crook of his elbow. As ever, he was clad in buckskins, with an ammo pouch, a powder horn, and his possibles bag crisscrossing his chest. A pair of pistols was tucked under his leather belt, a Green River knife sheathed at his waist.

Every now and again Shakespeare felt a twinge of pain in his left hip, but he ignored it and concentrated on the beauty of the day. He breathed deep of the breeze that stirred his long beard. Both the beard and his hair were as white as the snow that capped several of the mile-high peaks.

A fish leaped and splashed down. Ducks quacked and a goose honked. To the south a bald eagle soared, to the north a pair of ravens. A doe and her young ones grazed at the edge of the woodland and higher up an elk bugled.

"The wonder of it all," Shakespeare said to the world at large. He touched a hand to his hip. Then he noticed someone ahead and his mouth quirked in a grin.

Nate King wore the same style of buckskins and was similarly armed, but his hair and beard were a deep black. At the moment he was pacing back and forth and muttering and angrily gesturing.

"This is too rich for words," Shakespeare said. Raising his voice, he called, "How now, Horatio? What bodes this unseemly behavior?"

Nate paused in his pacing and glared and said, "Go away."

Placing a hand to his chest as if stricken, Shakespeare teased, "Is that any way to greet your best friend and the man who taught you everything you know? Crows and daws, sir. Crows and daws."

"You won't believe it," Nate said. "You just won't believe it." He resumed his pacing and muttering.

Shakespeare regarded the King cabin, situated west of his along the lake. "Methinks I detect the whiff of female."

"You think you know someone and then they go and do something like this."

"Care to share, Horatio, or should I guess from now until Armageddon?"

Nate stopped. "How many times have I told you to stop calling me that?"

"At least a million."

"You listen as good as she does."

"Aha. Then I was right. What has the beauteous Mrs. King done to put you in such a dither?"

"She wants to have a baby."

Shakespeare was genuinely shocked. Nate and his Shoshone wife, Winona, had two grown children. The oldest, Zach, was married to a woman named Louisa, who was in the family way. "At your age?"

Nate gestured at the cabin. "That's exactly what I said to her. All it did was make her mad."

"Spill, son," Shakespeare said.

Taking several deep breaths, Nate leaned on his rifle. "We were having breakfast. The subject of Lou came up, and how she was doing, and Winona put down her spoon and looked at me and said she had been thinking about having another baby herself."

"Good Lord."

"You could have floored me with a feather. I thought she was joking, so I said that at her age she might as well go and wrestle a grizzly because that's how much fun it would be."

"You didn't."

"And she got mad."

"Imagine that."

Nate took up his pacing once more. "If I live to be a thousand, I will never savvy women."

"You and the rest of the male gender. Maybe it's a mood," Shakespeare suggested. "Women have them in droves."

"Whatever it is, we're not having another baby and that's final."

"Uh-oh," Shakespeare said.

"What?"

"You didn't tell her that, did you?"

"No. Why?"

"Never tell a female anything is final, or she will take it into her head to prove to you it's not."

"Then what do I do? I'm too old for changing diapers and burping."

"Oh, hell," Shakespeare said. "You're barely half as old as me. But that aside, I happen to agree. Winona will, too, once she has time to think about it. My advice is to not bring it up again and wait for her mood to pass."

"I hope you're right."

"Do you see these white hairs? I'm always right."

Nate chuckled and gazed out over the lake. "All right. I'll take your advice. And it's nice to see you in a good mood of your own for once."

"How's that, Horatio?"

"You've been a bit of a grump lately. Even your wife says so. Blue Water Woman was over visiting Winona yesterday and said as how you wake up grumpy and spend the rest of the day becoming grumpier."

"She did, did she?" Shakespeare said, flustered, and launched into a quote. "She's the kitchen wench, and all grease, and I know not what use to put her to but to make a lamp of her."

"I won't tell her you said that."

"I tell her myself," Shakespeare declared. "Grumpy, indeed. If she was as old as me, she'd start the day in the same frame of mind."

"That again," Nate said.

"Excuse me?"

"You've been going on for a while now about how old you are and it's becoming tiresome."

"*Excuse me?*" Shakespeare said with more emphasis.

"So what if you have white hair? So what if you're past eighty?"

"When your joints creak and your muscles are always stiff and sore and you can't hardly get out of bed in the morning, then you can talk to me about age. Until then you will kindly grant me some consideration."

"You still get around better than most," Nate mentioned. "You're as spry as a kitten and as randy as a goat. Blue Water Woman said that, too."

"A pox on all women." Shakespeare would have gone on berating the fairer sex, but just then a rider leading a packhorse came out of the forest. "I do declare, Horatio. It appears we have company calling."

Nate turned and his eyebrows arched in surprise. "What in the world? He looks just like you."

# Chapter Three

The three Numa had come a long way. They would not have come so far were it not for the horse. They were not rich in horses as were some of the other tribes, so when the Appaloosa ran off, Yahuskin went after it. He would take as long as necessary to find it and bring it back. He was the first of his people to own one of the magnificent mounts bred by the Nez Perce. He valued it more than anything.

For fourteen sleeps, the three warriors followed the Appaloosa ever deeper into unknown country. Esa was the best tracker in the band, which was why Yahuskin asked for his help. Kiduto was a fierce fighter, which was why Yahuskin asked him to join them.

Twice they lost the trail, and Esa had to backtrack. Each time he found it again.

The delays ate at Yahuskin. He constantly worried that a mountain lion or a bear or wolves would feast on his prized possession, and he constantly urged his companions to greater haste.

On the fifteenth day, after Esa had again briefly lost the sign and picked it up again, Yahuskin grunted in exasperation.

"The winter snows will fall before we find my horse," he complained.

Esa was on a knee examining a hoof print. "You are welcome to do the tracking if you want."

"No," Yahuskin replied. "I could not do it as well as you."

"Then I do not care to hear about the winter snows," Esa said. He was doing his best and resented the criticism.

"I am anxious to find him," Yahuskin said.

The other two already knew that all too well. They looked at each other and Kiduto, who did not speak a lot, spoke now.

"We have been after your horse a long time. If we do not find him soon, I must turn back."

"You would abandon us?" Yahuskin said.

"I did not expect to be away this long," Kiduto said. "My wife and children will worry."

"I, too, did not think it would take this long," Esa echoed.

Yahuskin would have no choice but to go with them should they head back. He couldn't do it alone. "I am grateful both of you have stayed as long as you have."

"I like to see new country," Kiduto said.

"Or old country," Esa said as he rose, and when they looked at him questioningly, he encompassed the high peaks and timbered slopes with a wave of his arm. "Have you forgotten? Do you not know where we are?"

"Far from our own land," Kiduto said.

Yahuskin gazed out over the vast expanse of wilderness that stretched to the horizon in all directions. A nearby peak caught his eye. It was shaped like the beak of bird of prey. His memory stirred, and he blurted, "No."

"Yes," Esa said.

"Yes what?" Kiduto demanded.

Esa pointed at the peak. "Did you not hear of Eagle's Beak and the old times?"

They fell silent. All the Numa had heard the tales. Mothers imparted them to their children, and the storytellers told them at gatherings. Tales of the time when the earth was different, when there were creatures alive that were not alive now.

"The Si-Te-Cah," Yahuskin said, and involuntarily shuddered.

"The People Eaters," Esa said.

Kiduto made a sound of mild contempt. "The story scared me when I was a boy, but now I am a man. I have put the fears of a child aside."

"It is said the Si-Te-Cah were not like us," Esa said. "They did not think like we do or look like we do or move like we do. It is said they were the last of the old ones and that instead of eating animals, they ate the Numa."

"That was more winters ago than anyone can remember," Kiduto mentioned. "And they were long since destroyed."

The tale related around the village fires was a testament to Numa bravery. The Si-Te-Cah had preyed on the Numa as the Numa preyed on deer and buffalo. They dug pits and covered the holes with branches and leaves. A grisly fate awaited the unwary Numas who fell into them and were taken captive. They were eaten alive. For many winters this went on, until the Numa couldn't take it any longer.

They rose and waged a great war that ended with the extermination of their inhuman enemies.

It was whispered, though, that a few of the Si-Te-Cah escaped. That they went off into the country around Eagle's Beak and lived there to this day. Mothers warned their children that if they strayed off into the forest, they ran the risk of being snatched by a Si-Te-Cah and eaten. Few children strayed.

Now, staring worriedly at Eagle's Beak, Yahuskin remembered it all, and suppressed another shudder. "The old stories do not scare me, either."

"We will keep after the Appaloosa, then," Kiduto said.

Yahuskin couldn't help noting that soon they would be in Eagle Beak's shadow.

# Chapter Four

As the newcomer neared the lake, Nate saw that he had been mistaken. The rider had white hair like McNair, but there the resemblance ended. Shakespeare was well muscled and had a vitality about him; the rider was thin as a rail and so pale as to seem ill. Shakespeare had a lot of wrinkles, but amazingly, the rider had more. The rider's buckskins were so worn and faded they looked fit to fall apart at the seams if he stretched.

"He looks old enough to be your pa," Nate joked.

Shakespeare began to laugh, then gave a start. "My word. It can't be, but it is. Methuselah Jones!"

"Who?"

"He was here when I showed up. I thought he was dead."

"By here you mean the mountains?"

Shakespeare nodded.

"I thought you were the very first."

"Methuselah, there, might have that honor. He was living with the Piegans when I met him."

Now it was Nate who was startled. "The Piegans? They're part of the Blackfoot Confederacy. I thought they hated whites."

"Not until Lewis and Clark came along and killed

a Blackfoot." Shakespeare smiled and held up a hand. "Methuselah, as I live and breathe."

The rider wearily drew rein. He looked at McNair and blinked in surprise. "Can it really be? After all this time? Pudgy McNair?"

"Pudgy?" Nate said.

Shakespeare looked as if he had swallowed a lemon. "I was stouter back then. It was my nickname before I took up the Bard."

*"Pudgy?"*

"Hush."

"I figured you to be long gone under," Methuselah said. "Who's this man-mountain beside you?"

"Meet Nate King. Could be you've heard of him or his son, Zach. They're getting right on to famous in these parts."

Nate inwardly flinched. It was Zach who was more well known—for killing white men who were selling guns to the Indians to stir up a war, and for being taken into custody by the army and being put on trial.

"Can't say as I have, no." Methuselah scanned the lake shore and frowned. "Never expected to come on so much civilization this far in. Four cabins, and what is that at the east end of the lake? A lodge?"

"We are as far in as anyone has come," Shakespeare said. "And yes, it's some Nansusequas." He motioned. "Why don't you light and sit a spell? My missus will fix us something to eat if you're hungry."

Methuselah put a hand to the small of his back and arched his spine. "I reckon I could use some rest, at that. I've been riding for pretty near a week now." He stiffly dismounted and let the sorrel's reins dangle. "A missus, you say? Anyone I know?" he jokingly asked.

"Blue Water Woman."

Nate didn't know what to make of Jones's reaction: Methuselah stiffened and his face clouded and his wrinkles became crags.

"You don't say."

"I truly do. And I've never been happier. How about you? Do you have a woman somewhere?"

"No," Methuselah said in a small voice. "My last was pretty near forty years ago. I lost interest about the time I turned sixty."

"My God," Nate said. "Are you saying you're pushing one hundred years old?"

"A hundred and one, to be exact," Methuselah responded. "Why do you look so flabbergasted? People live to my age all the time."

"Not out here," Nate said.

Methuselah pursed his lips. "True. The wilds are a scythe that cuts us down with no mercy. I've lasted as long as I have because I've been luckier than most."

"Where have you been keeping yourself?" Shakespeare asked. "How is it I haven't come across you in a coon's age?"

"I got tired of people, of their petty ways, of no one able to get along. I got tired of the killing between red and white. So I went off into the mountains, farther than anyone has ever been, and I found me the Garden of Eden."

"I thought that was on the other side of the world," Nate said, grinning.

"I'm serious, boy. I found a valley where no one

else had ever been. A valley just like it was back at the dawn of creation. A valley like the good Lord intended things to be."

Methuselah smiled with the recollection. "The water so clean and pure. The animals so tame you can practically walk up and touch them. Trees that never knew an axe. Grass that was never trampled by the hoof of a horse. It's the most beautiful spot on earth."

"That's where you've been all this time?" Shakespeare asked.

Methuselah nodded. "I'd still be there except my time is short, and I'm heading back to the States to look up my sister and my brother. I'd like to see them one more time before I pass on to my reward. If they're still alive."

"Are you sickly?" Nate said.

"Whether I am or I ain't, it's personal and none of your business."

"I didn't mean to pry."

"That's all right," Methuselah said, but he sounded as if it wasn't. He grinned crookedly at McNair. "How about you reacquaint me with the prettiest gal ever born?"

"She'll be pleased to see you," Shakespeare said. "Horatio, you can come along, too."

Methuselah took hold of the reins and the lead rope to his packhorse. "Lead the way."

Nate fell into step behind them. Their visitor was too easily irritated to suit him, but any friend of McNair's was always welcome.

"Tell me more about this valley," Shakespeare prompted. "I'd like to set eyes on it myself."

"I already told you. It's the Garden of Eden all over

again. And I'm not sharing where it is with another living soul."

"I thought we were friends."

"We knew each other fairly well," Methuselah said. "Did some trapping together, went on buffalo hunts, shot that griz that attacked our horses."

"Those were good days," Shakespeare said. "I miss the trapping. It was a shame when the beaver trade dried up."

"A shame, hell. The fur companies about wiped the beaver out. For a while there you couldn't find a bucktooth anywhere. Then I stumbled on Eden."

"There are beaver there?"

Methuselah beamed. "So many, it reminds you of the old days. Big ones, like they were before the trapping."

"God, I'd love to see that," Shakespeare said.

Nate would have, too. The beaver had returned to many of the waterways, but it wasn't the way it had been.

"You'd think you had died and gone to heaven," Methuselah said. "Everything is bigger, not just the beaver. The deer. The elk. The grouse. You name it."

Nate wondered how much of this was true and how much was tall tale. The old trappers were notorious for exaggerating.

"How is it I missed it in all my wandering?" Shakespeare asked.

"It's hidden behind a cliff and ringed by mountains so high they touch the sky," Methuselah claimed. "There's only one way in or out. It was a fluke I discovered it. I was hunting a buck and saw it walk into the cliff and got curious."

"You could draw me a map."

Methuselah started to answer, but just then they neared McNair's cabin. The front door opened and out came McNair's wife. A Flathead by birth, she wore her long hair loose and had on a beaded doe hide dress.

Blue Water Woman was one of the kindest, sweetest women Nate knew, which was why he was taken aback when she glared and said, "I should stick you with my knife."

# Chapter Five

The meadow was lush with grass and wildflowers. A stream gleamed blue in the bright sunlight.

The three Numas drew rein and stared out over it.

"The tracks are fresh," Esa said. "The Appaloosa must be near."

Yahuskin hoped so. His companions had talked more and more of returning to their village. He could not keep them at the search much longer. They had already come farther than any Numa in more winters than any of them could recall.

Kiduto craned his neck back and bobbed his chin at Eagle's Peak, which reared high above. "This will be something to tell our people about. No one has been this close since the old times."

Esa started across the meadow but drew rein again. "Flies," he said.

"What did you say?" Yahuskin thought he had misheard.

"Flies," Esa repeated, and pointed.

A small cloud of black insects rose above the middle of the meadow. Whatever they were hovering over was hidden by the high grass.

Yahuskin poked his mount with his heels. A disturbing feeling had come over him. He passed Esa and straightened to try and see better.

Suddenly a larger black shape rose into the air, dispersing many of the flies. Flapping its long wings, a vulture gained altitude in ever-widening spirals. After it came another and then a third.

Yahuskin's dread worsened. The stench hit him and he nearly gagged. He had to hold his breath. His horse stopped and shied, but he goaded it on. When his lungs began to hurt, he took a single shallow gulp of air through his mouth and held it again.

Yahuskin's mount whinnied and came to another stop and wouldn't go on. He didn't force it. One look was enough to confirm his dread.

A pool of dry black blood covered a wide area. Here and there lay bones stripped white. Other pieces still had flesh that crawled with maggots and more flies. The legs had been ripped off, the belly disemboweled. The neck and the head were mostly intact. The eyeballs were gone, and the soft tissue of the nose had been eaten, but that was all.

"Your Appaloosa," Esa said.

Yahuskin could scarcely stand to look. He had traded a rifle and furs and a new steel knife and more for the animal that lay in bits and parts.

"I would guess a bear," Kiduto said.

Yahuskin thought so, too. The big cats didn't tear their prey apart, and wolves ate the neck and the head as well as the rest.

Esa slid down. He walked in a circle around the head, the dry blood crunching under his moccasins. Abruptly stopping, he squatted and bent low, studying the ground.

"What have you found?" Kiduto asked.

"Tracks."

"Was it a bear?"

"No," Esa said.

"What, then?" Yahuskin asked. Not that it mattered. His prized possession was gone and it would take him half a dozen winters to acquire enough to trade for another.

"I do not know."

Yahuskin and Kiduto glanced at each other and Kiduto said, "You know every track there is."

"I do not know these."

Yahuskin dismounted and walked around the head. The empty eye sockets compounded his dismay.

A sharp exclamation burst from Kiduto. Hunkering, he touched the impression in the blood. "I have never seen anything like them."

Neither had Yahuskin. Something had stepped in the blood when it was set and left two clear tracks. "What can have made these?"

Kiduto placed his foot next to one of the tracks. "It is like ours and yet it is not."

Esa stood and roved from piece to piece. "Here is another. And another. There was more than one. I would guess five or six."

Yahuskin avoided a loop of intestine. The coil bore marks that suggested the teeth of the biter were razor sharp. The belly, too, bore bite marks, as well as a red print on the hide. "Do you see?" he said in consternation.

Esa and Kiduto came to either side. Esa couldn't hide his shock. Kiduto pressed his hand to the belly alongside the print.

"Longer than ours," Yahuskin said.

"No bear ever left a paw print like that," Esa said.

"What can it have been?" Yahuskin wondered, although deep down he had a suspicion he refused to accept.

"The Si-Te-Cah," Kiduto said, and laughed.

"Perhaps so," Esa said.

Kiduto looked at him as if expecting him to laugh or smile. "You are not serious?"

"These tracks are unlike any others," Esa said. "The creatures that made them walked on two legs and then again on four. What animal does that other than bears? Yet these are plainly not bear tracks."

"People made them," Kiduto said. "Maybe not people like us but they have hands and feet."

"Hands and feet different from any others," Esa said.

"They look human enough for me," Kiduto insisted.

Esa turned to Yahuskin. "We should leave. Whatever these things were, they might come back."

All three of them glanced at the sun to see how much daylight was left.

It was halfway below the horizon.

# Chapter Six

Shakespeare was momentarily speechless. He assumed his wife was speaking to him, and for the life of him, he couldn't think of anything he had done to raise her ire. "Did I leave my dirty socks lying on the floor again?"

"Blue Water Woman," Methuselah said, and smiled warmly.

"Jones," she said.

"This is a pleasure. I never thought to set eyes on you again."

"Life plays tricks on us."

Shakespeare was glad she had stopped glaring. Clapping their visitor on the back, he declared, "Can you imagine him showing up after all these years?"

"Imagine," Blue Water Woman said.

Methuselah spread his arms. "Do I get a hug?"

"No."

Shakespeare laughed. "She's not much for affection in front of others. She only ever hugs me behind closed doors."

"Lucky you," Methuselah said.

"I invited him in," Shakespeare informed her. "I hope you don't mind. Figured we could talk over old times."

"Some old times are best forgotten," Blue Water Woman said.

Turning to Nate, Shakespeare poked him with an elbow and whispered, "See what I mean about females and their moods?" To his wife he said, "As for you, woman, I will quote the Bard. Eat my leek!"

"Your what?" Methuselah said.

"He recites William S., as he calls him, every chance he gets," Nate explained.

Blue Water Woman stepped aside. As Shakespeare went past she lightly punched him on the arm and he stopped.

"What was that for, wench?"

"Eat your own leek."

"I don't even know what a leek is," Nate remarked.

"I doubt we want to," Blue Water Woman said.

Shakespeare harrumphed and leaned his rifle against the wall and took the chair at the head of their table. "Make yourself at home," he addressed their guest. "Maybe the woman of the house will see fit to grace us with coffee."

"Grace your own. I'm going to fetch eggs from the chicken coop," Blue Water Woman announced, and shut the door after her.

"The nerve," Shakespeare said, and got back up and went to the counter. "Pay her no mind, Methuselah. She's been ornery since the day she plopped out of the womb."

"Plopped?" Nate said.

Methuselah set his rifle on the table, turned a chair around, and straddled it. "You haven't changed much, McNair, in all these years."

"I'll take that as a compliment." Shakespeare began filling a coffeepot with water from a bucket.

Methuselah drummed his fingers on the table. "I could use something to eat. I have some pemmican on my packhorse. I'll go get it." He stood and walked quickly to the front door.

"I have pemmican, too," Shakespeare said.

"You're already sharing your home and your coffee," Methuselah said. "Let me contribute a little."

"Suit yourself."

* * *

Blue Water Woman heard the front door open and close. She knew who it would be and when she came out of the coop with eggs in a basket, he was waiting.

"It pleases me no end to see you again," Methuselah said.

"It doesn't please me."

Methuselah reached out to put his hand on her arm, but Blue Water Woman drew back.

"Touch me and I'll knife you."

"That's a little harsh, ain't it?"

"I trusted you once," Blue Water Woman said. "I'll never make that mistake again."

"You sure hold a grudge."

"Some things a woman never forgets," Blue Water Woman said, "or forgives."

Methuselah smiled and folded his arms across his chest. "I'm impressed. You learned to speak the white tongue as good as most whites."

"I could not care less what you think," Blue Water

Woman said flatly. "Visit with my husband if you must and then be on your way."

"You never told him, did you?"

"If I had," Blue Water Woman said, "he would have shot you on sight."

"Not Pudgy. He was always too damn decent for his own good. Always so noble and pure of heart. About made me sick to my stomach."

"It would."

Methuselah colored and his cheeks pinched inward. "I'll only abide so much."

Blue Water Woman stepped in close and put her hand on the hilt of the knife on her hip. "Be careful how you talk to me. I would slit your throat here and now, but Shakespeare would want to know why and I will spare him that if I can."

"It's been, what, sixty years, for God's sake."

"Sixty or six, it would be the same." Blue Water Woman went around him, then stopped. "I mean it. Not a word to my man. Be on your way before the sun goes down. If he asks you to stay over, say you can't."

"I don't like being bossed around."

Blue Water Woman half drew the knife from its sheath. "You do not seem to understand, so let me make my feelings plain. I want you gone by nightfall or you will not leave here at all."

"Bold talk. I'm not about to sit still and let you do me in."

"You are a vile creature, Methuselah Jones."

"Hell, I could show you some creatures that would really raise your hackles."

"I would never go anywhere with you. You will leave or you will die."

"All right, all right," Methuselah said. "I'll jaw awhile with your idiot of a husband and then I'll light a shuck. Would that make you happy?"

"Very." Blue Water Woman wheeled and carried the basket inside.

Methuselah stared at the front door and swore. "How dare she talk to me that way? I have half a mind to teach her a lesson." A crafty look came over him, and he grinned. "And I know just how to do it."

# Chapter Seven

The three Numas had a decision to make. Riding at night was dangerous. It was only done when it could not be avoided.

They knew that if they started down the mountain they would soon be shrouded in darkness and have to stop.

"I say we stay here until morning," Kiduto proposed. "There is grass and water. You can make camp near the trees while I hunt for our supper."

Yahuskin gestured at the black blood and the tracks. "What about those?"

"What about them?" Kiduto rejoined. "I do not believe in stories meant to scare little children."

"We will go with you," Esa said. "It is not wise for any of us to be alone."

"Listen to your words," Kiduto said. "Are we Diggers, afraid of our own shadows? We are not. We are men. We are warriors. He unslung his bow from his shoulder, slid an arrow from his quiver, and notched it to the string. "I will not be long."

Kiduto broke into a jog and crossed to the verdant woodland. The shadows were long and dark and growing more so as the sun continued to sink. He glided almost soundlessly through the vegetation until movement alerted him to an animal ahead. He caught a flash of brown and froze, thinking it might be a deer.

The movement stopped. Nothing appeared, and Kiduto advanced on cat's feet, the arrow drawn to his cheek and ready to fly. He came to where the animal had been and scoured for sign, but there wasn't any.

Kiduto moved on. He was a skilled hunter. His family never went hungry. He had every confidence in his ability, and it was only a matter of time before he could go back to his friends with meat to eat.

The shadows were deepening, though, and soon it would be too dark to see well. Kiduto moved faster. He had spent all day on the trail of the Appaloosa and was famished.

Kiduto felt sorry for Yahuskin. The Appaloosa had been a fine animal indeed. Kiduto had envied him, owning such a horse. But now look. Yahuskin traded much and lost it all.

Another movement caused Kiduto to turn to stone. Whatever the animal was, it was closer and to his right instead of in front of him. He wondered if it was circling. A doe wouldn't, but a meat-eater would. He drew the arrow to his cheek.

All Kiduto wanted was an unobstructed view. An arrow to the heart or lungs would be enough.

Again a bush moved ever so slightly even though the wind had died. But this time it was to his left and not his right.

Kiduto stopped. It occurred to him that there must be more than one. Coyotes, he thought, but no, they wouldn't let a human get this close. Wolves, then; but no again, wolves were even more wary than coyotes unless it was the cold of winter and they were starved. What did that leave? he asked himself. He took several cautious steps and eased around a pine. He heard a slight sound behind him and started to turn when his head exploded in a burst of pain and a black pit yawned before him. His last sensation was of falling.

* * *

Kiduto returned to the world of the living with a start. His head ached and he was nauseated. He became aware that he was swaying. Shock set in. He was being carried. He opened his eyes but all around him was pitch-black. Vague shapes suggested trees and other growth. He tried to move his arms and couldn't. He tried to move his legs and it was the same.

A strange chattering came from in front of him and behind him.

"Who are you?" Kiduto demanded. "Why did you take me captive?"

The answer was more clicking and clacking.

"I am not your enemy," Kiduto told them. "I do not even know who you are." They weren't Blackfeet or Piegans. Their language was not like any he ever heard.

The thought jarred him. Kiduto strained to see his captors, but they were darkling forms without features. "It cannot be," he said. "Your kind died out long ago."

There was no response.

Kiduto licked his lips and swallowed. "Tell me," he said. "Are you Si-Te-Cah?"

The things stopped.

Kiduto felt a light touch on the back of his neck, like the brush of a finger yet not quite the same. "Si-Te-Cah?" he said again. He tried to bend toward the shape in front of him.

A blow to the head rocked him. Kiduto jerked back, his mind awhirl, struggling to stay conscious. He was going to ask them why they had struck him, but he lost his struggle and once more the pit claimed him.

\* \* \*

When next Kiduto opened his eyes, all he saw were stars. He was on his back. His arms and legs wouldn't move. He attempted to roll onto his side and couldn't. He sensed rather than saw movement. Creatures were closing from all sides. Starlight gleamed in otherworldly eyes.

"What do you want?" Kiduto asked, although he knew.

The eyes lowered and under each pair opened a maw with needle-sharp teeth. The mouths spread wide and the eyes gleamed brighter.

# Chapter Eight

Nate King noticed that Methuselah Jones was a lot friendlier when he came back in than he had been when he went out. It was with keen interest that he sat and listened to the two old-timers tell tales of the old days.

"It was a lot different back then," Methuselah commented at one point. "The Indians had met so few whites they didn't hardly know what to make of us. More tribes were friendly than were hostile and we roamed pretty much where we pleased."

"It was the beaver trade that changed everything," Shakespeare said ruefully. "Hundreds came west to make their fortune in plews only to find they'd be lucky to make ends meet."

"You trapped, too," Nate reminded him.

"Back then I was as fond of the dollar as the next gent," Shakespeare admitted. "But more than the money I loved the life. The wilderness was in my blood."

Methuselah sipped coffee and bit off a piece of pemmican and chewed. He glanced toward the rocking chair, where Blue Water Woman sat knitting, and then at McNair. "I've been thinking. Maybe I was too hasty a while ago. After all, I'm heading east, never to return."

"Hasty about what?" Shakespeare asked.

"About the Garden of Eden, as I call it." Methuselah sat back. "It's not my home anymore. What do I care if you pay the place a visit?"

"It would bring back the old days," Shakespeare said with an eager grin.

"Tell you what," Methuselah said. "If you have paper and something to write with, I'll draw that map you wanted."

"You hear that, Horatio?" Shakespeare said excitedly. "We have an adventure in the offing."

Nate was torn. On the one hand, the valley piqued his curiosity. On the other, he'd have to ride for a week to get there and he didn't relish being away from his wife.

"This is damned nice of you," Shakespeare told Methuselah.

Jones shrugged. "We're the last of our breed. We should look out for each other."

Nate watched closely as the map was drawn. It was in a part of the mountains he'd never been to. Nor had anyone he knew, for that matter.

"The Indians call it bad medicine, but they've always been superstitious," Methuselah related. "I lived there for years and never had a problem."

Blue Water Woman stopped knitting and looked up. "How is the valley called?"

"It doesn't have a name," Methuselah said.

"You said that some tribes know of it," Blue Water Woman persisted. "It must have."

Methuselah continued to draw as if he hadn't heard her. Finally he answered, "I seem to recollect that one tribe calls it the Valley of the Se-at-co."

"Se-at-co?" Shakespeare repeated. "I've heard that somewhere."

Nate hadn't, but then he didn't have his mentor's vast experience.

"Se-at-co is a Yakima word," Blue Water Woman said. She lowered her knitting. "It means Stick People. But other tribes have their own names. Some call them People Eaters."

Chortling, Shakespeare said, "Did you come across any people made of sticks while you were there, Methuselah?"

Blue Water Woman didn't look amused.

"There aren't too many people at all. But the few I saw were flesh and blood like you and me," Methuselah said. "Mostly the valley is full of critters like those you'd find right here in your own valley. Deer and elk and such and a heap of them."

"What do you say, Horatio?" Shakespeare resorted to another quote. "Over hill, over dale, through brush, through brier, over park, over pale, through flood, through fire. You and me on a grand adventure."

"We'd be gone most of a month."

"So?"

"I'd miss Winona."

Shakespeare tilted his head. "Are you joined to her at the hip? I swear, you've been whipped into bowing at the altar of her every whim."

"I think I resent that," Nate said.

"We can trap a few beaver in honor of the old days and do some hunting."

"I don't know," Nate hedged. "She might not like me being gone so long."

"Good God, Horatio. Do you need her consent to

visit the outhouse?" Shakespeare thumped the table. "Be a man, mouse, and say you'll come."

Methuselah cleared his throat. "Might I make a suggestion? Why not take your families with you? Or at least your wives? They might enjoy it as much as you."

Shakespeare turned to Blue Water Woman. "What do you say, love of my life? Just the four of us. No cares. No kids. No cleaning or washing. And we'll help with the cooking."

"I will go if Winona does. But I am not so sure it is wise."

"Why not?

"The Stick People."

"Be serious," Shakespeare scoffed. "There's no such thing. We'll have the entire valley to ourselves."

Methuselah slid the paper across the table. "Here's the map. I'm not much of an artist, but it should do the job."

Shakespeare studied it. "I know some of these landmarks." He put a finger on a squiggly line. "Is this the west fork of that stream the trappers used to call Culver Creek after that fellow the Bloods staked out?"

"It is."

"And is this Burnt Mountain?"

"It is," Methuselah said again. "But the vegetation has grown back since then."

"This will be fun. I can't thank you enough."

They drank more coffee and ate pemmican and made small talk until shortly before sunset. Then Methuselah stood and announced he would be on his way. Shakespeare tried to persuade him to stay the night, but Methuselah looked over at Blue Water Woman and declined. They followed him out and Nate and Shakespeare shook his hand. Methuselah smiled at Blue Water Woman, but she didn't smile back.

"It was a treat running into you, McNair," the ancient mountaineer said as he mounted. "I hope you find the Garden of Eden to your liking."

"I'm sure we will."

Methuselah touched his brow and tapped his heels against the sorrel. He rode east along the shore and when he was out of earshot he glanced over his shoulder and laughed. "The damned fools. They have no notion of what they're in for."

# Chapter Nine

The sun had been down a considerable while when Esa said, "He should be back by now."

"Yes," Yahuskin agreed. "One of us should go look for him."

Esa added a stick to their fire and peered into the darkness. "We do not separate. That was Kiduto's mistake."

Yahuskin's stomach reminded him that he had not eaten since dawn. "We will go together."

"And leave the horses?"

Yahuskin changed his mind. Should the animals be taken, it would be two moons if not more before they reached their village. "We will ride."

"At night?"

"What else can we do? Sit here and hope he returns?"

Yahuskin was annoyed by his companion's objections.

"We wait for the sun to rise. Then we search for him."

The logic of it made Yahuskin realize he must give in. He also realized he was so upset at the loss of the Appaloosa, it was affecting his judgment. He fell into a sulk and sat with his knees tucked to his chest and his arms across them. Resting his chin on his wrist, he stared into the flames and for the hundredth time since it happened, wondered why the Appaloosa had run off. Horses ran off all the time, it was true, but that was small consolation.

Night hid the mountains in a black veil. Here a wolf howled. There a mountain lion screamed. The cry of a female fox calling for a male was borne on the wind and carried toward the divide.

Yahuskin's eyelids grew heavy. He dozed and woke. He should lie down and sleep, but he was too distraught. He had liked how everyone would look at him when he rode about on his new horse. He had liked the envy of the other warriors and the admiring glances of the women.

"We are not alone," Esa said.

Yahuskin raised his head. "What?"

"We are not alone," Esa said again. He was idly poking the fire with the tip of a stick.

"What makes you say that?"

"Look toward the peak, but do not let on what you see," Esa quietly directed. "We do not want them to know that we know."

"Them?" Yahuskin gazed at Bird's Peak, a gigantic silhouette against the stars, and then down across the benighted slopes below and the meadow. Not an arrow's flight away were two pairs of unblinking eyes. They made him think of a cat's, only they were somehow different.

"Do not stare at them."

Yahuskin tore his eyes from the others. "What are they? I have never seen eyes like those before."

"I do not know," Esa said. "Or perhaps I do and I am afraid to admit it."

"You are not afraid of any animal alive."

"I did not say they are animals," Esa said. "And they are not men."

"What, then?" Yahuskin asked, and the answer leaped into his mind of its own accord. He stiffened and had to stop himself from looking at the eyes again. "You are not suggesting . . . ?"

"Si-Te-Cah."

Yahuskin's mouth went dry. "It cannot be."

"You said that at the way your Appaloosa was torn apart, too. Same with the tracks we found near it. Now, those eyes cannot be. Yet they are, and now we know why Kiduto has not returned."

"There are only two," Yahuskin said.

"No. Now there are five."

Yahuskin glanced up and fear spiked through him. Five pairs of eyes glistened back at him. He quickly turned away and swallowed hard.

"We are in trouble," Esa said.

"Do you still insist we sit here until daylight?"

Esa set down the stick and placed his hand on the bow at his side. "If we do we will be dead by then."

"How can you sit there so calm?" Yahuskin could barely keep from jumping up and springing to his horse.

"We have time. They will wait until we lie down to sleep to attack."

"You hope," Yahuskin said. "But if they are Si-Te-Cah, and the tales are right, they do not think like we do. They think in the old ways."

"Try to stay calm yourself."

"They will eat us, Esa. I do not want to be eaten. We must flee."

"Be patient. The eyes have not moved. But now there are seven of them."

Yahuskin pretended to stretch and peered over his arm, and Esa was right. "If enough come they will surround us. We must go now."

"We hobbled our horses. As soon as they see us go to remove the hobbles, they might attack."

"Then we must remove the hobbles quickly."

"I have a better idea. I will go over to them and rub them down and feel of their legs as if I am examining them, and slip the hobbles off. If I do it slowly and without any sign that I know they are there, they might not suspect."

"It might work."

"Do you have a better plan?"

"No," Yahuskin admitted. He peeked over his shoulder. Now there were eight sets of eyes. "Let's do it."

\* \* \*

Esa left his bow on the ground as he rose and walked to the horses. He patted his horse and ran his hand along its side and leg. With his back to the eyes in the dark, he removed the rope hobble.

Yahuskin turned and attempted to string his bow while it was flat on the ground. It was made of ash and strong, and he couldn't bend it far enough.

Esa went to the next horse. He rubbed it and talked to it and slid his hands down a leg to the hobble.

Trying to conceal the bow with his body, Yahuskin picked it up and put one end on the ground and bent the ash with his knee so he could hook the string.

Esa was at Kiduto's horse. There was no one to ride it, but horses were too valuable to be left behind. He moved it close to his own and walked to the fire and squatted. "The horses are ready."

"So am I." Yahuskin had notched an arrow and held his bow low down.

"There are ten of them now."

Yahuskin didn't care to look. The glowing eyes were too unnerving.

"Two of them are on the side of the meadow behind you."

His skin crawling, Yahuskin shifted and glimpsed them out of the corner of his eye. "They are spreading out to surround us."

"Yes."

"Then why are we sitting here?"

"Do not panic," Esa cautioned. "There are not enough of them yet."

"I am not afraid," Yahuskin lied.

Esa slung his bow over his shoulder. "We will get up slowly and walk to the horses and I will point at one of the legs of mine as if something is wrong with it. When I say to, jump on yours and ride as the wind."

Yahuskin grunted in assent. He rose and followed Esa and dared to glance at the eyes from under his brow. They were bigger. The creatures were coming closer. "Esa?"

"I see," the other warrior whispered. "Stay calm."

Yahuskin was anything but. He gripped his bow until his knuckles were pale.

Esa pointed at his horse's leg and said, "I will count to three. Don't worry about Kiduto's horse. I'll bring it."

Impatient to be off, Yahuskin gritted his teeth.

"If we are separated, I will meet you at the river we crossed two sleeps ago."

"Let us just *go*."

"One," Esa said.

Yahuskin couldn't wait any longer. He gripped his mount's mane and swung up and slapped his legs. Esa called to him, but he didn't look back. He was out of the firelight and into the darkness, riding for dear life.

Two pairs of eyes swept toward him, seeking to cut him off. A clacking sound accompanied them.

Yahuskin drew back his arrow. He was not as skilled as some of the other warriors when loosing a shaft on horseback, but he let it fly anyway and then concentrated on getting away.

Esa shouted his name, but it was every warrior for himself. He reached the end of the meadow and was swallowed by the forest and immediately slowed. It wouldn't do to have his horse break a leg.

A tree loomed and then another. Yahuskin narrowly missed both. He plunged down a short slope and remembered a large boulder in time to avoid it. From behind him came the noise of Esa's horse.

Yahuskin glanced right and left. There were no eyes. The creatures were not after them. He grinned and yelled to Esa to stay close to him. They would have a grand story to tell when they got back. Their people would regard them as the bravest of the brave. It wouldn't make up for the loss of the Appaloosa, but it would increase his standing in the band and that was something.

The wind was cool on Yahuskin's skin. Like the

others, he wore only a loincloth and moccasins. A limb stung his leg. His shoulder was cut by another. They were minor. He was alive, and that was what mattered.

Yahuskin rode until he came to a smaller meadow much lower down. He drew rein and wheeled his animal, smiling at their triumph. "We did it," he exclaimed.

A riderless horse trotted up to him.

"Esa?" Yahuskin realized the animal was Kiduto's. He waited for Esa to appear, but the woods were silent and the night still. Cupping a hand to his mouth, he shouted Esa's name. He received no answer.

"No," Yahuskin said. His conscience pricked him. He shouldn't have run off. He should have stayed at Esa's side.

But he was alive, and his people would look up to him even more as the only one to survive. He gripped the reins of the other horse and turned his own to go.

All around him were eyes, glowing, hideous, unblinking eyes.

They swept toward him and Yahuskin screamed.

# Chapter Ten

Winona King was excited. It had been much too long since she enjoyed a holiday, as the whites called it, alone with her husband. Their son, Zach, and his wife had offered to look after their daughter, Evelyn, and a Digger girl who was staying with them, Bright Rainbow. Now, hurrying from their bedroom to the main room and back again as she packed a parfleche, she grinned and exclaimed, "I am looking forward to this. It is just what we needed."

Nate was at the table cleaning his pistols. He'd half expected her to say no to the idea and almost wished she had. He didn't share Shakespeare's enthusiasm for reliving the old days by trapping a few beaver. "It is?"

"To get away for a while and relax, yes."

"I was pretty relaxed right here."

Winona came briskly out of the bedroom carrying a folded blanket. She stopped and hefted it and said, "We don't really need this, do we? The six blankets I already have on the packhorse should be enough."

"Six?" Nate marveled. "Is everyone in the valley coming with us?"

"Funny white man," Winona said, and whisked back into their bedroom. Her voice floated merrily out. "Blue Water Woman and I have talked it over. If this other valley is everything that man said it is, we'll set up camp at one end and they'll set up camp at the other."

"Why so far apart? We'll have to ride a piece just to talk."

Winona poked her head out and stared at him.

"Oh," Nate said sheepishly. He wrapped a cleaning cloth around the end of a ramrod and jammed it down a flintlock's barrel. When he slid the cloth out, it was black with powder.

Winona bustled to the table and added a dress to her pile. "In case I fall in the stream."

"Don't you have three or four packed already?"

"You don't understand females, husband."

"I know that some white women pack practically everything they own to go on a three-day trip. I never realized Indian women were the same."

"Female is female, and male is male," Winona said.

"That sounds like something Shakespeare would say."

The clatter of hooves brought Nate out of the chair. He commenced to reload as he strode out into the glare of the morning sun. "I see you're raring to go."

Shakespeare was on his white mare. He wriggled in the saddle and grinned from ear to ear. "I feel like I'm twenty years old again."

Behind him, Blue Water Woman calmly sat her chestnut.

She was leading their packhorse.

"And you?" Nate prompted.

"I am not as giddy as my husband. If he were to change his mind I would not be disappointed."

"That's not going to happen, wench," Shakespeare said. "This is just what I needed to shake off the doldrums. To be away in the wilds. To live a little." He snickered. "To love a little."

"I would not count on that love part so much," Blue Water Woman said.

"Did you hear her, Horatio?" Shakespeare said. "Here's a large mouth, indeed, that spits forth death and mountains, rocks and seas."

"Spit a mountain?" Blue Water Woman said. "That's preposterous."

"Did you hear her, Horatio?" Shakespeare said. "Insulting the Bard. It's what we get for teaching our wives our tongue."

"They speak it better than we do," Nate said.

"Speak for yourself," Shakespeare said. "I am well acquainted with your manner of wrenching the true cause the wrong way."

"Was that more William S.?"

"You can't tell his golden prose from the chaff of common speech?" Shakespeare drew himself up to his full height. "I do frown on thee with all my heart. And if my eyes can wound, not let them kill thee."

"This trip should be fun," Nate said.

Winona emerged with her arms laden and her face lit with delight. "Blue Water Woman! Shakespeare! Are you as excited as I am?"

"Verily," Shakespeare responded with a flourish.

"So excited I have goose bumps," Blue Water Woman said with no enthusiasm whatsoever.

"Pay her no mind," Shakespeare advised Winona. "She got up on the wrong side of the bed this morning." Sliding down, he hastened to help Winona with her burden. "Permit me, my dear."

Winona shot Nate a look that would wither a cactus. "It is nice to know there is *one* gentleman in this valley."

"I can't win for losing," Nate said as the pair went around the corner to the corral.

"I do not want to do this either," Blue Water Woman said.

"Talk Shakespeare out of it, then," Nate suggested. "He'll listen to you."

"No."

"But you just said—"

"That I don't want to, no." Blue Water Woman cut him off. "But you saw his face. You saw how happy he is. He has some of his old zest again."

"I could use some of that myself."

Nate went back in and finished cleaning his guns. He had packed the night before. When Winona was done, he went to the corral and brought his bay and her brown mare and their packhorse around. He gave her a boost, forked leather, and lifted his reins.

"Hear ye, world!" Shakespeare gaily hollered. "Hang out our banners on the outward walls. The cry is still, 'They come!'"

"Oh, brother," Nate said.

They headed out, Shakespeare in the lead with his map, Nate bringing up the rear so he could keep an eye on their back trail. Jaunts in the Rockies were not like jaunts east of the Mississippi. Back there, the worst a person might contend with was rude service.

Out here, the law of fang and claw and blade and bullet held sway.

It took most of the morning to climb to the pass Nate's daughter had discovered not long ago, and once through it they spent most of the afternoon descending to the next valley and winding along it to a mountain covered in spruce and fir.

Shakespeare was in fine fettle and quoted the Bard of Avon liberally.

Winona chirped like a wren about this and that and the scenery.

Blue Water Woman said little.

Nate said nothing at all. He wasn't keen on their outing, but with his wife and his best friend both eager and happy, he held his tongue. It annoyed him, though, that he was the only one who appeared to be alert for danger.

Twilight was mantling the mountains in shades of gray when they stopped for the night in a clearing high in a stand of aspens. The phalanx of tall trees shielded them from the brisk wind and roving eyes, and they could sit by the fire and enjoy themselves. Even Nate, although he sat where he could see the horses and would notice right away if they acted as if something, or someone, was out there in the dark.

Shakespeare behaved more like his old self. He ribbed the ladies, he joked, he quoted, and quoted, and quoted. Along about ten he sat back against his saddle and spread his arms wide to the sky and declared, "Look at all those stars. It has always dazzled me that the Almighty saw fit to make all of that and us bugs, besides."

"Speak for yourself, husband," Blue Water Woman said. "I am not an insect."

"Would you settle for an actress?"

"The white women who pretend they are other people and walk out onstage and recite lines? Like the play we saw in St. Louis?"

Shakespeare wagged his hand in a flourish. "All the world's a stage, and all the men and women merely players. They have their exits and their entrances, and one man in his time plays many parts."

"Here we go again," Nate said.

"His acts being seven ages. At first the infant, mewling and puking in his nurse's arms. Then the whining schoolboy, with his satchel and shining morning face, creeping like a snail unwillingly to school. And then the lover, sighing like a furnace, with a woeful ballad made to his mistress's eyebrow. Then a soldier, full of strange oaths, and bearded like the pard, jealous in honor, sudden and quick in quarrel, seeking the bubble reputation even in the canon's mouth. And then the—"

"How do you remember all of that?" Winona interrupted.

Shakespeare scowled at her. "A moment, madam, while I wax eloquent."

"Where is some candle wax when I need it?" Blue Water Woman said.

Nate threw back his head and started to laugh but stopped when he saw his bay and several of the other horses raise their heads and stare. He shifted to look in the same direction, and his skin crawled.

Staring back was a pair of gleaming eyes.

Nate had seen all sorts of eyes by firelight. Coyote

eyes, wolf eyes, fox eyes, deer eyes, elk eyes, buffalo eyes, bobcat eyes, mountain lion eyes, and others. He had seen so many, so often, that he could tell one set of eyes from the other by their shape and how high they were off the ground. These eyes were bear eyes. Worse, they were so high off the ground that unless it was a black bear standing on its hind legs, they could only belong to one animal. Grabbing his rifle, he quickly stood. "We have a visitor."

The others looked, and were fast to follow suit.

"A griz!" Shakespeare exclaimed.

All of them raised their rifles, but no one fired. It took more than one shot to bring a grizzly down. To wound one was foolhardy; it might drive the griz berserk.

This bear sniffed and lumbered into the circle of dancing light.

"My God," Shakespeare said.

Nate felt a chill run down his spine. It was immense, one of the largest he had come across in years, an enormous brute capable of ripping them to bits and pieces if they weren't careful.

"We should give it some food," Winona whispered.

"Might put ideas into its noggin," Shakespeare said. He took a step and gestured. "Shoo!"

"Husband," Blue Water Woman said.

Nate sighted down his Hawken at the grizzly's eye. The skull was inches thick and proof against most slugs. The heart and lungs were protected by layers of muscles and fat and next to impossible to penetrate.

"Shoo, consarn you!" Shakespeare shouted, and took another step.

The grizzly growled.

A horse whinnied in fright, and the bear swung its immense head.

"No," Nate said breathlessly. The horses were hobbled and wouldn't be able to escape. He started to sidle between them and the bruin.

"What are you doing?" Winona whispered.

"Maybe if all of us shoot at the same time . . ." Blue Water Woman proposed.

To their mutual astonishment, Shakespeare raised his arm over his head and bellowed, "And then the justice, in fair round belly with good capon lined, with eyes severe and beard of formal cut, full of wise saw and modern instances, and so he plays his part. The sixth age shifts into the lean and slipper'd pantaloon, with spectacles on nose and pouch on side, his youthful hose, well saved, a world too wide for his shrunk shrank. And his big manly—"

The grizzly snorted and shook its head and took a step back.

"Don't stop," Nate whispered.

Shakespeare nodded. "And his big manly voice, turning again toward childish treble, pies and whistles in his sound. Last scene of all, that ends this strange eventful history, is second childishness and mere oblivion, sans teeth, sans—"

Uttering another snort, the grizzly turned and melted into the ink of night as silently as it had appeared.

Shakespeare lowered his voice to normal and ended with "Sans eyes, sans taste, sans everything." He chuckled and said, "I'll be damned."

"You bored it so much, it left," Blue Water Woman said.

"Such slanders," Shakespeare retorted.

"Listen!" Winona said.

All of them did, and Shakespeare said, "I don't hear anything."

"Me either. Do you think it is truly gone, or is it standing out there making up its mind whether to attack us?"

"How would I know, madam? I don't have a bear's brain."

"Or any other," Blue Water Woman said.

Nate didn't think they were taking the grizzly seriously enough. He moved to the edge of the firelight and peered into the aspens.

Winona's elbow brushed his. "Anything?"

"It could be ten feet away and I wouldn't know it," Nate remarked.

"How something so big can be so quiet?" Winona marveled.

"I wish it would give my husband lessons," Blue Water Woman said.

In tense dread they waited, but the grizzly didn't reappear. Nate finally lowered his rifle and straightened. "I reckon it's gone."

"We're liable to run into more the farther we go," Shakespeare said.

"So long as they are like this one," Winona replied.

Nate had tangled with more than his share of the monarchs of the mountains. His Indian name, in fact, came from his first clash with a griz. A Cheyenne warrior witnessed the fight and bestowed the name Grizzly Killer on him. Since then, he'd killed a number of others and the moniker had stuck, but he'd just as soon go the rest of his life and never tangle with another.

Shakespeare returned to the fire and sat. "Now, where was I?"

"About to turn in," Blue Water Woman said.

"Was that a hint?"

"My ears have had enough of William S. for one night."

Mumbling, Shakespeare sat back. "It's a fine how-do-you-do when a man's own wife treats him as if he is addlepated."

"You are."

"What I want to know," Winona said, "is how you remember all those words."

McNair shrugged. "I have a knack, dear lady. Just like you do for languages. You are a natural-born linguist."

Blue Water Woman winked at Winona and then said to Shakespeare, "Does that make you a natural-born blowhard?"

Flushing with indignation, Shakespeare bellowed, "Did you hear her, Horatio? Did you hear her pierce me to the quick?"

Nate sighed and hunkered and added a branch to the flames. "I'll keep first watch."

"Do you think the bear will come back?" Winona wondered.

"Let's hope to God it doesn't."

# Chapter Eleven

That high up, the hour before dawn was chill.

Blue Water Woman moved closer to the fire for the extra warmth. Around her the others slept, Shakespeare snoring loud enough to topple trees. She remembered how frisky he had been a few nights ago, and smiled. She loved that man dearly, and it warmed her heart as the fire warmed her body that he was so excited about the trip to the Garden of Eden, as Methuselah Jones had called it.

*Methuselah Jones.* The name pricked at her mind like a thorn. Blue Water Woman was not spiteful by nature. She didn't hate for hate's sake or hold mistakes against those who made them if they were honest mistakes. But she had meant it when she said she would never forgive him for what he had done.

She should have foreseen, she told herself. There had been signs. The looks he gave her. The touches when she had made it clear she did not want him to touch her. That terrible day in her father's lodge, she had learned an important lesson.

The crack of a twig brought Blue Water Woman out of her reverie. She pushed erect with her rifle ready. Something moved in the trees, something big. She went to shout to wake the others but changed her mind. Maybe if she was quiet it would go off and leave them be.

The thing came nearer, a block of beige color against the black. If it was the grizzly and it attacked, she would shoot it and run to lure it away from the others.

The shape acquired form, and Blue Water Woman let out a puff of breath. The horselike head, the long body, the thin legs; it was only an elk. It stood staring at them as if curious and then turned its pale rump to the fire and trotted away.

Blue Water Woman walked in a circle to stretch her legs. Shakespeare was always complaining about how old he was getting, but he wasn't the only one feeling his years. She had lived almost as many winters as he had, and while she complained less, she felt the same aches and pangs.

Winona's blanket moved and her head poked out. "Good morning."

"Did I wake you?" Blue Water Woman said. "If so I am sorry. It is a while until dawn."

"I haven't slept all that well." Winona stretched and fluffed her hair and stood. "I have become too soft." She grinned and rubbed her arm. "The ground is not as comfortable as my bed."

Blue Water Woman squatted. "I will heat the coffee." The pot had been half-full the last she checked. She added water from their water skin until it came to the brim.

"Tell me true," Winona said. "Your heart isn't in this, is it?"

"It is good for Shakespeare, but I cannot help worrying."

"About things like the grizzly that we might run into?"

"About Methuselah Jones."

Winona sat cross-legged with her rifle across her lap. "I didn't get to meet him. Why should he worry you?"

Blue Water Woman hesitated. She had never told anyone. But Winona was her best friend and the person she trusted most besides her husband. "He is not as he seems," she began, but could not bring herself to reveal the rest. Friend or not, it was too painful. "He is not to be trusted."

"You know him, I take it?"

"Many winters ago he was a guest in our village and a friend of my father's."

"What did he do that you don't trust him?"

"All I will say is don't ever be alone with him."

"I wish you would tell me, but I respect your decision not to." Winona sobered. "You have me worried, though. Why would a man you dislike so much be so nice toward your husband?"

"Too nice," Blue Water Woman said. "When he offered to draw a map to this Garden of Eden, I was suspicious."

"From what I hear, he told Shakespeare and Nate all about it before it ever came up about them going."

"A mystery," Blue Water Woman said. "All I know is the man has a bad heart and speaks with a forked tongue."

"A mystery," Winona agreed.

A sudden sharp squawk in the forest caused both of them to tense and reach for weapons.

"Just a jay," Winona said, and grinned.

"It is up early."

The sky to the east was still dark. Stars by the thousands sparkled in the vault of the firmament. Far off amid the peaks, a wolf howled and the lonesome wail echoed and reechoed.

"I had forgotten how beautiful the night is," Winona said quietly.

Blue Water Woman could not get her mind off her worry. "When we reach this Garden of Eden, we must not let down our guard."

"Agreed."

"My husband is a big child. All he will think of are the beaver. I must be his eyes and ears."

"And my husband will follow him like a puppy. They cannot help themselves, those two. They are men."

Blue Water Woman laughed. "You are fortunate to have Grizzly Killer. There are days when if I hear one more word of the Bard's, I want to pull out my hair."

"If Shakespeare heard you say that, he would be crushed."

Smiling, Blue Water Woman gazed at her sleeping man, who was on his back with his beard on top of his blanket. "He is the great love of my life. We were apart for so many winters, I treasure each moment we are together. I would be the one crushed if I lost him."

"Don't talk like that. The whites call it a jinx."

"What do they know?" Blue Water Woman joked. "They carry rabbit's feet and think it will protect them from bad medicine."

Winona nodded and chuckled. "Everyone knows a hawk's talons or a rattlesnake's rattle is better."

Blue Water Woman touched the coffeepot. It was only warm.

"I would give my life for that man."

"If it came to that, I would give mine for Nate."

"Sisters in love," Blue Water Woman said.

High above them, the wolf howled its lament.

* * *

The more he thought about it, the more it bothered him, and the more it bothered him, the more he thought about it.

It got so, Methuselah drew rein on a knobby ridge and swore. He shifted in the saddle and looked back up the mountain and said to himself, "No. It would be stupid." He clucked to the sorrel and yanked on the lead rope and descended a few hundred feet and again drew rein.

"It would be damn stupid," Methuselah said to the empty air, and did more swearing.

He had been lucky to get out of there alive. He should have known they would try to stop him. They had preserved their secret for untold ages and were afraid he would give them away.

They knew what would happen if the surrounding tribes learned of their existence. Which was why no outsider had ever entered their secret valley and lived to tell of it. He owed his survival to a fluke. Had it not been for a rock slide that pinned the young one he freed, they would surely have killed him.

In his mind Methuselah relived that day. He had stumbled on the notch and ridden through it into a wondrous world where time stood still. To view it better, he had climbed to a high slope, and it was there he heard the mewling cries that made him think of a cat. He had come on the rock slide and when he saw the . . . thing . . . that was uttering the cries, his skin had crawled and he had nearly jerked his rifle up and shot it. Why he didn't he would never know. Instead he had climbed down and warily moved a boulder that pinned its broken leg. It had sniffed him and limped off, more broken than alive, and he had assumed that was the last he would ever see of whatever it was, and gone on.

Little did he know there were more, or that the valley was their home. Three mornings later they paid him a visit. He awoke to find himself surrounded. In his fear he had almost grabbed for his rifle, but he had been too scared to move, and it saved his life. Their leader came close with the one he had saved and through signs he was given to understand that they wouldn't harm him.

All the years he stayed in their valley, they never touched him. It got so he took them for granted, almost. One look at them, with their rapier teeth and their clawlike fingernails, and he could never fully trust them.

Their leader was as curious about him as he was about them. They spent many hours talking with their hands. Bit by bit he learned some of their language. Their tongue was hard on the human throat, no more so than the white tongue was on theirs. Otherwise they left him alone. He was permitted to visit their village, such as it was. They never stayed in one place for more than a few moons, and their lodges were the most peculiar he ever saw. But nowhere near as peculiar as they were.

Secretly, Methuselah loathed them. They were hideous. Abominations that should have died out when the world was young.

The worst was how they moved. God, he couldn't stand that.

Methuselah gazed up the mountain. There was no sane reason for him to go back. He had gotten away. Leave it at that, he told himself. He had kin to find.

But there was Blue Water Woman. She had treated him like scum, and it bothered him. It reminded him of that day long ago when she had held a knife to his throat and made him leave her father's lodge and warned him that if he was still in the village by sundown, she would tell her people what he had tried to do and they would make him run a gantlet of knives and tomahawks. He'd had to turn tail and hated it.

"The bitch," Methuselah said, and without warning pain flared. Groaning he doubled over. The attacks were a lot worse. He didn't have long. He might not even make it to the States, might not get to see his sister and his brother again. If they were even alive.

It got him thinking. Why go to all the trouble to try to find kin he hadn't seen in ages? Why not treat himself to a last dab of pleasure and get back at the bitch who had held that knife to his throat so long ago?

The pain faded and Methuselah sat up. Reining around, he started back.

There was nothing sweeter than vengeance.

# Chapter Twelve

Shakespeare had no trouble following the map. By the fourth day they reached the fork of the Culver and by the sixth they came to Burnt Mountain. "It won't be long now."

"You sound like you cannot wait," Blue Water Woman said.

"I can't." Shakespeare was feeling younger than he had in years, and reveling in it. He breathed deep of the high country air and said, "I can't wait to lay a trap. How about you, Horatio?"

Nate wasn't as eager. Trapping had been a job, that was all. He never really liked killing beaver, just as he never really liked to kill anything. He would have been perfectly content to go through life without killing, ever, but life hadn't let him. "It will be like old times," he said.

"Yes, it will," Shakespeare happily agreed. "Now let's find that cliff with the notch."

"We are seeing a lot more wildlife," Winona commented as they climbed a steep spur.

"Virgin land," Shakespeare said. "This is how it was when I first came West. Creation untouched by the hand of man. I'd about forgotten how grand it is. Methuselah's valley might just be the paradise he claims."

"If he did not deceive us," Blue Water Woman said.

"Why would he do that?"

"I do not want you to be disappointed." Blue Water Woman avoided the question.

"Look around you. This is glorious."

As Shakespeare rode he was stirred by memories. The indelible impression of his first days in the Rockies; his amazement at how high they thrust into the sky, his rapture at the abundance of wildlife, his sheer delight in feeling more alive than he'd ever felt.

Shakespeare toyed with the notion that if the Garden of Eden was everything Jones claimed, he would move there with Blue Water Woman. But no, he'd never leave the Kings. They were his family, and he was as devoted to them as if they were his own flesh and blood.

That night Shakespeare sat around the fire with the others and tingled with anticipation. "Tomorrow is the day."

"Just don't get your hopes too high," Blue Water Woman cautioned.

Shakespeare was growing exasperated with her. "Why do you persist in dashing them?"

"I care for you. I do not want you hurt. And I do not trust Methuselah Jones."

"Why not?"

"Call it women's intuition," Blue Water Woman said, and let it go at that.

"I was pricked well enough before, and you could have left me alone," Shakespeare quoted.

"I love you, McNair."

Shakespeare turned to Nate. "I ask you, Horatio. What is a man to do?"

"Grin and bear it," Nate said.

* * *

The next day dawned brilliant and clear. They saddled their mounts and tightened the packs on their pack animals and were under way shortly after sunrise. Not an hour later they drew rein before a sheer face of solid rock.

"The cliff!" Shakespeare exclaimed.

Nate scoured it intently. "I don't see an opening."

"Jones said it was well hid." Shakespeare gigged his mare up to the seemingly solid wall—and there it was, a gap wide enough for a horse, hidden by an overlap. "Forsooth!" he cried, and entered. On either hand rose hemming walls.

Enough light filtered down that he could see the pockmark of old horse prints and a jumble of other tracks he didn't pay much attention to. He went around a bend and was out of the notch. Dazzled, he drew rein and blurted, "My God."

Before him spread a verdant valley aglow with the golden tint of the sun. Rimmed by ramparts crowned in ivory, every slope was rich with timber. Thick grass and splashes of red, yellow, and blue wildflowers mantled the valley floor. The air had a crystal quality. To breathe it was to invigorate the lungs.

Everywhere there was life. Butterflies flitted among the flowers. The melody of a multitude of birds rose in avian chorus. Deer and elk grazed the tall grass and were drinking at a stream as blue as the sky. A beaver swam in a broad pool.

"Oh, wonder!" Shakespeare quoted. "How many godly creatures are there here?"

"It is everything Jones claimed," Blue Water Woman said in disbelief.

"This is a sacred place," Winona said softly.

Nate was as stunned as the rest. He never imagined a valley like this existed. He'd heard the tales, of course, mostly Indian legends about how different the world had been before the coming of man, and here it was, the proof right before his eyes. He saw another beaver join the first. "It's a good thing the trapping brigades never came across this place."

"I have found heaven," Shakespeare declared.

Blue Water Woman pointed. "What is that?"

An arrow's flight from the notch stood a dwelling, a small cabin built crudely from logs and chinked with clay to keep out the wind.

"Must have been Methuselah's," Shakespeare reckoned, and made for it. "We'll have a roof over our heads tonight."

Blue Water Woman wanted nothing to do with anything that had to do with Methuselah. But he was long gone, and it would be safer in there than out on the ground, so she didn't object.

Nate came alongside Winona. "If I'd seen this before I found King Valley, we'd be living here."

"It would not be right," Winona said.

"Why not?"

She encompassed the valley with a sweep of her arm. "Do you not feel it, husband? The Great Mystery is strong here."

The cabin door was ajar. It hung on elk-hide hinges stiff with age. Nate had to push hard to open it. Inside was a bed frame made of saplings with thin interwoven branches instead of springs. There was a wooden bucket and a tree stump for a table and boulders for chairs. The floor was dirt. Next to the door was a trimmed oak branch evidently used to prop against it so nothing could get in.

"This is all Jones had?" Nate said.

"He always was peculiar," Shakespeare replied. "Never gave a lick about possessions or money or any of that."

"The root of all evil."

"No," Shakespeare amended, "the *love* of money is the root. Not that I give much of a hoot about it myself."

Winona moved about the room, her nose crinkled. "I don't like the smell. Let's prop the door open and air it out." She stepped to the lone window and moved the dirty cloth that hung over it. "And we will need a new curtain."

"I'll unpack the animals," Nate volunteered.

"I will help you," Blue Water Woman offered.

The corral had three rails and a water trough. Nate hung their saddles over the top rail, which threatened to break under the weight, and draped their saddle blankets over a lower one. Blue Water Woman unfastened their packs and placed them in a pile. The beaver traps were in a burlap sack that clanked as she set it down.

"Are you all right?" Nate asked when it hit him how uncommonly quiet she was being.

"I do not like it here, Grizzly Killer."

Nate gazed out over the pristine wonderland. "How can you not?"

Blue Water Woman followed his gaze; the forest, so green and serene, the grass waving in the wind, the peaks that had towered since the dawn of time. It was truly beautiful, yet inside her a tiny voice warned that Methuselah Jones had induced them to come and Methuselah Jones was evil.

"Look at the size of those beaver," Nate said, with a nod at the stream. "In the old days their pelts would make a free trapper drool."

"It will be a shame to kill them," Blue Water Woman said.

Nate frowned. He was thinking the same thing. He closed the corral gate, which consisted of three long poles he had to slide through buckskin hoops, and turned to help her carry their provisions inside. She was staring at the ground with a strange expression and he thought she might not be feeling well. "What is it?"

Blue Water Woman pointed. "You tell me."

The ground was bare earth churned by hooves and marked by the moccasin prints of Jones as well as animal tracks. Deer prints were everywhere. A raccoon had visited the cabin recently. But it was the other prints that gave Nate a start.

"What in the world?"

Sinking to a knee, Blue Water Woman touched one. "What can this be?"

"I don't know," Nate admitted.

The tracks were made by naked feet. The toes and the heels were plain and their general shape was human, but they were so narrow as to suggest it was only half a track. Yet Nate counted five toes. He placed his own foot next to the clearest. His was three to four times as wide. "Jones must have made them and they shrunk somehow."

"That is silly and you know it."

Yes, Nate conceded, it was. Yet he could not account for them any other way. He roved about and found more. "Whoever it was, they've been all over."

"They are not the tracks of whites."

"Indians, then," Nate suggested. Most tribes used moccasins but not all. The Diggers, for instance, often went without footwear in the summer.

"They must be the thinnest Indians alive," Blue Water Woman made mention.

"Whoever they are, they didn't bother Jones while he was here." Nate shielded his eyes from the sun with his hand. "There must be a village somewhere. We'll have to be on the lookout." He hefted a pack from the pile. "I'll tell Winona and Shakespeare."

Blue Water Woman absently nodded. She was recalling a tale told of the old times, and was deeply troubled. Picking up a parfleche, she turned to go inside and thought she spied movement in the trees on the other side of the corral. "Is someone there?"

No one answered.

Unease came over her, and she almost bolted inside. "If someone is there, say something," she said in the white tongue and then in her own.

The silence gnawed at her nerves.

Her unease growing, Blue Water Woman moved to the front door. They had only just arrived and already she wished they never came.

# *Chapter Thirteen*

Shakespeare McNair stood on the bank of the beaver pond and fondly regarded the domed beaver lodge in the middle. It rose some six feet out of the water and was nearly forty feet from end to end. "This takes me back, Horatio."

It took Nate back, too, to cold mornings waist-deep in icy water, to the smell of the castoreum used to bait the traps, to the blood and the gore of skinning the beaver for their pelts.

"We'll set our traps tomorrow," Shakespeare proposed.

"Do we have to?" Nate asked.

Shakespeare tore his eyes from the pond. "I thought that's why we came."

"Look at them."

"I am. They are healthy and plump and their fur is prime. So?"

"Not one slap."

Beaver showed alarm by smacking their tails on the water. But these beaver weren't showing any alarm at all. One swam within a few dozen feet and stared at them and swam off again.

"They are as tame as can be," Nate remarked. "I don't feel right laying traps for them. It would be like trapping babies."

Shakespeare stared at them a while and then said, "Damn it all."

"Is that the Bard or you?" Nate joked.

"Go hang yourself, you naughty mocking uncle," Shakespeare quoted.

"What about the beaver?"

"Yes indeed. What about them?" Shakespeare scratched his beard in contemplation. He had looked forward to trapping a few for old times' sake. "But where is the challenge in trapping creatures so trusting?" he asked aloud.

"We can explore and decide later," Nate proposed. "The day is young yet."

They collected their wives and hiked deeper into the valley along the stream. The gurgling water, the singing birds, the multitude of animals, were a marvel. A bull elk watched them go by with no more fear than if they were cows.

"Friendliest critters I ever did see," Shakespeare exclaimed.

"There aren't many young," Blue Water Woman observed.

Nearly all the animals they had seen were adults.

"Probably hiding," Shakespeare said. "There have to be plenty of predators."

Nate began to study the ground more intently. The mention of meat-eaters made him realize he hadn't seen a single track of a wolf or coyote or bear or mountain lion.

In a quarter of a mile, they came to another beaver pond. On the far side a beaver gnawed at a tree. Others were swimming or repairing the dam.

"I could watch them all day," Shakespeare said.

Not Blue Water Woman. She was of the opinion that when you saw one beaver you saw them all. She was more interested in the wealth of other wildlife.

Around them the grass moved to the breeze. Blue Water Woman gazed up the valley and suddenly it hit her that there wasn't any breeze; the wind had temporarily died. "We are being shadowed," she announced.

"By who?" Nate asked in alarm.

"It might be a what," Blue Water Woman said. She pointed but the grass was suddenly still.

"I don't see anything," Shakespeare said.

"Something was there, I tell you. Coyotes maybe," Blue Water Woman guessed.

Nate moved past the others. "I'll have a look." He began to rove in a circle, seeking sign.

"I will help, husband," Winona said.

The grass came as high as their waists. Here and there the blades were flattened as if by the passage of a heavy form or repeated use by smaller game. Or so Nate assumed.

"We won't be able to sleep tonight for all the howls and roars."

"You could sleep through an earthquake," Winona said. The times she'd tried to wake him in the middle of the night, she had to shake him until her arm about fell off.

Minutes passed, and Nate came to a stop.

"Nothing," Winona said. They were near the trees. She perched on a log and leaned back. "Let's rest a bit."

Nate wasn't tired, but he humored her and sat.

"We should bring Zach and Evelyn and Lou here one day," Winona said. "They would love it."

"Evelyn would," Nate agreed. Their daughter adored flowers and butterflies and the like. Their son was more practical.

"The mountains are full of pleasant surprises, are they not?" Winona said.

"You're one of them," Nate said. He couldn't help thinking that the mountains were also full of unpleasant things, too.

Winona grinned. "Thank you, kind sir. Remind me of that when we are back in our own cabin and I will treat you to a back rub."

"You could treat me tonight."

"Not with Blue Water Woman and Shakespeare in the same room."

"Are you sure you're Shoshone?" Nate had spent many a night in the lodges of her family and cousins and friends and learned early on they weren't shy about expressing affection.

A couple of robins flew out of the trees and over their heads. Sparrows chirped in the undergrowth. Across the valley a buck stepped boldly out of cover and cropped at the grass.

"Want venison for supper?" Nate asked, and raised his Hawken.

"I would rather you didn't."

"I won't miss," Nate promised. He never fired unless he was certain.

"We have plenty of food," Winona reminded him. "Besides, there is something about this valley . . ." She let her voice trail off.

"Are you glad we came?"

"I suppose." Winona straightened and looked over her shoulder and came off the log in the blink of an eye with her rifle up. "What is *that*?"

Nate spun. "What is what?" All he saw were spruce and pines and a few oaks.

"I thought—" Winona said, and stopped. "It must have been an animal, but it moved strangely."

"Strangely how?"

"You will think I am crazy."

"Try me."

"It moved like a spider."

The dappling of shadow and light had played a trick on her, Nate reckoned. "How big was the thing?"

Winona held her hand at knee height.

"That would be one huge spider," Nate teased. He stepped over the log and started into the woods only to stop when Winona gripped his arm.

"No. Please. Don't bother."

"I don't mind looking," Nate said. His wife was the most levelheaded person he knew. If she said she had seen something, she had seen something.

"I'd rather you didn't." Winona smiled and pulled on his arm. "Let's get back to the McNairs."

"This isn't like you," Nate said.

Winona shrugged. "We came here to relax and have a good time, not to chase shadows." She rose onto her toes and kissed him on the cheek. "I must have been mistaken."

"I hope so," Nate said. "The last thing we need to run into is giant spiders."

# Chapter Fourteen

Night settled over the Valley of the Se-at-co. Overhead, a plentitude of stars sparkled.

The Kings and the McNairs sat around the fire they had kindled outside the cabin. The inside was too stuffy and had an odor the women disliked. They'd left the door open to admit the air, and had removed the dirty cloth from the window.

The men were drinking coffee and the women tea. Winona had made stew from pemmican and the flour she brought, and added salt and wild onions for seasoning.

Nate was ravenous and could have eaten the entire pot himself, but he limited himself to two helpings. As he dipped his wooden spoon, he listened for the keening yip of a coyote or the howl of a wolf or the rarer roar of a bear. But the valley was unnaturally silent. "Mighty peculiar."

Winona did not need to ask what he was referring to. "You noticed, too?"

"Noticed what?" Shakespeare asked between bites.

"This Garden of Eden of yours," Blue Water Woman said. "I have never heard anywhere so quiet."

"Eh?" Shakespeare tilted his head with his ear to the wind. "The racket will start up soon enough.

It has to. A valley this size has to be crawling with flesh-eaters."

"Then where are they?" Blue Water Woman said.

"Just wait." Shakespeare resumed eating. He felt a contentment he hadn't felt in a while and was at a loss to explain why the others didn't seem to like the Valley of the Se-at-co very much. He liked it a great deal.

"Have you thought about the beaver?" Nate asked.

"I have," McNair said, "and I agree. Trapping them would be like stomping on baby chicks. We'll explore instead."

Nate was relieved. His days of raising plews were well behind him and he wanted to keep it that way. He finished his stew and refilled his tin cup with hot coffee and sat back. "Do we tell anyone else about this valley?"

"We do not," Winona said quickly.

"Let's keep it our secret," Shakespeare agreed.

"We should not tell anyone at all," Blue Water Woman threw in.

"I was thinking of Zach," Nate said. His son loved the wilderness as much as they did and would be just as fascinated.

"Not even him," Blue Water Woman said.

Shakespeare stopped chewing. "It's Nate's son. He can do what he wants."

"It would not be wise."

"It wouldn't be right not to share either," Shakespeare said. "What harm can there be? Zach is family. He can come with us the next time we do."

"I will never visit here again," Blue Water Woman said.

"Why in blazes not? It's the Garden of Eden that Methuselah told us it was."

Winona was familiar with the white Bible. Nate read to her from it from time to time. There was much she did not understand, but she remembered all that he read, and she said, "Wasn't there a serpent in the Garden?"

"The devil," Shakespeare said. "Or so a lot of folks think." He chuckled. "I didn't see a single snake all day."

The light from their fire spread about forty feet. Nate gazed toward the timber and for a few heartbeats saw eye shine. The eyes were there and they were gone. Deer, he thought, although it could have been just about anything.

Shakespeare set down his tin plate and patted his belly. "That sure hit the spot."

"It's nice to have my cooking appreciated," Winona replied.

"Hey, now," Nate said.

Over the next hour they talked about this new valley and King Valley and the weather. Nate was about to suggest they turn in when one of the horses whinnied and there was the stomp of hooves.

"Must have caught the scent of a cat or a bear," Shakespeare speculated.

"I'll go see." Nate needed to stretch his legs anyway. He gripped the end of a burning brand, and holding it in front of him, went around the corner to the corral. To his surprise the horses were in the middle and facing the ink-shrouded forest. "What is it?" he said, and walked to the end of the rails. He raised the torch higher and for a fleeing moment caught eye shine low to the ground. He thrust the torch out, but the eyes were gone. Whatever it was, it was god-awful quick. He took a few steps and spied more eye shine, only this time in a tree. He raised the torch high and those eyes disappeared, too. "Raccoons," he guessed.

Another horse nickered, and they commenced to mill nervously about.

Nate elected to stand there awhile. The raccoons might show themselves, and he could shoo them off. He yawned and rubbed his beard and put his hand on a pistol. Come to think of it, he reflected, raccoon meat was tasty.

Far back in the trees eyes appeared again, gleaming faintly, staring right at him.

"I see you," Nate said, and laughed. The eyes were the right height for a raccoon standing on its hind legs. But as they went on staring, a sense came over him that they weren't the eyes of a coon. Their shape was wrong, and they were larger than a coon's would be. "What *are* you?" he said, and took a few steps into the timber.

The eyes stayed where they were, fixed, unblinking.

Nate went through his mental catalogue of all the eyes he had ever seen and couldn't come up with a match. It wasn't a deer. It wasn't a possum. It wasn't a mountain lion or a bear.

"What are you?" he said again, and strode closer. He heard an odd scuttling noise he couldn't account for, sounding as if it was right behind him. He whirled, but nothing was there. He faced the eyes again, only they had vanished.

Nate backed to the corral. "I'm too old to be as skittish as you," he said, and grinned at his foolishness.

"I'm skittish, am I?" Winona said, coming up behind him.

"I was talking to the horses."

"Did they talk back?"

Nate laughed. He put his arm around her shoulders and held her close against his side, savoring her warmth and the scent of her hair. "I saw something."

"What?"

"It could have been anything."

"That narrows it down." Winona kissed him on the chin. "Our fire will scare off most anything. Why don't you come back and we'll turn in?"

"Changed your mind about the back rub?"

"You wish."

Yes, Nate did. He let out an exaggerated sigh. "There was a time when you couldn't keep your hands off my body."

"Zach is proof of that."

"Not Evelyn?"

"She was that evening you brought home a jug of wine. Remember? We drank until we were giggling and tipsy and then you had your way with me."

Nate hadn't forgotten. They didn't drink very often. "As I recollect, it was you who had your way with me."

"The wine affected your memory."

"Uh-huh."

"My goodness. You are almost as eloquent as Shakespeare."

Nate grinned and kissed her. "If we ever visit St. Louis again, let me do the talking."

"Why, may I ask?"

"I don't want everyone to know you speak English better than I do."

"I can't help it. Languages come easy."

"What comes easy to me," Nate said, and nuzzled her neck, "is loving you."

"Flattery, handsome husband, will still not get you that back rub with the McNairs under the same roof."

"I can ask them to sleep outside."

"You will do no such thing."

"How about if we sleep outside, then?" Nate suggested. "We can spread our blankets near the corral and keep an eye on the horses while you give me that back rub."

Winona snorted. "You expect me to believe you will behave yourself?"

"It could happen."

Winona chortled and plucked at his sleeve. "Come on, liar. We'll sleep inside with Shakespeare and Blue Water Woman."

"I'm not above begging," Nate said.

Winona stopped and gazed at the dark woodland and gave a slight shudder. "Any other place, I might agree."

"You don't like it here?"

"Something . . ." Winona paused. ". . . bothers me." She bobbed her head. "Listen. It is still so quiet. Not a sound anywhere."

"Spooky," Nate said, only partly in jest.

"Yes," Winona said. "It is."

# Chapter Fifteen

Shakespeare McNair was up before the rest. That was unusual. Normally Blue Water Woman was the first to rise. Most days, by the time he got out of bed she had coffee on and was preparing breakfast. But today he was up before the sun. He'd slept fully clothed save for his moccasins, and he tugged them on, grabbed his rifle, and stepped out into the predawn chill.

Not a solitary sound broke the tranquility. It was so quiet, he could hear the murmuring of the stream.

"God, I love it here." Shakespeare smiled and stretched and walked toward the pond. Beaver were early risers, too, and while he no longer cared to trap them, he did delight in their antics. They reminded him of the old days, and he hadn't realized how much he missed them.

The surface of the pond was as still as the valley. Not a single ripple or splash.

To the east the sky was turning gray. A grosbeak trilled and a frog croaked.

On the bank of the other side of the pond, something moved. A beaver, Shakespeare suspected, until he realized it was moving too fast. He thought it might be a coyote or a fox, but then it came to a tree and whisked up into the branches.

"What on earth?" Shakespeare wondered. He wanted to investigate, but he would have to wade across or go all the way around. Puzzled, he retraced his steps to the cabin. Suddenly a figure filled the doorway, and he took a swift step back.

"Jumpy, are you?" Nate said. He emerged and rubbed his shoulder. "I miss my bed."

"You've grown weak in your young age," Shakespeare said.

"The forties aren't young. And I can still lift an anvil over my head."

"But can you sleep on one?"

Nate chuckled. "I swear. Sometimes you make no sense whatsoever."

Shakespeare peeked inside. "The women aren't up yet? Why, the lazy wenches. Have they no shame?"

"I heard that," Blue Water Woman said from under her blankets.

"Rise and shine, dumpling. Your lord and master needs his nourishment."

"Your idea of a holiday is for me to wait on you hand and foot?"

"I couldn't have put it better."

"Not in this life or any other."

"Dang, woman, that was harsh," Shakespeare said in mock indignation.

"Tell you what," Blue Water Woman said sleepily. "Heat coffee for me and when my blood is flowing I will make you those flapjacks you love so much."

"Deal," Shakespeare said.

They had used most of their firewood the night before, so Nate and Shakespeare went into the forest for more. The spreading gray of impending dawn did not penetrate that far and downed limbs were hard to see.

Nate was groping under an oak when a thicket rustled and something hissed. He glanced up. A shape, too vague to identify, was rapidly retreating. An animal, he thought. He watched until it was out of sight and went back to looking for downed limbs. When his arms were full, he rejoined McNair. "Did you see or hear anything?"

"Just my stomach growling."

Painted by the master brushstroke of a celestial artist, the eastern sky was ablaze with vivid streaks of pink and red and orange. Half the stars were gone and soon the rest would be.

Shakespeare rekindled the fire and put coffee on. He held his hands out to warm them and gazed up the valley. "Do we ride today or walk?"

"We can cover more ground on horseback."

"Then ride it is. I want to see as much of this valley as we can before we leave."

The long night of quiet was finally broken by a chorus of avian warbles and chirps. The birds were coming alive to greet the new morning.

Now that the darkness was evaporating, Nate let himself relax. The strangeness of the night was forgotten in the brightness of the day.

Presently the wives were up. After a leisurely breakfast, they saddled their mounts and followed the stream, coming across more and more beaver the farther they went. Deer showed no fear. Elk treated them like fellow elk. Grouse took dirt baths and not panicked flight. A wren circled Winona's head, merrily singing.

"The Garden of Eden is a fitting name," Shakespeare said when they stopped at midday.

"It's not like anywhere I've ever been," Nate mentioned.

"I do not understand why there are no meat-eaters," Blue Water Woman said.

Shakespeare turned. "Now, how would you know that?"

"Did we hear a single roar or howl all night? No. Nor have we come across a single track of those that eat meat."

Winona spoke up. "And think of the animals, how unafraid they are. They have no fear of anything. As if they've never been hunted by man or beast."

"Ridiculous," Shakespeare said. "Wherever there is prey, there are predators."

"Find tracks and I will believe you," Blue Water Woman said.

Shakespeare spent the rest of their ride to the end of the valley and back again searching. He concentrated on the bare spots and soft soil along the stream, reasoning that meat-eaters, like everything else, needed to slake their thirst. He found tracks, scores upon scores, but always deer or elk or bird or fowl and never, not once, the print of any animal that ate other animals.

By late in the afternoon they were at the cabin. They put the horses in the corral and Winona offered to make a new batch of stew.

"No," Nate said. "All that talk of meat-eaters has

me hungry for the real article." He was hankering for venison.

"Won't you feel guilty?" Winona asked.

"Whatever you shoot will just stand there and look at you," Blue Water Woman said.

"Makes it easier." Nate walked off and his mentor fell into step.

"I'm with you, son. If these animals haven't learned to fear man, it's high time they did."

"I just want a steak," Nate said.

Not fifty yards from the cabin stood a big doe. She saw them but went on cropping grass.

"Maybe I should walk up and bash her over the head," Shakespeare said.

Nate pressed the Hawken's stock to his shoulder. He fixed a bead and cocked the hammer, then lightly pulled the rear trigger to set the front trigger. He held his breath and was about to shoot when a buck rose out of the grass next to the doe and stared at them with the same unconcern. Shifting, he aimed at the buck, and when the sights were squarely where he wanted them and his arms were as steady as they could be, he fired.

The buck snorted and leaped into the air and came down on its side and didn't move.

The doe looked at it and went on grazing.

"I'll be damned," Shakespeare said.

Reloading as they advanced, Nate saw the doe sniff and recoil. The scent of blood had finally done what the shot and the buck's death hadn't. With a bound she was off into the trees.

"The Garden of Eden is no more," Shakespeare

said with mock gravity. "And you, Horatio, are the serpent."

Nate didn't find that the least bit funny. But he refused to feel bad. Venison was a staple on the frontier. He had lost count of the number of deer he'd shot over the years. It had to be in the hundreds.

Several more doe were across the way. They went on feeding as if nothing had happened.

"How about I do the honors?" Shakespeare said, starting to draw his knife.

"I shot it." Nate handed his rifle to McNair, drew his bowie, and bent to the task. He rolled the buck on its back and slit each hind leg. He cut from the chin to the tail down the middle of the belly, then cut each front leg from the knee down and peeled back the hide.

"We should smoke some of this," Shakespeare said. "Otherwise a lot will go to waste."

"Let the women know," Nate said, and went on working. By the time he was done, Winona and Blue Water Woman had rigged drying racks from trimmed tree limbs.

There was a lot of meat to slice and hang. They were at it most of the morning. At last Nate straightened and walked to the pond. Kneeling, he rolled up his sleeves and dipped his arms in. The blood turned the water red and bits of gore floated to the surface.

Winona came up. She had her rifle and his. Squatting, she watched two beaver gaily swimming. "I think we are being watched."

"You *think*?"

"It is only a feeling but a strong feeling." She gave him the Hawken.

Nate remembered to reload. He opened his powder horn and poured black powder into his palm and fed the powder down the barrel. From his ammo pouch he took a ball and patch and tamped them down the barrel with the ramrod.

Winona waited until he was finished to say, "Shakespeare loves it here, but Blue Water Woman and I are uneasy. She confided in me last night that she thinks this valley is bad medicine. She wants to leave. I'm willing to stay longer but not more than a day or two."

"Shakespeare will be disappointed."

"And you?"

Nate gazed out over Eden. "The luster is wearing off. It's not natural, the animals the way they are. It's not natural that we haven't seen any sign of meat-eaters. Whenever you ladies are ready to leave is fine by me."

"Good. I knew I could count on you." Winona pecked him on the chin.

Shakespeare took the news with a squawk of protest. "Two more days? That's all? We could stay for a month of Sundays and it wouldn't be enough for me."

"Please, husband," Blue Water Woman said.

"But there's so much we haven't seen yet."

"Please."

Shakespeare muttered, but he gave in. They spent the afternoon climbing the mountain behind the cabin. From a grassy shelf, they were treated to a vista of nature as legend had it the earth had once been: vital and green and rife with living beings.

Breathing deep, Shakespeare said reverently, "If this is how heaven is, I reckon they can count me in."

"You will be around awhile yet," Blue Water Woman said.

"Dream on, fair one, dream on."

They descended by a different route and were a short distance from the cabin when Shakespeare drew up and said, "What in God's name is that?"

Nate was as confounded as his mentor.

Under a giant spruce sat a bizarre cone five feet wide and almost as high. Woven from limbs with the needles left on, it resembled an upside-down basket. The needles were brown, the branches brittle, leading Nate to say, "Whoever made this, it was a while ago."

"But who?" Winona wondered. "And why?"

"I don't see any openings," Blue Water Woman said.

Nate lifted one side and brown needles rained down. He was at a complete loss.

"How curious," Shakespeare said.

The horses were dozing, so they didn't think anything was wrong until they came to the front door.

"I thought I shut it," Winona said.

Nate went in and flared with anger. "We've had visitors," he gruffly informed them.

In their absence, their parfleches and packs had been opened and their effects scattered. So had their pots and pans and blankets. The flour had been upended. The coffee tin had been partially crushed.

The water skin had a hole in it and most of the water had drained out.

Nate squatted and examined the hole. "Teeth marks."

"A bear, you reckon?" Shakespeare said.

"Or raccoons," Winona said. Those devious little devils delighted in sticking their noses into everything.

Blue Water Woman was swatting flour from one of her dresses. Suddenly she stopped and turned. "The meat!"

They ran outside and around the cabin and Nate indulged in a rare streak of swearing.

The racks had been pushed over and most of the strips were gone. The trampled grass gave no clue to the identity of whatever was to blame.

"It has to be raccoons," Winona insisted.

Nate was disinclined to agree. It would take an army of raccoons to eat all the venison he had cut up. He said as much.

"What else, then?" Winona said.

Shakespeare had been roving in ever-wider circles and now he called out and pointed at a patch of bare earth. "Take a gander."

The short hairs at the nape of Nate's neck prickled.

Clearly imprinted in the dirt was another of the strange thin tracks of a humanlike foot.

"What *are* these things?" Winona said.

No one could answer her.

# Chapter Sixteen

By nightfall they had cleaned up the mess and repacked and were eating what was left of the venison.

Blue Water Woman had little appetite and presently set her tin plate down. "I would like to leave in the morning, husband."

"So would I," Winona said.

To Nate it didn't matter. He liked the valley, but he was growing as uneasy as the women. "If we're taking a vote, I vote with them."

Shakespeare frowned. He loved his wife dearly and nearly always did whatever she asked, but he had been having a fine time until the mess was made. "We're letting a pack of raccoons scare us off?"

"That track wasn't made by any coon," Nate said.

"I know. It's just that—" Shakespeare stopped. He didn't know if he could make them fully understand how young the valley made him feel, and how invigorating that feeling was.

"Please," Blue Water Woman said.

"If it means that much to you, fine," Shakespeare said. "We'll head out at first light."

Once again the night was eerily still. It was so quiet that they all heard a splash from over in the pond.

Nate knelt at the small stone fireplace and added firewood. "We should take turns keeping watch."

Shakespeare, Winona, Nate, and Blue Water woman—that was the order they agreed to.

Shakespeare had no trouble staying awake. He drank enough coffee to drown a fish. It made him feel restless, but it kept him wide-eyed until it was his turn to turn in. Nothing of note occurred except that once he thought he heard the pad of feet outside the front door. He went to the window but saw nothing to account for it.

Winona filled her own coffee cup and sat near the fire. She was not as fond of the brew as the men. She'd much rather drink tea. But it helped keep her alert, so she sat and sipped and thought about the events of the day and what they might mean and before she knew it, it was time to wake her husband.

Nate was slow to rouse. He was finally enjoying a good solid sleep. Sitting up, he shook his head to clear the cobwebs, but his mind was mush. His remedy, as theirs had been, was coffee. Cup after cup. He was on the fourth when what he could only describe as scuttling noises came from outside. Putting down the cup, he gripped his Hawken and opened the front door. Nothing was there. He shut the door and sat back down and went on sipping. He was reaching for the coffeepot when he happened to glance at the window and his heart nearly stopped.

The silhouette of a head was framed in the opening.

Leaping to his feet, Nate drew a pistol and ran to the door. He yanked it open and stepped out—but no one was there.

He looked left and right and off toward the stream and into the forest. Again, nothing.

Thinking it must have been his imagination, Nate closed the door and took a seat. He wedged the pistol under his belt and placed his rifle across his lap.

Nate thought of the strange tracks. They appeared to be the prints of people, yet they were so thin, the people had to be sticks. He gave a mild start. What was it Blue Water Woman had said back when Methuselah Jones told them about the Valley of the Se-at-co? Her words came to him in a rush: *It means Stick People.*

Nate glanced at the window and frowned. Indian legends often had kernels of truth. And he was well aware that for every tribe most people had heard of, there were half a dozen others that no one knew existed. He had run into some of those tribes. They tended to shy from white men, with good cause. Whites often brought disease, with disastrous results. Just look at what happened to the Mandans. But if there was a tribe of Stick People in the Garden of Eden, where was their village? There had been no sign of lodges or trails made by the tribe's comings and goings. He thought of the odd cone made of pine boughs, and shook his head. Whatever it had been, it sure wasn't a lodge.

Nate sipped and pondered. The sooner they got out of there, the better. He'd lost all enthusiasm for exploring. The Garden of Eden, like its biblical namesake, had a serpent in its midst and that serpent had ungodly thin feet.

Sudden sounds came through the door, a rapid pattering and a light thump as if something had brushed against it.

Darting over, Nate jerked it open. Once again nothing was there. He glimpsed a shape gliding along the ground and raised his rifle, but the figure disappeared. Something that low had to be an animal. But what? he wondered. It had been too big to be a coon and too small to be a bear. Closing the door, he returned to the fireplace.

Nate didn't need more coffee to stay awake. His raw nerves sufficed. When it came time to wake Blue Water Woman, he didn't. He let her sleep and went on keeping watch.

Half an hour went by. Nate yawned, and was surprised he could feel tired with so much coffee in him. He rubbed his eyes and put a log on and was settling back when piercing whinnies and squeals of terror shattered the night, along with the crack and crash of wood and then the pounding of hooves. He was to the door and raced out and around the corner and reached the corral in time to see the last of their horses galloping madly off into the forest.

Behind him, Shakespeare and Winona and Blue Water Woman hustled up, Winona holding a brand aloft.

"Good God!" McNair exclaimed.

"What happened?" Winona asked. "What did this?"

The rails nearest the trees had been shattered and cast aside. Marks in the dirt and a red smear led from the corral, through the opening, and into the woods.

"Something killed one of our horses and dragged it off," Blue Water Woman said.

"But what?" Winona wondered. "A bear?"

"The Stick People," Nate said, and they looked at him. "Those tracks we saw. It has to be."

"It would take a lot of them to drag off a grown horse," Shakespeare said skeptically.

Nate hadn't thought about that. A horse weighed upwards of a thousand pounds. How had they broken into the corral and gotten the horse out of there in the short time it took him to run outside?

"We should follow the blood and see where it leads," Blue Water Woman said.

"I'll go," Nate volunteered, and reached for the burning brand.

# Chapter Seventeen

Winona swung the torch away from him. "You are not going into those woods alone"

"Listen to her," Shakespeare said. He gazed skyward. "It'll be daylight in a couple of hours. We should wait until then and go together."

Blue Water Woman nodded in agreement.

"Back inside, then," Nate said, and covered them while they filed in. He was last. As he was stepping over the threshold, a figure appeared at the edge of the trees. He couldn't make out much detail, as dark as it was, other than that the figure was as tall as he was, if not taller—and on two legs. He stopped and turned toward it, and it melted away.

"Get inside," Winona urged. She was afraid he was going to go after the horses without them. The moment he stepped past her, she shut the door and wedged the pole against it.

"So much for paradise," Shakespeare said.

Blue Water Woman sat with her back to the far wall. "The stories are true, then."

"What stories?" Shakespeare said.

"The Se-at-co are real. I never really believed, but they are."

"Let's not get ahead of ourselves."

Blue Water Woman was staring into space. "My

grandmother would gather us children and tell us tales. About Amotken and how the world was made. About the animal people, who could think and talk like us. About how Coyote taught us to make bows and arrows and to hunt buffalo." She paused. "She told us of the little people who buzz like bees and the hairy giants who take women and mate with them, and she told us of the Stick People. They are from the old times. They are like men and women and yet they are not men and women. She always said there were few of them left. These might be the last."

"Men and not men?" Nate said.

"My grandmother said that Amotken gave them their own land with plenty of deer and elk to hunt, but the Se-at-co were not content. They hunted humans, too, and did terrible things to those they caught."

Shakespeare turned from the window. "What kind of terrible things?"

"Torture. Mutilation. And worse."

"What can be worse than that?" Shakespeare said.

"It is said they ate them."

"God," Nate said.

"For many winters the Se-at-co hunted our people, until a great warrior gathered all the humans and waged war on them. Most were killed. The few who lived fled into the mountains and have not been heard of since. Although there have been rumors of unusual tracks and of people who have gone missing."

"You're saying these Stick People have been killing humans all along?" Nate said.

"If all of this is true," Winona said, "they will try to catch and eat us, too."

"Let's not jump to conclusions," Shakespeare said.

"It could be they're just a tribe of skinny Indians. The Apaches are known for being stocky and muscular. The Nez Perce are tall and lean. Maybe if we try to talk to these Se-at-co—"

"We can't take any chances," Nate broke in. "From now on we stay together. No one goes anywhere alone. Is that understood?"

Winona and Blue Water Woman both said yes.

Nate faced his mentor. "What about you? Why are you balking?"

"Maybe they're not the threat we think. They killed one of our horses, yes. They stole some of our meat and made a mess of our effects. But they haven't harmed *us*. Maybe they're not as vicious as the stories make them out to be."

"Or maybe they're wary of our guns," Nate said.

"All I'm saying is that we shouldn't kill them on sight," Shakespeare said. "Let's try to make friends and avoid bloodshed if we can."

"I don't know," Winona said.

"Methuselah Jones did. This cabin is the proof. He lived here for years and they didn't harm him."

Nate pursed his lips. McNair had a point.

Shakespeare wouldn't let it drop. "If they truly are the last of their kind, think of what that means."

Blue Water Woman raised her head. "The old stories say they are not to be trusted."

"That was long ago," Shakespeare argued. "They deserve the benefit of the doubt."

"And if you're wrong?" Nate said

"We defend ourselves if we have to. But until they give us cause, we shouldn't rush to judgment."

"Oh, my," Nate said.

"What?"

Nate grinned. "You said all that without once quoting the Bard."

Shakespeare put his hands on his hips. "Thou half-penny purse of wit. I shall not excuse you, you shall not be excused, excuses shall not be admitted, there is no excuse shall serve you, you shall not be excused."

"I knew it was too good to last."

Winona smiled at their banter, but not Blue Water Woman. She stood and went to her man and placed her hand on his arm and looked him in the eye. "I think we are making a mistake."

"By not wiping the Stick People out? God, you're a bloodthirsty wench."

"I am serious."

"What can it hurt to—" Shakespeare began, but he got no further.

The last thing any of them expected happened.

There was a knock on the door.

# Chapter Eighteen

The Kings and the McNairs looked at one another in surprise. It was Nate who moved to the door and demanded, "Who's there?"

"Methuselah Jones. The door won't open. Let me in."

Nate kicked the pole aside, yanked the door open, and grabbed hold of Jones's shirt. Before the startled old-timer could think to stop him, Nate pulled Jones inside, pivoted, and shoved him so hard, Jones stumbled halfway across the room. He would have fallen if he hadn't thrust the stock of his rifle at the ground to brace himself. "I should bust your skull."

"What on earth?" Methuselah blurted.

"Our horses have been stolen, our meat has been taken," Nate said angrily.

"You didn't tell us there were people here," Shakespeare said.

"If they *are* people," Blue Water Woman interjected.

Methuselah straightened and rubbed his chest where Nate had grabbed him. "Why do you think I came all the way back? I was on my way to the plains when it hit me that I'd mentioned the Se-at-co but hadn't made it plain they live here. We got too busy joking about sticks."

"A strange thing to overlook," Winona said.

"Not at all, Mrs. King," Methuselah said politely. "Fact is, I hardly ever saw them. They never gave me any problem. Whole months would go by and I wouldn't so much as catch of glimpse of the things."

"Things?" Winona repeated.

Methuselah gave Nate a solicitous look. "I'm sorry to hear about your horses and your meat. They never stole anything from me."

"Never?" Shakespeare said.

"Like I said, they left me pretty much alone. Maybe you did something to make them mad."

"Hold that thought." Nate shut the door and wedged the pole and turned. "Now, then. What could we have done that you didn't?"

Methselah shrugged. "That was just a guess. It could be they're upset about there being so many of you. I was just one man."

"So you have no idea why they took our horses?" Winona said.

"No, ma'am, I don't." Methselah stifled a yawn. "But I'm more than willing to talk to them on your account and see what I can do about getting your animals back."

"You would do that for us?"

"I'm here, ain't I?" Methselah smothered another yawn. "And I'm mighty tuckered out. I rode all night."

"It was very considerate of you to rush back to tell us," Winona said.

Blue Water Woman frowned.

"Thank you. Now, if it's all the same to all of you, I'd like to turn in. I need a few hours of sleep."

Methuselah moved to the north wall and eased onto his side with his back to them. He lay with his head on his arm and said, "Don't mind me none." Almost immediately he was breathing deeply as if in sleep.

The four stared at his back for a full minute before Nate said, "Well."

"Well what?" Shakespeare replied.

"He's done the right thing by us. If he can recover our horses, I'll be in his debt."

"It is his fault they were taken," Blue Water Woman said.

Shakespeare put his hands on his hips. "How do you figure? He wasn't even here."

"He didn't tell us about the Se-at-co living here."

"And he explained about that."

"Why do you defend him?"

"He came back, didn't he? That right there shows me his heart is in the right place."

"He has no heart."

"Blue Water Woman," Winona said.

"He doesn't," Blue Water Woman said. "And he speaks with two tongues."

"Now he's a liar?" Shakespeare said.

"I do not believe a word he told us, no. We cannot trust him."

"First you want to wipe out the Se-at-co. Now this. What's gotten into you?"

"I think we should take his horses and go."

Shakespeare didn't hide his shock. "Whoa there. You want to *steal* his animals and strand him here afoot?"

"The Se-at-co stole ours."

"But they're not him," Shakespeare said, and shook

his head in bewilderment. "After all these years I thought I knew you."

"He is not to be trusted," Blue Water Woman said again.

"I, for one, would like my horse back," Nate said. "I'm willing to let him try on our behalf."

"As am I," Winona said.

Shakespeare nodded. "Makes three of us."

The hurt on Blue Water Woman's face was plain. "Fine. You are my husband and my best friends. I will do as you want even though you are making a mistake." Turning, she went to the opposite side of the cabin from Jones and lay with her back to him with her rifle in her hands. "I am going to try to get some sleep. You should, too. We will need our wits about us this day."

"Blue Water Woman—" Shakespeare began.

"Hush, husband. You have made your decision clear. I will abide by it even though I do not agree with it. Now let me get some rest."

Shakespeare went over to the far corner and beckoned for Nate and Winona to join him. "What do you make of all this?" he whispered.

"Blue Water Woman is not acting at all like herself," Winona whispered back.

"We've known her a good many years and she's always had a good head on her shoulders," Nate said. "She must have a reason for feeling like she does."

"I'll try to pry it out of her," Shakespeare proposed. "In the meantime, I guess she had the right idea. We should all of get some rest."

"I'll stand watch," Nate offered.

"You need sleep, too," Winona said.

"Someone has to, and I don't know if I could sleep if I tried."

Reluctantly, Winona lay down near the McNairs.

Nate went to the window. He was surprised to see that Methuselah Jones had left his mount and packhorse in front of the cabin and not in the corral. Jones had even left the saddle and packs on.

Nate realized that here was perfect bait. Whoever took his bay and the other horses might come after Jones's. He strained his eyes into the dark, seeking to distinguish shapes and movement. He did it for so long, his eyes began to hurt. The two horses stood with their heads hung in exhaustion, another fact in Jones's favor; the man had practically ridden his animals into the ground to get there.

An uneventful hour crawled by and then two. Dawn wasn't far off. Nate gave his head a toss to shake off the mental cobwebs. He was tired to his core. He should have listened to Winona and gotten some sleep.

One of the horses raised its head and nickered.

Nate was instantly alert. The horse was looking toward the corner of the cabin nearest to the corral. Nate craned his neck to see better—just as *something* came around the corner.

# Chapter Nineteen

Anticipation mixed with dread rippled through Nate King. He wanted the thing to come to the horses, but it had stopped, evidently wary of showing itself. All he could tell was that it was on two legs and tall and exceptionally thin—just like the figure he'd spotted before. He remembered Shakespeare speculating that the Se-at-co were nothing but skinny Indians, and it appeared his friend had been right.

Or was he? Nate wondered. It was too dark to be sure, but he would swear the figure wasn't wearing clothes. No buckskins, no moccasins, not even a breechclout. And there was something about the toothpick arms and legs and the shape of the head that didn't seem right. The head seemed to be swiveling back and forth on an impossibly long neck.

Then it happened. The stick figure glided toward the horses.

Nate was struck by the shape of the head. It was twice as long from top to bottom as most human heads would be, and the jaw jutted like a spike. But what was most bizarre was that there didn't appear to be a nose. A trick of the shadows, he reckoned.

The Se-at-co stopped after only a few steps. With each stride, Nate noticed, the head bobbed up and down, as a pigeon's might do when it was feeding, or a snake's. He didn't know what to make of it. Hardly breathing, he waited for whatever it was to come closer. But the figure stayed back.

Nate wanted to see it better. Ducking from the window, he moved to the door and quietly removed the oak pole and set it down. He leaned his Hawken against the wall and drew a pistol.

Girding himself, he wrenched the door wide and sprang outside.

The Se-at-co wasn't there.

Nate glimpsed a rail-thin form going around the corner. He flew after it, but when he reached the corner it was gone. He stopped in bewilderment. There hadn't been time for the thing to reach the forest. The corral was empty. He looked up, thinking it might be climbing onto the roof. He looked down, thinking it might have heard him and dropped flat.

Something rose out of the high grass half a dozen yards away, something on four legs, not two. In a blur, it shot toward the woods, scrabbling like a giant crab.

Rooted in amazement, Nate was slow going after it. He galvanized into a sprint, but the thing was ungodly fast. Nate burst into the forest and halted. He might as well be at the bottom of a well. It was pitch-black. The undergrowth crackled, and he whirled but saw no one. He took a step, and suddenly his left leg was seized above the ankle. It felt like iron cords wrapped tight. He tried to turn, but his leg was pulled out from under him. Crashing onto his back, he rolled toward his attacker. No one was there. He pushed to his knees, only to have something slam into his back.

Rigid bands clamped around his back and chest. He heaved but couldn't break the grip. Something hissed in his ear and spittle flecked his skin.

Nate couldn't decide if it was a man or an animal. He imagined teeth sinking into his neck, and panic lent him strength. He surged against the bands. He could use his forearms, and swung his flintlock. It was like hitting rock. Suddenly he was released.

Nate spun. For a few heartbeats he was virtually face-to-face with his attacker. In the dark all he could make out was that the face was as flat as a board. Copper eyes were fixed on him with inhuman intensity. Then there was a shout and the flare of light, and whatever had had hold of him whirled and was gone with incredible speed, moving on all fours.

Nate rose as the light became bright and Winona was there, a torch held high, a pistol in her other hand.

"What was that? I only caught a glimpse."

"I don't know," Nate said.

"Are you all right? A noise woke me and I saw you were missing, so I rushed out and heard sounds of a struggle."

"I saw one of the Se-at-co out the window and when I came outside this—thing—jumped me."

From the darkness beyond the ring of torchlight came rustling sounds. Sounds that came swiftly closer.

"We should go back inside, husband," Winona advised.

Nate didn't want to. He wanted to stay there and draw whatever was out there into the light so he could see what had attacked him. But for her sake he said, "Back to back. Shoot anything that comes at us."

They moved toward the corral, the breeze fanning the torch and causing the light to writhe and flicker. Nate hoped it wouldn't go out. He had a feeling that if it did, they would be set on. Just as they made it out of the trees and into the open Winona whispered, "Look!"

Nate saw them. Eyes. Lots of eyes, low to the ground, eyes unlike those of any animal he had ever seen. They stared without blinking, baleful stares, fierce stares, as if the creatures yearned to close and tear them apart. It made his skin crawl.

"What *are* they?" Winona whispered.

"Keep going." Nate wanted her inside where they were safe. They backed around the corner of the cabin and more light washed over them.

"How now, Horatio. And the fair Ophelia. Have you two been off courting?" Shakespeare teased.

"Something is out there," Winona said.

McNair sobered and came to their side. He had his rifle. "I don't see anything."

Neither did Nate. The eyes were gone. "Inside," he urged, and was glad when the door was closed and the oak pole propped against it. He leaned against the door, trying to make sense of what had just happened.

Blue Water Woman sat up, yawning. "What is all the commotion?"

Shakespeare answered her with, "Winona and Nate were off making babies and a raccoon came along and scared them."

"You are not the least little bit amusing," Winona said.

"I have been saying that for years," Blue Water Woman said.

"Teeth hadst thou in thy head when you were born," Shakespeare quoted, "to signify thou cam'st to bite the world."

"You four sure are lively," said a voice from across the cabin. "A fella can't hardly sleep for all the ruckus." Methuselah Jones rolled over. "It's not dawn yet, is it?"

"An hour or so," Nate said.

"Then do you suppose you'd let me sleep until it is? I have a busy day ahead if I'm to convince the Se-at-co that you're friendly."

"And persuade them to give back our horses," Shakespeare reminded him. "Don't forget that."

"Of course." Jones rolled back over. "And put out those torches, if you would be so kind. I can't sleep with it so bright."

"I reckon we should all try to get a little more rest," Shakespeare said.

Nate couldn't sleep if he tried. "Go ahead. I'll keep on standing guard."

"So long as you stand it in here and not out there," Winona cautioned. "I want your word that you won't go outside again without letting us know first."

"I'm not a child," Nate said.

"Your fairer half is being sensible and reasonable, Horatio," Shakespeare said. "I want your promise, too."

"Very well."

"Let me hear you say the words," Winona said.

"Define, define, well-educated infant," Shakespeare quoted.

"I won't go out that door without asking your permission," Nate said.

The torches were extinguished and Winona and Shakespeare lay down. Nate stayed by the window, looking out. When feet brushed the ground and an arm brushed his, he shifted to make room, thinking it was his wife.

"Mind company?" Blue Water Woman whispered.

"You have to give your word not to step out the door without telling the white-haired word spout and his partner in tyranny," Nate said.

Blue Water Woman laughed lightly. "Word spout? Oh, I like that. I will use it on him sometime soon just to see how red his face gets." Her smile died and she looked worriedly out the window. "What are we up against out there?"

"I wish to God I knew."

"If they had not taken our horses, I would urge that we leave right away."

"If they hadn't taken them, I'd go."

"I hope you will take me seriously about Jones," Blue Water whispered.

"Something happened between you two, didn't it? A long time ago?"

"No matter how long, a person doesn't forget." Blue Water Woman took a deep breath. "He tried to rape me, Nate. He got my dress up and—" She stopped and trembled. "If I hadn't gotten hold of a knife—" Again she stopped.

"No need to go on," Nate said softly.

"Do you understand why I dislike him so?"

"Let me put it this way. He so much as touches you, I'll break his arm."

"Thank you. You are a good friend."

# Chapter Twenty

The day dawned clear and beautiful. The sky was azure, the forest bright hues of green, the valley floor resplendent in the rosy wash of sunlight.

Methuselah Jones slept well past daybreak. It was the middle of the morning when he stirred and sat up and stretched. "Morning," he said to the Kings and the McNairs, who were clustered by the window.

"Good morning," Winona said.

Shakespeare grunted.

Neither Nate nor Blue Water Woman said anything.

"I reckon I should get up and about and see what I can do about smoothing things over with the Se-at-co."

"That would be kind of you," Winona said.

"The important thing is to get our horses back," Shakespeare brought up again.

"I'll try my best," Methuselah said, and inwardly smiled at his lie. Retrieving their mounts was the last thing he wanted to do. He sniffed and said, "Any chance of having some of that coffee I smell?"

"Help yourself," Nate said, with a nod at the pot by the fireplace.

"I'm obliged." Methuselah went out to his own

mount and rummaged in a parfleche. He found his tin cup and came back in and filled it to the brim. "This is a treat. For years I had to go without."

Winona and Shakespeare came over and Winona said, "If you don't mind my asking, why did you stay here for so long all by yourself?"

Methuselah shrugged. "I've never had any problem with being alone. Fact is, I prefer it."

"You like the wilds," Shakespeare said.

"And I don't care to be around people one damn bit," Methuselah saw no harm in admitting. "They carp, they whine, they're too nosy, they're too bossy, they put on airs, they cheat, they lie, they hurt others, they kill."

Blue Water Woman broke her silence. "What a strange thing for you to say."

"Live a year in any city and tell me I'm wrong."

"That is not what I meant."

Methuselah sipped and gave her his best smile. "I'm not the man I used to be," he lied again. "When we're young we do and say things we'd never do or say when our hair is gray and we're long in the tooth."

"True," Shakespeare said. "We mature despite ourselves."

"Not everyone," Blue Water Woman said.

Methuselah hid his smirk by raising the cup to his mouth. He swallowed and enjoyed the pleasant warmth that spread through his belly. "I only hope the Se-at-co will listen to reason."

"You speak their tongue?" Winona asked.

"A little," Methuselah said. "It's damn hard to

learn. Nothing like the white tongue or any Indian tongue, for that matter."

"I am good at tongues," Winona said. "Maybe I should go with you."

Both Methuselah and Nate said "No" at the same time.

"I beg your pardon?" Winona said, glancing from one to the other.

"You wouldn't go marching into an Apache village, would you?" Methuselah said. "Odds are you'd never march out again."

"Are you saying they are as fierce as Apaches?"

"I'm saying they can be worse. They don't know you. They won't trust you. Go near their young and they'll rip your heart out."

"Surely you exaggerate."

"No, ma'am," Methuselah said. "I sure as blazes do not."

He drained his cup and stood. "Enough jabber. I'd better get on with it."

"We're grateful," Shakespeare said.

Methuselah smiled at them, but only Shakespeare and Winona smiled back. He went out and put the cup in his parfleche and climbed on the sorrel. "I'll leave my packhorse with you. If I don't come back you're welcome to him."

"Where is their village?" Nate asked.

"They don't have one. They move around a lot and camp in a different spot every night." Methuselah told yet another falsehood. "Be seeing you, I hope." He jabbed his heels and rode past the corral and into the forest. Since he knew what to look for and where, he spotted two of the Se-at-co right away, perched where they could spy on the cabin unseen. He dipped his chin to each of them and they let him pass.

Methuselah had his rifle across his saddle and his brace of pistols, but he would only use them as a last resort. They wouldn't do him much good anyway, he reflected, as hard as it was to hit the damn things.

A pair of sparrows flitted past. Robins were warbling and jays were playing in a bush. Ground squirrels scampered from the sorrel and a rabbit bounded off.

It never ceased to amaze Methuselah, how rich the valley was in wildlife. The Se-at-co had a lot to do with it. They killed every meat-eater that wandered in. Didn't like the competition, Methuselah reckoned.

He rode slowly so word would reach them he was coming long before he got there. They might wonder why, and that alone should keep him alive. He grinned sadistically at the fate that would befall the McNairs and the Kings if all went well.

It was a big "if," Methuselah told himself. The Se-at-co were unpredictable as hell.

Out of the corner of his eye he caught movement. One of them was pacing him thirty feet out. As long as he had lived there, he still wasn't used to how they moved. It was—unnatural. That was the word. There was much about the Se-at-co that was unsettling, but how they moved was the worst.

Another one appeared on the opposite side. They showed no emotion. But then, they rarely did. Something to do with the muscles in their faces, Methuselah suspected. All their muscles were so hard, it was a wonder they could move.

Two more had joined his little parade, one behind

and another staying ahead of him. They had him surrounded, Methuselah realized.

The forest rolled on. Midway along the valley Methuselah came to the rift and suddenly there were a dozen of them, some hissing their displeasure, others curling and uncurling their exceptionally long fingers as if they couldn't wait to wrap them around his throat. The sorrel snorted and shied, but he goaded it down in.

Ages past, the earth had split. Tall trees graced the rims, but brush was scant and the bottom was mostly open. Here, where the high trees kept out the sun and perpetual shadow reigned, dwelled the valley's inhabitants.

Scores of large cones, woven from tree boughs, were scattered like so many giant acorns. In some of the cones Se-at-co were sleeping, curled into bony balls as was their habit. Most were empty because they were waiting for him, as he'd expected, many on all fours, their long jaws and horrid eyes enough to give most folks unending nightmares.

Methuselah sat straight in the saddle and tried not to show the fear that lurked deep in his heart. They could easily slay him and there would be nothing he could do except scream.

Their leader was on two legs, his copper eyes empty of clues that would betray his intent.

Methuselah drew rein. He stayed on the sorrel. The horse was his only prayer of escape. He looked around for the animals taken from the Kings and McNairs, but they were nowhere to be seen. With great effort, constricting his throat so as to reproduce the Se-at-co tongue, he said, 'I back.'

'It bad you leave nest,' was the guttural reply. 'We not like.'

'I friend Se-at-co,' Methuselah said.

Their leader didn't respond.

For the hundredth time Methuselah wondered if it was male or female. It was impossible to tell. 'I come help Se-at-co.'

'Help how?' the leader wanted to know.

'Other people come nest,' Methuselah said.

'We see. We take food.'

'Where food?'

The leader headed deeper into the rift, the others scrabbling to either side. Beyond the adults were the young.

Precious few, as Methuselah had learned. The Se-at-co had only themselves to blame. In the harsh weather of winter they ate them.

Then the stench hit him. Methuselah nearly gagged. He had forgotten how abominable the reek was. Their feeding area, the Se-at-co called it, where they gathered to gorge on prey. The sight made his stomach churn.

Countless bones covered a wide area. Most had long since been stripped bare, but bits and pieces of rotting flesh clung to more recent kills. On top of the heap, and only partially devoured, was a horse, its glazed eyes wide with the fright it had felt when it died. The head and neck were intact, but the belly had been eaten away to the backbone, with a few loops of intestines and half a liver swarming with flies. Several Se-at-co were feasting and looked up. Their long chins slick with gore, they chomped their mouths with relish. Like all their kind, they ate with their mouths open and Methuselah could see the squishy clumps they were chewing. Bile rose in his throat, and he swallowed it down.

On the other side of the feeding area, tied to trees, were the rest of the horses. The Se-at-co wouldn't feed or water them. One by one, over the next week or so, they would be slain and gorged upon.

'Food good,' their leader said, and looked pointedly at Methuselah's sorrel.

'Other people stay nest,' Methuselah said, his throat practically hoarse.

That took the leader's mind off the sorrel. His head snapped up and he clacked, 'Live here?'

'Yes.'

'We not let.'

Struggling to remember the right sounds, Methuselah touched his chest and said, 'You need know so I come.'

'Bad them here.'

'I help you,' Methuselah offered.

'They have sticks that kill.'

Methuselah made a pouncing gesture with his hand, his fingers like claws. 'You attack when people—' He couldn't remember the sounds, so he twisted and pointed at his back.

'When?'

'Soon.'

'When?' the leader pressed him.

'Soon. Keep watch. You know when can,' Methuselah said.

Once the McNairs and the Kings were taken care of, he'd head for the States.

The leader was staring at him with the inscrutable expression of their kind.

'More?' Methuselah said.

'You not go.'

'I came back,' Methuselah said. 'Prove I am friend.'

In a staccato burst, the leader said something to the others too fast for Methuselah to follow. Some showed their pointed teeth in what for them were grins.

'You kill people?' Methuselah said.

'We kill.'

Methuselah reined the sorrel around and got out of there. There was only so much of their presence he could abide. He didn't care that half a dozen followed him. He had done what he set out to. He'd have his revenge on Blue Water Woman. So what if her husband and the Kings had to die as well? They were nothing to him.

Good riddance, he thought, and laughed.

# Chapter Twenty-one

In the bright glow of the afternoon sun, the Garden of Eden was deceptively peaceful. Nate stood on the bank of the pond watching the beaver industriously work and tried not to dwell on the fact that another night loomed. Half the day was gone, and Jones wasn't back yet. He'd not seen hide or hair of the Se-at-co, but he couldn't shake the feeling they were out there and that unseen eyes were on him. It put him on edge, and when a hand fell on his shoulder, he gave a start.

"You are jumpy, husband," Winona said.

"You would be, too, if you saw one of those things," Nate said.

"You told me you didn't get a good look at it."

"No, I didn't, but there was something about it . . ." At a loss as to how to describe his feelings, Nate fell silent.

"We will be gone soon. Jones will return with our horses, and by nightfall this valley will be a memory."

"I hope so," Nate said. He gazed toward the cabin. "Where's McNair?"

"Inside arguing with Blue Water Woman. She is upset with him, and he can't find out why. Do you know?"

Nate went on staring at the beaver.

"If you did, you would tell me."

"Unless I gave her my word I wouldn't."

"Ah." Winona crouched and dipped her hand in the water and splashed some on her neck. "This is a fine mess we are in. If Jones can't get our horses, we should leave on foot."

"It's a long way to our valley."

Winona patted the ground. "Would you rather be six feet under, as you whites like to say?" She didn't wait for him to answer. "When my time comes to shed this life, I want to die in my cabin with my loved ones around me."

"We don't always have a choice." Nate wouldn't mind dying peacefully in bed, but life in the wilderness was fraught with perils.

Up the valley, hooves drummed and out of the forest trotted Methuselah Jones.

"He's back!" Winona exclaimed. "But he hasn't brought our horses."

They walked to the cabin and got there just as Jones drew rein and dismounted.

"I bring good news."

"And nothing else," Nate said.

Methuselah frowned. "I'm sorry. They wouldn't hand your horses over. But I know where the Se-at-co are keeping them and I have an idea."

"We are listening," Winona said.

"I don't want to have to explain it twice. Where are Blue Water Woman and McNair?"

A loud voice in the cabin was followed by Shakespeare stomping out in a huff and slamming the door. "Why the good Lord created females I will never know," he grumbled. He looked up and saw them and his cheeks became red. "Oh. I didn't know you were there."

"Is there a problem?" Methuselah asked.

"Besides my wife telling me there is something important she must tell me and then refusing to tell me?"

"Strange," Methuselah said.

"Woo her, wed her, and bed her, and rid the house of her," Shakespeare quoted.

"Are you still talking about your wife?"

"I will praise an eel with the same praise."

Methuselah shook his head. "You're making no damn sense. Are you mad at her?"

"No more so than the moon at the sun."

Jones appealed to Nate. "Is it me or is he addlepated? What in God's name is he talking about?"

"Pay attention," Shakespeare said, and quoted anew. "A horse, a horse, my kingdom for a horse."

"You're asking about the horses, aren't you?"

"Here comes the trout that must be caught with tickling."

"Enough!" Methuselah declared. "My head is spinning. What in hell do fish have to do with anything?"

"The issue is horses, sir," Shakespeare said. "Or the lack thereof."

"Addlepated isn't the half of it," Jones retorted. "But to answer your question, I've found where the Se-at-co have your animals hid. We should wait until the sun goes down and sneak in and get them."

"Why wait?" Nate said. "Let's do it now while we have the light."

"They'd spot us," Methuselah said. "Your horses are well guarded. Which is why we need a distraction to draw most of the Se-at-co away."

"What kind of distraction?" Nate asked.

"We set the cabin on fire."

"And you said I was addlepated," Shakespeare said.

"It will work," Methuselah said. "The Se-at-co never learned how to make fire. They were always fascinated by mine. We set my cabin alight, and it will lure them from all over the valley."

"The idea has merit," Shakespeare said. "What do you think, Horatio?"

"We'd have to cache our saddles and saddle blankets and parfleches where we can get to them quick," Nate mentioned.

"I know just the place, near the cliff," Methuselah said.

He looked at each of them. "What do you say?"

"You don't mind losing your cabin?" Winona said.

"I'm heading for the States, remember? And I'm never coming back."

"Then let's do it," Shakespeare said. "I'll let my crustier half know."

"I'll go with you," Methuselah said.

Nate watched them go into the cabin and balled his fists.

Now that Blue Water Woman had confided in him, it was all he could do not to slug the man.

"Why are you scowling, husband? Don't you like Jones's plan?"

"It's as good as any other," Nate said.

"I sense you are uneasy. Care to share why?"

Nate touched her cheek.

"Oh. You are concerned for my welfare. So far the Se-at-co haven't harmed us. All they've done is steal."

"So far," Nate said.

# Chapter Twenty-two

At the base of the cliff about fifty feet from the cleft was an erosion-worn niche large enough for their saddles and blankets and supplies. Methuselah Jones helped carry their gear, commenting at one point that, "Your stuff is as safe here as anywhere."

Nate had his doubts. He couldn't shake the persistent feeling that they were being watched. It could well be that as soon as they walked away the Se-at-co would steal everything.

Their possessions, though, were of small consequence compared to their lives. He could always replace a stolen saddle. He could never, ever, for as long as he lived, replace Winona.

Nate listened to the plan Methuselah laid out with heightened suspicion. He knew the man once tried to rape Blue Water Woman. It was possible Jones had changed since then. After all, it had been decades since the incident. Then again, it had been Nate's experience that few people ever really changed. They were who they were. The tides of life washed over them with no more effect than the tides of an ocean on the boulders that littered its shores. People with no regard for others early in life often had no regard for others later in life. So he was skeptical.

At the moment Methuselah was saying, "If this

works, you can slip in, get your horses, and be gone from this valley before the Se-at-co catch on."

"It sounds good to me," Winona said.

"Time hath not yet so dried this blood of mine," Shakespeare quoted, "nor age so eat up my invention." He left out a couple of lines and finished with "But they shall find, awakened in such a kind, both strength of limb and policy of mind."

"What does that even mean?" Methuselah asked. "And how in hell do you remember all that stuff?"

"It means I am with you," Shakespeare translated. "And I've read the Bard a million times. Nay, a million times a million."

"You are as strange a son of a bitch as I have ever met."

"Thank you. I'll also thank you to speak more politely. Ladies are present, in case you've forgotten."

Methuselah glanced at Winona and then at Blue Water Woman.

"I would never forget."

"Good. To battle, then," Shakespeare said. "And may the whims of war be in our favor."

"I thought we're trying to avoid a fight," Nate said.

Methuselah gazed at the sky. "It's a couple of hours until sunset. We should gather the firewood and be ready."

Collecting downed branches and piling them inside the cabin took a while. Methuselah offered to scour the vicinity on horseback to be sure the Se-at-co were nowhere around, and rode off. Blue Water

Woman excused herself and walked away deep in thought. Shakespeare excused himself and followed her.

"That leaves us," Winona said. She clasped Nate's hand and made for the beaver pond. "Are you ready for tonight?"

"Why do you ask?" Nate rejoined.

"You seem preoccupied."

"I have a lot on my mind."

"Not so much that it will slow you down, I hope," Winona said. "It promises to be dangerous."

"Very," Nate said. He guided her to a grassy hump and they sat with their arms and hips brushing. "Have I mentioned today how much I love you?"

"You are worried, aren't you?"

"Silly goose. You're not?" Nate plucked a blade of grass and tossed it into the breeze. "We don't know what we're up against. There's something about these Se-at-co, something that's not normal."

"Remember our visit to Santa Fe?" Winona brought up. "They remind me of the Apaches. They are just as stealthy."

To Nate's way of thinking, that's where the resemblance ended. "Apaches, at least, are men."

"What are you saying? These aren't? What do you know that I don't?"

"About the Se-at-co, nothing," Nate said. "Except that I fought one in the dark and the whole time I had this . . . feeling."

"What kind of feeling?"

"That what I was fighting wasn't human."

"Oh." Winona fell quiet.

Out in the pond two beavers were swimming from the dam to their lodge, their round heads cleaving the water smoothly.

"No matter what the Se-at-co are," Winona said, "if they live and breathe they can be killed."

"I won't let them harm you," Nate said.

"I know that. Your love is the one constant in my life. Our two hearts are one."

"Stay close to me tonight."

"And you to me."

Nate kissed her and she responded with ardor. When they broke apart, she leaned her head on his shoulder and sighed.

"Why can't life be moments like this, one after the other, our whole life long?"

"Ask God, not me."

"The Great Mystery is just that. I wish I were smarter so I could understand."

"You're the smartest person I know," Nate said proudly. "A lot smarter than me."

"You are too modest. And I am not nearly as smart as Shakespeare."

"Come again?"

"Do you not realize how intelligent he must be to memorize so much of his beloved William S.? I could never do that."

"You learn languages quicker than he does," Nate noted.

"I was born with the knack, as you whites would say. He was born with his gift. You have yours."

Nate chuckled. "What would that be, exactly? The gift of skinning hides?"

"Why is it you can praise others but not yourself?

You have the gift of being a good husband and a fine father."

"A lot of men do that," Nate said.

"A lot try their best. You do it well. You have always been there for me, and for your children. As gifts go, quoting the Bard and learning new tongues can't compare."

"I don't do anything special."

"Now who is the silly goose?" Winona kissed him on the mouth and rested her head again. "I love you with all that I am. Remember that, no matter what happens."

"Don't talk like that. We're getting out of this."

"That's my Nate."

They sat quietly as beaver swam and dived and came up again.

"There is one thing," Nate said.

"Yes? You adore me from my hair to my toes and when we are home you will ravish me?"

"Jones once tried to rape Blue Water Woman."

Winona sat up.

"I promised her I wouldn't say anything, but you should know. Just in case. She wouldn't give me the particulars, but it must have been pretty bad. She hates him and I have never known her to hate anyone."

"Well," Winona said. "When this is over I should take my knife and cut him below his belt."

"Now, now."

"What?"

"You'll have to wait your turn."

"Seriously, husband. As Shakespeare would put it, this does not bode well."

"No," Nate King said. "It doesn't bode well at all."

# Chapter Twenty-three

A sliver of sun hung on the cusp of creation. The shadows had lengthened and spread, and soon darkness would descend.

Nate stood with his wife and friends outside the cabin. A small fire crackled at their feet.

"It's taking him an awful long time," Shakespeare said. "He should have been back by now."

No sooner were the words out of his mouth than Methuselah Jones rode out of the woods. "I didn't see hide nor hair of them," he announced as he drew rein. "And that worries me."

"Maybe they've decided to leave us be," Winona said.

"This is their valley, their home, their nest, as they think of it," Methuselah said. "They're out there, all right. I just can't say where." He alighted, his saddle creaking under him. "It doesn't change anything. We go through with the plan. As soon as the sun is gone, we set the cabin on fire."

"We're ready," Nate said, with a nod at the brand.

"I can see that." Methuselah opened a parfleche and took out a bundle of pemmican. "Anyone hungry?" He offered it to each of them. Only Shakespeare took some.

"My husband and I were talking earlier," Winona said, and Nate gave her a sharp glance. "Are these Se-at-co much like Apaches?"

"Why would you think that?" Methuselah asked between chews. "They are as different as night from day."

"They are as secretive as Apaches," Winona said.

"Oh. That." Methuselah bit off another piece. "I reckon they are. But that's the only thing the two have in common. You've got to remember. The Se-at-co have been around since the dawn of creation. From a time before our time. They are as unlike us as people could be and still be called people."

Now it was Winona who shot Nate a glance. "My husband says he thinks they're not human."

"Does he, now?" Methuselah said. "I don't know what else you'd call them. They're not exactly animals."

"*In*human?" Nate said.

"I guess. All I can tell you is they can walk on two legs when they want and they think and act like us in a few other ways." Methuselah turned to the west. "The sun is down. Ready to start this?"

For an answer, Nate bent and gripped the unlit end of a burning brand and carried it into the cabin. He thrust it at the waist-high pile of limbs. The limbs caught almost immediately. Small fingers of fire became large spires of flame that gave off coils of smoke. He turned and thrust the brand at another spot and more of the branches ignited. Coughing against the smoke, he dropped the brand and backed out.

"All right," Methuselah said. "Stay close. We'll do this exactly as we talked about." He grabbed the reins to his sorrel and hastened toward the beaver pond.

"Arm, arm, my lord. The foe vaunts in the field," Shakespeare quoted, and trailed him.

"I'll bring up the rear," Nate said, and did, behind his wife.

They crossed the stream where it narrowed past the pond.

On the other side they hugged the bank until they came to a stand of cottonwoods. Venturing in, Methuselah tied off the sorrel and the five of them moved to the edge of the trees. From there they had a clear view of the cabin.

Smoke was pouring from the doorway and window, and flames licked skyward from the roof.

"That should bring them," Methuselah said.

The flames grew. Soon the cabin was fully ablaze, its glow made brighter by the black of descending night. The blaze lit the ground for dozens of yards, the light nearly reaching as far as the pond. The crackle and pop of burning wood was near continuous.

"No sign of the Se-at-co yet," Shakespeare said.

"Give it time," Methuselah replied.

Nate was watching behind them and around them as well as the fire. He already had the Hawken's hammer pulled back and his finger around the trigger.

With a loud crash and a hiss, part of the roof buckled. Sparks rose in a multitude of fireflies and were borne away on the wind.

"Pretty, ain't it?" Methuselah said. "I always did like fire."

"Look!" Winona whispered.

Figures moved in the darkness that bordered the light.

Furtive forms, there one instant and then gone, as if they were insubstantial ghosts briefly given substance.

"I told you!" Methuselah said.

Nate thought he heard a step behind them and turned, but no one was there.

"I can't see them clearly," Winona said.

"You don't want to," Methuselah said.

Nate did. He was keenly anxious to learn what they looked like. One of the figures tantalized him by almost stepping into the light. He had an image of a moving broom handle and then it was gone.

"How long do we wait?" Shakespeare asked.

"We want as many of them there as possible," Methuselah said. "So there are fewer near the horses."

Nate shifted so he could both see the fire and cover behind them. By now a ring of coppery eyes were fixed on the cabin in what might be rapt fascination, exactly as Jones had said they would be. There was something about those eyes, even from a distance, something so unworldly, that they sent a shiver down his spine.

"It's working," Methuselah said.

Nate scanned the cottonwoods. The sorrel was a dark block against the pale trunks. He heard his wife gasp and Shakespeare blurt, "Stars and garters," and he turned.

A Se-at-co had stepped out of the dark into the firelight.

Well over six feet, it was impossibly thin, its arms and legs sticks of bone. Its hands were twice as long as Nate's, with fingers that had to be nine or ten inches in length. The face was hideous: flat as a board, with a slit for a mouth and a spike jaw. Its copper eyes were slightly slanted and glowed as bright as the fire.

"My God," Shakespeare exclaimed.

"I told you they were different," Methuselah said.

By Nate's reckoning there were more than twenty Se-at-co partly visible, with twenty more pairs of eyes farther back. "The horses," he said.

"Yes, yes, of course." Methuselah ran to the sorrel, untied it, and stepped into the stirrups. "Keep up with me," he said, and brought his mount to a brisk walk.

Nate fell into a jog. Once out of the stand, they made for the woodland that fringed the valley floor to the north and traveled along it until they were midway down the valley. In the distance, the cabin was a column of fire and smoke that reached to the stars.

"So far, so good," Shakespeare said when Jones came to a stop. "No sign of any of those things after us."

Methuselah pointed his horse toward the forest on the other side. "That's where the rest of them will be."

"And our horses?" Nate said.

"It's why we're here, ain't it?" Methuselah swung down and handed the reins to Winona. "I'll go over and see how many we have to deal with. The four of you stay put until I get back."

"You might need help," Shakespeare said. "I should tag along."

"And maybe be taken?" Methuselah shook his head. "They know me. They won't think twice, me showing up at their camp. I've been there many a time."

"You're taking a big risk," Shakespeare said.

"It's my way of making amends. I should have told you about the Se-at-co back at your place. Because of me, all of you are in danger." He started across. "I won't be long. If you hear a gunshot, get the hell out of here."

"We won't abandon you," Shakespeare said.

"You're a good man, McNair," Methuselah said, and was swallowed by the darkness.

"There goes a brave coon," Shakespeare said. "We'll owe him when this is done."

"I owe him already," Blue Water Woman said.

"What do you mean by that?" Shakespeare asked.

Nate prayed most of the tribe was at the burning cabin so that they could get their horses back without much trouble.

Winona turned to Blue Water Woman and said quietly, "You should tell him."

"Tell who what?" Shakespeare said.

Blue Water Woman shifted toward Nate. "You gave your word."

"I'm sorry," Nate said.

"Your gave your *word*."

"His word about what?" Shakespeare asked.

"You should tell him," Winona repeated.

"I thought I could trust you, Grizzly Killer."

"You can. But she's my wife and I never keep secrets from her and she's your best friend and you shouldn't, either. Plus she's a woman."

"Being female has nothing to do with this," Blue Water Woman said.

"Being female has everything to do with it," Nate responded.

Shakespeare was looking at them in mild exasperation. "Will someone tell me what in Hades you three are talking about and why you picked *now* of all times to talk about it?"

"Later, husband," Blue Water Woman said.

"I had rather chopped this hand off at a blow and with the other fling it at your face," Shakespeare quoted. "Don't treat me like a simpleton. I demand to know what is going on since apparently it involves you and it's something you don't want to tell me."

"Nate," Winona said.

"I don't want to hear it from him," Shakespeare said, and jabbed a finger at Blue Water Woman. "I want to hear it from her."

"I would rather not," Blue Water Woman said. "It will make things worse."

"*What* will?"

"Nate," Winona said again.

"Will you please hush?" Shakespeare snapped at her. "This is between my lovely wife and myself. So out with it, wench."

"Not now."

"I do frown on thee with all my heart." Shakespeare resorted to the Bard. "Is this why you've been so moody? You're hiding something from me?"

"I did what I thought was wise," Blue Water Woman said.

"So did I," Nate threw in.

Shakespeare snorted and quoted, "Oh, there has been much throwing about of brains."

"*Nate, please,*" Winona pleaded with such urgency that they all turned in her direction. She was staring into the trees, her rifle to her shoulder.

Nate's skin broke out in goose flesh. He suspected what he would see before he looked—copper eyes, agleam with starlight, fixed on them with savage intensity. Half a dozen Se-at-co were spaced so as to prevent them from escaping into the woods. "Damn."

"Where did they come from?" Winona whispered. "Jones said they were across the valley."

"Jones lied," Blue Water Woman said.

"Either they followed us," Nate said, and he hadn't seen any sign of anyone behind them, "or they've been waiting here this whole time."

"But that means—" Shakespeare said, and stopped.

"Yes," Nate said. "It does."

# Chapter Twenty-four

Nate hated being played for a dunce, almost as much as he hated his wife being put in peril.

"Why are they just standing there?" Winona said. "Why don't they say something or do something?"

"They're waiting for the rest," Shakespeare said, and extended his arm.

Backlit by the bright glow of the burning cabin, a swarm of stick figures were rushing down the valley.

"We'll be overwhelmed," Winona said.

Not if Nate could help it. He trained the Hakwen on the foremost Se-at-Co. "Leave us be," he said. "Go away or I'll shoot."

"They don't savvy," Shakespeare said.

"Fight or run?" Winona asked.

Down the valley the Se-at-co were coming fast. At a guttural bark from one of those in the trees, the rest started forward.

"Fight or run?" Winona said again.

"There are too many," Nate said.

"Which way, then?"

Nate only saw one choice. The swarm was coming from the east. The Stick People were between them and the woods to the north. Methuselah Jones had gone off to the south claiming that was where the Se-at-co were most likely to be. "West!" Nate hollered, and gave Winona a push. She and the McNairs whirled and bolted and he raced on their heels.

"Husband!" Winona yelled.

"I'm here!" Nate glanced back just as the six Se-at-co emerged from the forest. The things weren't moving with any great haste, as if to them the outcome was a foregone conclusion. He was tempted to snap off a shot, but in the dark and with him moving so fast, he'd likely miss. He ran on and when next he glanced back he was bewildered to see that the Se-at-co that had come out of the trees were gone.

Ripples in the grass warned Nate where they were. "Faster!" he shouted, even though it was obvious his wife and the McNairs were running as swiftly as they could.

They would never reach cover, Nate realized. Winona was fleet enough that she might make it, but Shakespeare had his years against him and Blue Water Woman was matching his stride.

In an instant, Nate came to a decision; he'd gain the time they needed by holding the Se-at-co at bay. Accordingly, he stopped and spun. The ripples in the grass were almost on him.

He wedged the Hawken to his shoulder just as the grass parted, and out exploded a stick figure.

Nate's blood ran cold. In his travels to the Southwest and to the Pacific Ocean he had seen a lot of strange and marvelous and terrible sights, but he had never beheld a sight like this.

The Se-at-co was on all fours, its long hands and feet slapping the ground like paws. But it wasn't running as a human on all fours would do, in a loping motion similar to a dog or a cat. It scrabbled like a spider. Its bony arms and legs poked from its sides just like the legs of a black widow.

Lightning swift, the thing was on him before he could shoot. Its mouth gaped wide, exposing twin rows of razor teeth, and a tongue as long as one of its fingers flicked the air like a whip. The thing jumped as a spider would do and crashed into Nate's chest with such force, he was nearly bowled over. He staggered, and the creature hissed and snapped at his neck even as its spindly arms and legs wrapped around his torso and clamped fast.

It was akin to being gripped in a vise. Nate sought to break free, but the thing was too strong. He could barely move his arms. Its hideous face was mere inches away, its copper eyes fixed on his eyes as if seeking to bore into his brain. He inadvertently recoiled, tripped over his own feet, and went down. He landed on his back, the Se-at-co on top. He rolled to try to shake it off. The creature clung on. He rolled the other way and drove his knees at the Se-at-co. It had no effect other than to spark another hiss.

Nate had never fought anything like this creature. He slammed his forehead against its flat face and his own was spattered with wet drops. They could bleed, and as Winona had said, if they could bleed and breathe, they could be killed.

He tried to rise and a second creature was on him, its limbs around his legs. He kicked to no avail. Thrashing and struggling mightily, he collided with something that turned out to be a third Se-at-co. Its long fingers wrapped around his face and neck.

"No!" Nate wanted to roar, and couldn't. Its fingers were over his mouth.

Suddenly he was moving. The things were carrying him as effortlessly as he might a rag doll. The feel of their skin on his was like dry leather, and hot breath fanned his throat. He made one more try to cast them off, a Herculean heave that would have thrown them from him if they were human. But they weren't, and it didn't.

He was their captive.

# Chapter Twenty-five

So much had happened so fast that Shakespeare McNair was in a state of confusion. The revelation that his wife was hiding something from him was a shock. In all their years together she had never, ever kept anything from him.

Now the Se-at-co were after them. In his day Shakespeare had fought the Comanches and the Apaches, he'd tangled with the Blackfeet and the Sioux, he'd had to defend his life against Utes and Pawnees. He wasn't afraid of these so-called Stick People. They were all bone and no brawn. He pegged them to be as weak as kittens.

Then Shakespeare looked back and discovered Nate was no longer behind them. He went to shout Nate's name and thought better of it. Winona, in her alarm, might stop running, and they had to keep moving, if only so later they could help Nate if need be. He glanced at his wife, grimly keeping pace on his right, and ran on. His lungs protested. His chest hurt. But he gritted his teeth and bore it.

Without warning something came at them, something low to the ground and moving in a fashion that made Shakespeare think of a long-legged spider. For a few seconds he thought it *was* a spider, a giant one, until he saw its long face and its long hands with their long, long fingers. The jolt of recognition threw him off his stride. His foot came down wrong and he stumbled, and just like that, the thing was on him.

Shakespeare's legs were swept out from under him. He glimpsed Blue Water Woman still running, and he didn't yell for help. She might be caught as he had been. He slammed a fist against the Se-at-co's jaw, but it was like hitting rock. He punched where a cheek should have been and hit it on the mouth. He drew back his hand with blood flowing from his knuckles.

Shakespeare raised his rifle and went to bring it crashing down, only to have his arms seized by another Se-at-co. He wrenched and tugged, but the things weren't the weaklings he'd supposed; quite the opposite. They had iron in their thin sinews.

A third Se-at-co appeared and took hold of his legs. With remarkable rapidity they bore him to the south. He was helpless in their grasp. A sense of doom came over him. Out loud he said the name that meant more to him than life itself.

"Blue Water Woman."

* * *

Winona flew, the grass whipping around her legs. She worried she would trip. She focused on an island of trees ahead, thinking that if they reached them, they could find cover. She was almost to them when she slowed and glanced over her shoulder to check on the others and was stunned to only see Blue Water

Woman. Her friend reached her side, breathing heavily.

"I am too old for this."

"Where are they?" Winona said, fear clutching at her heart.

"What?" Blue Water Woman turned. "Shakespeare!" She started to go back.

"No." Winona grabbed her arm. "The Se-at-co must have them."

"Let me go," Blue Water Woman said, and pulled. "They could be dead for all we know."

"We didn't hear shots or shouts," Winona said. She couldn't conceive of her man going down without a fight.

"Please," Blue Water Woman said, pulling harder.

"Think," Winona urged. "We mustn't be caught ourselves. We may be the only hope our men have."

Blue Water Woman stopped resisting. "Shakespeare," she said softly.

"Come on. We must hide." Winona held on to her arm and moved into the trees. Mostly spruce, which was good. The limbs grew low to the ground, providing excellent cover. She went a ways in and spied one that suited her. Dropping to her knees, she said, "Under here." She flattened and crawled under the drooping branch laden with needles. There was barely room.

Blue Water Woman followed suit.

They lay side by side as around them the wind rustled the trees and from somewhere far over the mountains that hemmed the valley wafted the faint cry of a wolf.

"Where are they?" Blue Water Woman whispered.

Winona knew she wasn't referring to Nate and Shakespeare. "I don't know."

"They were close behind us. Why haven't we seen them?"

"We should be quiet in case they are hunting us," Winona advised.

For the longest while they lay and listened and heard nothing to suggest pursuit.

Blue Water Woman broke the silence. "I do not understand."

"We will wait for daylight and search for our men."

"By then they could be dead if they aren't already."

"It will do us no good to blunder around in the dark," Winona whispered. "The Se-at-co would find us."

"I don't want to wait," Blue Water Woman said.

Before Winona could respond, hooves thudded. She stiffened as the rider approached and the thudding stopped.

"Blue Water Woman? Winona? You in there?" Methuselah Jones hollered.

"Don't answer him," Blue Water Woman whispered.

Winona had no intention of doing so. She suspected he had a hand in the ambush and craved to bury her knife in him.

"Come on out if you are," Jones yelled. "It's safe."

"Before this is done, I am going to kill him," Blue Water Woman vowed.

The horse nickered, and Jones began making the oddest sounds, as if he were trying to talk while being strangled. Something answered him in the same strange tongue. Then the hooves thudded and Jones rode on.

"He was talking to them," Blue Water Woman said, venom in her voice. "He is helping them."

"This is what we get for trusting him," Winona said. "You should have told us sooner that he once tried to rape you."

"I was too ashamed."

Winona put her hand on hand on Blue Water Woman's shoulder. "We are friends. We will be friends until the day we die. You need never feel shame around me."

"Thank you," Blue Water Woman said with great emotion. She took a deep breath. "I think you are right. We should wait until morning. We will find our husbands, I will kill Jones, and we will go home."

"You're forgetting the Se-at-co."

"No," Blue Water Woman said. "I'm not."

# Chapter Twenty-six

Methuselah Jones was fit to burst a blood vessel. He had made it as easy as could be for the Se-at-co to take the Kings and the McNairs captive. He had explained about the fire, and how he would lead them to a certain spot, and the Se-at-co were to wait in ambush and jump them. But in their arrogance the Se-at-co got overconfident. They sent only six when there should have been twenty.

Jones had just finished going to the end of the valley and calling out to Blue Water Woman and Winona every so often. They never answered. He was furious they had gotten away and vented his spleen on the Se-at-co scrabbling beside the sorrel. 'You make mistake,' he complained. 'Not catch females.'

'We will,' the creature boasted. 'This our nest. We know it better than they.'

Forgetting himself, Methuselah said in English, "They're not stupid, these gals. And they can be damned tricky. You were jackasses to let them get away."

'What you say?' the Se-at-co asked.

'Which one are you?' Methuselah asked. He never could tell the damn things one from the other. The creature made sounds that the best he could translate was 'Hu-mac?' So it was their leader. 'You must catch other two.'

'I say we catch, we catch,' Humac said. 'They only two. Se-at-co more.'

In disgust Methuselah said in English, "You've made it harder for me, you bastards." He decided not to say any more. He mustn't anger them or they might turn on him.

Methuselah couldn't let the two women leave the valley. That they hadn't answered his shouts suggested they suspected he was in cahoots with the Se-at-co. They couldn't be allowed to get word of that to their people. They must die. He had no qualms about it. He never did about killing. It was something that had to be done sometimes, like swatting flies and stomping snakes.

Most of the Se-at-co had returned to the rift. Methuselah rode in among their cones and over to where two figures were being guarded by four Se-at-co.

"You," Nate King said.

"Where did your squaws get to?"

Shakespeare McNair swore and heaved up off the ground. He lunged for Jones, but two Se-at-co seized him and slammed him down.

"Better watch yourself, McNair," Methuselah warned. "Make them mad and they'll break every bone in your body."

"They aim to kill us anyway," Nate said.

"That they do but in their own good time," Methuselah confirmed. "They have a—what do you call it?" He had to think. "A certain way they like to do it."

"A ritual?" Nate said.

"That's the word. They do it when the moon is full and go through a lot of rigmarole."

"You've seen them do it?"

"A couple of times. Once it was a couple of Nez Perce. Another time it was a white man, a trapper."

"You didn't help them?"

"Why should I? They were nothing to me." Methuselah leaned on his saddle. "Besides, it's not like they've adopted me into the tribe. I'm an outsider. They tolerate me because I saved one of them once. That, and I think they're as curious about us as we are about them."

"So that's why they let you live here."

"From what I can gather, our kind and their kind have been killing each other since forever. I'm the only human being they've ever been halfway friendly with."

"They sure picked a sterling specimen," Shakespeare said. "Heap of wrath, foul indigested lump. Would thou wert clean enough to spit upon."

"Don't start with that nonsense," Methuselah said.

"Thou art baser than a cutpurse."

"I won't tell you again. Spare me your insults or I'll shoot you where you sit."

"The Se-at-co won't mind?" Nate said.

"Not as long as I don't kill you and spoil their fun during the full moon." Methuselah straightened and raised his reins. "I'm going to go bed down for the night. Need to get an early start looking for your women." He reined around, and stopped. "I wouldn't try to escape were I you. They're a lot faster than us and a hell of a lot stronger and they can see in the dark like cats."

"Away, you cutpurse rascal, you filthy bung, away," Shakespeare said.

"There you go again," Methuselah said. "Will you spout that stuff as they're crushing you, I wonder?"

"Crushing us?" Nate said.

"That's how they kill. They squeeze and they squeeze until your ribs burst." Methuselah chuckled. "Gives you something to look forward to." He clucked to his sorrel and made off into the night.

"I hate him," Shakespeare growled.

"Makes two of us," Nate King said.

# Chapter Twenty-seven

The crawl of light across the vault of sky turned the deep black of night to the gray of predawn. In the stand of trees on the valley floor, Blue Water Woman stirred and raised her head. She had fallen asleep. It surprised her, as worried as she was about Shakespeare. Beside her, Winona lay with a cheek on an arm, adrift in slumber.

Blue Water Woman rose onto her elbows and winced. She was stiff from sleeping on the ground and her legs were sore from all the running they had done.

A few birds were singing. Daybreak was near. She was eager for the sun to rise so they could begin their hunt for the men. And for Methuselah Jones. She should have shot him the moment she saw him.

The others didn't understand. They hadn't realized how treacherous he was. He could look someone in the eye and smile and pretend to be a friend, all the while scheming behind the person's back. She hadn't realized herself, until that day he came into her father's lodge. The flap had been down, a sign to others she did not want visitors, but he pushed it aside and swaggered in as if the lodge were his. She had been brushing her hair with the new brush her mother had traded for and didn't see him until he was almost on her. His image in the mirror had startled her so badly, she dropped the mirror and it broke. She had turned and demanded to know what he was doing there and he prattled something about how he had long admired her and how he would like for them to be "friends."

In her youth and inexperience Blue Water Woman had not recognized his vulgar meaning. She had said that friendships must grow naturally, and if he wanted, he could return to visit her when her parents were there. Suddenly he had changed before her eyes. His smile became a scowl and the feigned friendliness in his eyes became a fierce hunger. He was on her before she could collect her wits. He had borne her to the ground and groped her.

She'd fought. Oh, how she'd fought. She clawed and hit and kneed him. She'd inflicted cuts and pain, yet he still sought to hike her dress up and have his way. In their struggle they rolled about, this way and that, and came up against the side of the lodge where her father kept his bow and quiver and spare knife. Jones was so aroused and enraged, he was unaware she had the knife until she pressed the blade to his throat.

Her mistake, Blue Water Woman mused, was in not slitting it then and there. He'd frozen, and she had demanded he leave and forced him out at knifepoint. She warned that she would tell her parents and they would rouse warriors to punish him. She fully meant to do so. But after he'd fled, she had sunk next to the broken mirror and cried her heart out, cried that a man would do such a thing, cried at how close he had come to succeeding, cried at the hideousness of it all.

In her grief and shame, she had decided not to let anyone know. Jones had left their village, and that was what mattered. She'd dried her eyes and pulled herself together and when her parents came back she apologized for accidentally breaking the mirror and promised her mother she would get a new one.

Later she heard that Jones had gone to stay with other tribes and caused constant trouble to where none of the tribes wanted anything to do with him. Eventually, word had it, he disappeared, and she'd imagined he had either gone back to the land of the whites or been killed in the wilds.

Now here he was.

Blue Water Woman burned with hate. Once again Methuselah Jones had brought heartache upon her. This time she would not forget. This time she would not go her way until she was sure beyond any doubt that he would never cause her heartache again.

Winona mumbled in Shoshone and stirred. She slowly rolled onto her back, opened her eyes, and blinked. "I was hoping it was a dream."

"Don't you mean a nightmare?" Blue Water Woman said.

"I can't believe I fell asleep with my husband's life in danger."

"I slept as well," Blue Water Woman said to put her at ease. "We needed the rest."

A robin warbled in a nearby spruce. Sparrows were chirping in abandon.

Winona turned onto her side, facing her. "It will be dawn soon. We must plan."

"It is as I told you last night. We find our men. We save them. I kill Jones. We go home."

"You have it all worked out, I see," Winona said, and grinned.

"What more is there?"

"The Se-at-co will try to stop us. Have you thought about how we can get the better of them in their own valley?"

"We kill them."

Winona arched an eyebrow. "Shakespeare is right. You *are* a bloodthirsty wench. But there are a lot of them and only two of us. We must do this carefully."

"Jones told us they are mostly abroad at night," Blue Water Woman remembered. "Something to do with their eyes. They don't like bright light."

"Maybe we can use that." Winona went to sit up and bumped her head on the branch. "Darn. I forgot."

"There is something else we can use."

"What?"

"Fire."

"To distract them? We don't know where they are."

"The whole valley," Blue Water Woman said. "Burn them out so that not one lives."

Winona stared at her for the longest while until finally Blue Water Woman said, "What?"

"I was teasing when I said you were bloodthirsty. I didn't think you wanted to kill *all* of them. There must be women of their kind and children."

"All of them," Blue Water Woman said. "They have lived past their time and are an enemy to all."

"Dear God."

Blue Water Woman smiled. "You sound like your husband."

"And you sound like my son. Zach never lets an enemy live if he can help it."

"Have I ever mentioned," Blue Water Woman said, "how much I admire him?"

# Chapter Twenty-nine

Nate nodded off toward dawn. He slept fitfully until the screech of a jay woke him at daybreak. In the rift it was chill and dark, which the Se-at-co seemed to like. Many were on all fours, chattering in their hard-to-fathom tongue. Four still stood guard.

"How you can sleep at a time like this is beyond me," Shakespeare remarked. He had his knees to his chest and his arms around his legs.

Nate stretched and rubbed his beard. "You've been up all night?"

"One of us had to work on a way to give these devils their due."

"And?"

Shakespeare sighed. "Nary an idea, I'm afraid. Short of killing a few and running for our lives."

"Not much of a plan."

"I am open to better. Just so you come up with it quick. Our wives are out there somewhere, and I don't know about you, but I'm worried sick."

"They're smart. They won't get caught," Nate said.

"What does that say about us?"

A whiff of foul odor drew Nate's gaze to a broad area covered with gleaming bones and the remains of a recently devoured horse. Past the bones were his bay and their other horses. "Look yonder."

Shakespeare swiveled at the hips. "I'll be. I didn't notice them. It's careless of these monsters to leave them so close to us."

"Monsters?" Nate said.

"What else would you call them?" Shakespeare rejoined, and gestured. "Look at them, for God's sake."

It was true, Nate had to admit, that the Se-at-co were abominable. Their inhuman faces and stick bodies were grotesque. Their young, he noticed, weren't scampering around and playing as most young would do. They were hunkered in a group on all fours and eyeing the adults as if they were wary of them.

"I've never seen the like in all my born days," Shakespeare said.

Nate turned to a guard and raised his hands. 'Question. You finger talk?' he asked in the sign language common among many tribes. There was no reaction. He tried again. 'Question. We be friend?' Again, he might as well have been swatting flies.

"You're wasting your time," Shakespeare said. "They don't understand a lick of sign."

"Jones talks to them."

"He's had ten years to pick up their lingo."

It was too bad, Nate reflected. He'd like to avoid spilling blood if he could. "What I don't get," he said, "is why they haven't tied us up."

"Could be they don't have rope."

"They could use Jones's."

"Don't put ideas in their heads."

The sun was almost up and sunlight was dispelling the shadows in the rift. Many of the Se-at-co were moving to the cones made of interwoven branches, lifting them, and crabbing under. Curling into balls, they closed their copper eyes.

"They sleep during the day," Shakespeare said. "There's hope for us yet."

Nate was thinking the same thing. If enough did the same, they could try for the horses.

Shakespeare nudged his elbow. "Look over there," he said, with a casual bob of his head.

Piled over near the bones were their rifles, pistols, and knives. The Se-at-co had let them keep their possibles bags and ammo pouches, which most Indians would never do.

"Yes, sir," Shakespeare said with a grin, "things are looking up."

That was when hooves drummed and down into the rift came Methuselah Jones. He rode straight to them and dismounted. The Se-at-co largely ignored him. A tall one scuttled over and clacked and Jones replied and the creature left.

"That was their chief, you'd call him. His name is Hu-mac. He says that they are looking forward to sending your shades into the land of the dead."

"The what?" Shakespeare said.

"That's the best I can translate it." Methuselah squatted just out of reach and smirked. "How are you feeling today, gents?"

Nate controlled his fury. "Go to hell."

Methuselah laughed and glanced at the sky. "Either of you have any notion when the next full moon is?"

"I don't keep track much anymore," Shakespeare said, a feeling of dread coming over him.

"It's tonight," Nate said.

Methuselah nodded. "That's right. Tonight the two of you die. Your women, too, if I can find them."

"Were you born scum or do you work at it?" Nate said.

"Now, now. Don't be petty. Frankly, I don't give a damn about yours. It's McNair's I came back for."

"Blue Water Woman?" Shakespeare said. "Why?"

"To finish what I started all those years ago," Methuselah said. "To finish it permanent."

"What in blazes are you talking about?"

Methuselah's smirk froze on his face and his eyes narrowed. "Are you saying you don't know?"

"Don't know what?" Shakespeare turned to Nate. "Does this have anything to do with the secret the rest of you are keeping from me?"

"I'll be damned," Methuselah said, and chortled. "Blue Water Woman never told you."

"Told me *what*, damn you?"

"He tried to rape her," Nate said.

And all hell broke loose.

# Chapter Thirty

Years ago, long before Nate met Shakespeare McNair, his mentor had been known by another name: Carcajou. It was given to McNair by French-Canadian trappers. It meant "wolverine."

Nate had often wondered why. Wolverines were famed for their ferocity, yet Shakespeare was about the most peaceable man Nate ever met. The nickname didn't seem to fit.

Now he found out different.

For a few seconds Shakespeare was perfectly still, as if the revelation had shocked him senseless. Then he uttered a growl worthy of his namesake and launched himself at Methuselah Jones in a blur of white hair and buckskins. The Se-at-co were taken by surprise and slow to react, and Shakespeare was on Jones before they could reach him. Jones tried to scramble back and level his rifle, but Shakespeare grabbed him and spun and hurled him bodily at the nearest pair of creatures. Then Shakespeare bolted for the weapons.

Nate dived at the legs of the other two guards and bowled them over. In a twinkling, he was up and running after McNair.

Other Se-at-co had seen and were converging.

Some dropped onto all fours so they could run faster than their brethren on two legs.

Shakespeare reached the pile. He snatched up a pair of pistols and wheeled. A Se-at-co was almost on him. Thrusting a muzzle at its face, he fired.

The result was spectacular. If it had been a human, the ball would have bored clean through and ruptured out the back of the head. But the Se-at-co's head exploded. It burst apart like a shattered melon, and the bony body collapsed like a puppet with the strings cut.

Shakespeare shot another, again in the face, again with the same result.

By then Nate was there. He grabbed his Hawken and spun. A creature was scrabbling at him, its teeth bared. He shot it in the mouth.

A din broke out, an unearthly keening. The Se-at-co under the cones were scrambling to get out. Others were seeking cover.

Nate scooped up his pistols. "Come on!" he cried.

Shakespeare had confronted another Se-at-co. His pistols were empty and he clubbed the thing over the head. The stick thing flung up its bony arms to protect itself and he battered them aside and brought a pistol crashing down on its head so hard there was a loud *crack*.

"Come on!" Nate cried again.

A creature was sliding out from under a cone almost at Shakespeare's feet. Raising a leg, he brought his foot slashing down.

"We have to go!" Nate bellowed. Running over, he

gripped the back of Shakespeare's shirt and hauled him toward the woods.

Their way to the horses was cut off by too many Se-at-co.

"Let go of me!"

"No."

"Damn it!"

"No."

The Se-at-co were closing in. Wary of the guns, they used the cones as cover.

Shakespeare struggled to break Nate's grasp. "I'm going to kill them! Every last one!"

"Think of Blue Water Woman," Nate said. They reached the vegetation. He flung Shakespeare ahead of him and turned.

The creatures were still keeping their distance. Whirling, he fled and caught up to his friend.

Shakespeare was calming. The red was fading from his face and the fierce gleam from his eyes. He started to slow.

"Keep going," Nate said, and gave him a push. He was alert for pursuit, but so far there was none.

"I lost control," Shakespeare said. "Haven't done that in so long, I forgot what it's like."

"You should do it more often."

"Did you see where Jones got to? I wanted to shoot him, but he wasn't there."

"He probably ran. Just as you should be doing."

After that they didn't talk until they had put half a mile of thick timber behind them. Climbing onto a boulder half as big as a cabin, they watched their back trail and rested.

Nate mopped his sleeve across his sweaty brow

and commenced to reload. "Not bad. We have four pistols and a rifle between us."

"Sorry," Shakespeare said. "I should have grabbed my Hawken, too."

"You were too busy killing."

Shakespeare opened his powder horn and went to pour, then looked up, his face stricken with hurt. "Why didn't she tell me?"

Nate shrugged.

"She told you. She told Winona."

"No, I told Winona."

"But why you and not me? She's never kept anything from me before."

"Shame, I would guess," Nate said.

Shakespeare bristled. "*He's* the one who tried to have his way. What does she have to be ashamed of?"

"I'm not a woman. I couldn't say."

"Don't play dumb. All that reading you do, you're smarter than you pretend to be. What am I missing? Give me a reason that makes sense."

"Love, then," Nate said.

"How in hell do you figure that?"

Nate checked their back trail again. He was surprised the Se-at-co hadn't given chase. Maybe it was their dislike of daylight. "Has anyone ever told you that you curse a lot when you're mad?"

"I shall laugh myself to death at this puppy-headed monster," Shakespeare quoted. "A most scurvy monster. I could find it in my heart to beat him."

"Jones or me?"

"I swear to God."

"All right. She loves you so much, she knew it would

hurt you and make you mad enough to murder Jones, and she wanted to spare you that."

"The hurt I can understand," Shakespeare said. "As for murdering him, mark my words. I am going to kill Methuselah Jones dead, dead, and dead."

"If the Se-at-co don't kill us first," Nate said.

# Chapter Thirty-one

"Do you hear that?" Winona asked, stiffening in excitement.

"Of course," Blue Water Woman answered, and broke into a run. "Hurry. They might need our help."

From across the valley came the boom of guns. Pistols cracked and a rifle blasted. Someone shouted.

"That was Nate!" Winona exclaimed. She was almost to the stream when she realized what they were doing and dug in her heels. They were out in the open in the glare of the sun where anyone, or any *thing*, could spot them. "Wait," she said. "We're making a mistake."

Blue Water Woman had a foot in the water. "They are our husbands," she said, and waded out.

"Come back. We're of no use to them if we're caught."

"I haven't seen a Se-at-co since last night." Blue Water Woman was looking at Winona and not ahead. "And I will not desert my man when he needs me."

The grass on the opposite side moved, framing a flat face with copper eyes and a mouth of razor teeth.

Winona shouted a warning, but she was too late. The creature launched itself at Blue War Woman. It rammed into her and they pitched into the water with a tremendous splash. Winona jerked her rifle up, but didn't have a clear shot.

Blue Water Woman kicked and scrambled to her knees.

She aimed her rifle at the Se-at-co, which was also rising, and there was the *click* of a misfire.

The creature hissed and sprang.

Winona came off the bank in a flying leap. She swung the Hawken in midair, timing her swing so that the stock smashed into the thing's flat face as it was about to bite Blue Water Woman's neck. The thing reeled back.

Blue Water Woman still had her pistols. Either might misfire, but she drew one anyway, jammed it against the stick man's body, and fired. There was a *snap*, as of a tree limb breaking, and a screech that tore at the ears like claws, and the creature collapsed, part of its torso, if it could be called that, in slivers.

"The others will hear and come," Winona said. "We must hide."

"I am through hiding." Blue Water Woman clambered up the bank and dropped to her knees. She was breathing heavily and her dress was soaking wet. As quickly as she could, she set to reloading.

"Listen to reason," Winona said, climbing after her. "The shooting has stopped. Whatever happened, we are too late to help them."

"Stay if you want."

"We are not warriors."

"No," Blue Water Woman said, opening her ammo pouch. "We are wives and they are our men and if this is my day to die it will be at my man's side."

"Will you listen to yourself?"

"I listen to my heart."

In the forest to the south was a break where the land sloped in on itself, and in the shadows of the trees that lined the break there was movement.

"Se-at-co," Winona said. "A lot of them."

"Good."

Winona bent and dug her fingers into Blue Water Woman's arm. "Please. This is folly."

"Do you see Jones?"

"What?" Winona looked again. "No. But he might be with them."

"Good."

"You scare me, sister."

Blue Water Woman was wrapping a ball in a patch. "Do you have your steel and flint?"

"Yes, but—"

"The wind is blowing from us to them."

"Now?" Winona said.

"Now."

Squatting, Winona put down her rifle. The grass was dry but not so dry that she was sure it would catch. She used tinder from her tinderbox and struck the steel against the flint and when a spot of bright red appeared, she puffed lightly. It went out. She tried again, working fast. The dot lasted longer but faded.

"Hurry," Blue Water Woman urged. "I think they are gathering to attack."

Again Winona struck the steel and flint. Again sparks rained on the tinder. Again dots blossomed. This time, though, her puffs ignited a flame. More puffs, and the flame grew and multiplied. She drew back, tingling with dread that the grass was too green.

There were puffs of smoke and a crackle, and flames fanned by the wind devoured the grass in a spreading line that moved toward the rift.

"Are you ready?" Blue Water Woman said. She had reloaded. Her pistols were under her belt, her rifle in her hands.

"I think it is a mistake, but I will not leave your side," Winona said.

"Then let's go find our men."

# Chapter Thirty-two

"A shot." Nate rose from the boulder. As best he could judge, it came from the valley floor, out toward the stream.

"Our wives," Shakespeare said, and was in motion before the echo died. With a bound worthy of a man half his age, he was off the boulder and sprinting down the slope.

Nate flew hard after him. Winona must be in trouble. He would reach her or die trying. A thicket barred their way and Shakespeare veered to go around. Nate lowered his shoulders and plunged in, heedless of the scratches and tears, plowing like a mad bull. He was out the other side and ahead of McNair when he smelled the acrid scent of smoke. Below, through the trees, flashes of red and orange were mixed with the green of the grass. To his right was the rift, the shadows alive with Se-at-co. Not a lot of them but enough that anyone with any sense wouldn't do what he did; he charged them.

They were looking toward the spreading fire and chattering excitedly, their backs to him. Before they knew he was there, Nate was in among them. He slammed the Hawken's stock into the back of a skull, drove it at a cheek, rammed it between a pair of copper eyes. A creature on all fours rushed at his legs and he shoved the muzzle into its face and fired. He heard Shakespeare's gun go off. Suddenly he was amid a throng of Se-at-co.

He swung and shot a pistol and clubbed and blew off a hideous face and swung some more. Shouts and keening shrieks mingled with shots and blows. The fire was close and smoke got into his eyes and nose. He was a dervish, whirling and hitting and spinning and smashing. Something brushed his shoulder. He spun, ready to bring a pistol slashing down, and beheld the loveliest face there had ever been or ever would be. No words were necessary. Back to back they stood and fought. A few yards away Shakespeare and Blue Water Woman were battling, but he couldn't worry about them. The smoke thickened even as the creatures thinned, and suddenly there was only the smoke and Winona's hand on his arm.

"We have driven them off."

"Shakespeare?" Nate hollered.

"Here, Horatio." McNair had a gash on his brow, and Blue Water Woman's dress was torn.

"The horses," Nate said.

"Which way? I got turned around."

Nate thought he knew. He barreled into the smoke but slowed at a tug from Winona.

"Have a care, husband. There are many left."

On cat's feet and with hawk's eyes, Nate stalked past smoke-shrouded oaks and brush. His eyes stung terribly.

A gust of wind momentarily cleared the smoke, and almost at his feet was a cone. It was empty. Quickening his pace, he wound through more of them.

Shakespeare let out a yip of joy; he had found his rifle.

They came to the barrow of bones and the carcass of the dead horse, thick with flies. The stink was worse than any stink ever. Their feet crunched with every step.

"What manner of creatures are these?" Winona said in horror.

The bay and McNair's white mare and the rest of the horses were where Nate had seen them last. They were skittish from the commotion and the smoke, but they calmed readily enough.

Shakespeare was giving Blue Water Woman a boost. "She sprained her leg," he said.

"We do not have a rope for the packhorse," Winona noticed.

"I'll bring it," Nate said so her hands would be free for riding. He kneed the bay behind it. "Everyone ready?"

Shakespeare climbed on his white mare. A drop of blood trickled down his brow and over his cheek into his beard. "This isn't over yet, Horatio."

"No," Nate said. "It isn't."

# Chapter Thirty-three

Nate led them out of the forest and over to the stream so the horses could drink. They stayed on, Nate and Winona scanning the grass to the south of the stream, Shakespeare and Blue Water Woman watching the grass to the north.

"When do you think it will be?" Shakespeare said.

"They'd be stupid to rush us in the open," Nate reckoned.

Both he and McNair glanced toward the far-off cliff.

"How are you holding up?" Winona asked Blue Water Woman.

"I have my man back."

An eerie silence had fallen. The birds, the squirrels, everything had gone quiet. In the stillness, the buzz of a bee on a wildflower seemed unnaturally loud.

The land was an inferno of burning trees and brush. From out of the flames came horrid squeals and screeches.

"The horses have had enough," Nate said, and started down the valley.

No Se-at-co appeared to try and stop them. No wildlife was anywhere to be seen. Even the beaver were absent from the pond.

Wisps of smoke rose from the charred ruins of the cabin.

Nate drew rein and gazed at the cliff and loosened his pistols under his belt.

"Hard or slow?" Shakespeare said.

"Slow," Nate said. "We stick together no matter what."

He tapped his heels. "If one of us goes down, the rest stop to help."

"It won't be long."

Heavy vegetation grew between the cabin and the cliff.

The trail worn by game and by Jones's horse was only a few feet wide.

Nate was tense with expectation. They had twelve guns among them. Whether that would prove enough remained to be seen.

Under the trees on both sides, shadows moved. Hints of copper glinted. They would all attack at once.

Nate brought the stock up. "Make each shot count," he said over his shoulder. When he looked back, the Se-at-co were exploding from the forest like a horde of giant crabs, all of them on all fours, their hissing and their teeth enough to freeze a person in fear.

Nate sighted on a head and fired, and it exploded. He drew a pistol, drilled a face with a gaping maw, shoved the pistol under his belt. He drew his other pistol and fired into a creature about to launch itself at the bay's legs. Behind him guns thundered and a horse squealed. He turned. Winona's horse was down, and she was wielding her rifle like a club. He nearly broke the bay's ribs, he used his legs so hard in wheeling around. Then he was at her side and his hand was down and she grasped it and he pulled her up behind him.

The firing stopped.

A lot of Se-at-co were down and would never rise. From their wounds oozed blood more brown than red.

"Reload," Nate commanded, and was the first to finish. When the rest were ready he assumed the lead.

The cliff rose, bleak and sheer. At its base the undergrowth that hid the niche appeared darker than it should.

Nate halted twenty feet out and raised his rifle.

"Again?" Winona said in disbelief.

"I almost feel sorry for them," Shakespeare said.

Nate didn't. When the things charged out he shot them as he would rabid dogs, first one, then a second and a third. Others guns boomed.

The Se-at-co did the unexpected; they turned and fled.

Swiftly as they could, the mountain men and their wives threw on saddle blankets and saddles and slipped on bridles.

At the cleft Nate drew rein. It was a good spot for another ambush. "Nose to tail," he said. "And watch your backs."

The precaution proved needless. They made it through, and stopped.

"At last it's over!" Winona said in delight.

"You're forgetting someone," Nate said.

"He'll be riding like a bat out of hell," Shakespeare predicted.

"He won't get away." Nate was set to ride on when Blue Water Woman brought her horse around in front of them.

"I am going on alone."

"Over my dead body," Shakespeare said.

"I must," Blue Water Woman said.

"The both of us or not at all."

To nip an argument in the bud, Nate intervened. "He tried to kill all of us. We all have a stake."

"I am the one he tried to rape," Blue Water Woman said. "I have more right."

"That raven won't fly," Shakespeare said. "It was so long ago my hair was brown."

"Why are you being so stubborn?" Blue Water Woman asked.

Shakespeare reined close to her and jabbed a finger at her chest. "You listen to me, woman, and you listen good. This is me and only me. Not the Bard." He paused. "I love you. I've always loved you. Fate played a dirty trick on us and we didn't get together until late in life. But we're together now and we're going to stay that way." He motioned when she went to speak. "Don't interrupt. I can't tell you how hurt I was that you told Nate about the rape before you told me. He says you wanted to spare me the hurt. Fine and dandy. That works both ways. I don't want you hurt, either. So if you're fixing to go after that son of a bitch, you're taking me along. That's final."

"But, husband—"

"Don't you dare. Are our hearts entwined or are they not?"

"It's not as simple as that."

"Answer me, you contrary filly. Are our two hearts one?"

"They are," Blue Water Woman said softly.

"End of discussion."

Nate cleared his throat. "Where my best friend goes, I go. If he happens to be heading for the prairie, I reckon I'll tag along."

"And where my husband goes, I go," Winona said.

Blue Water Woman averted her face. "I love you all very much."

"Then what are we sitting here for?" Shakespeare said gruffly. "There's a coyote that needs exterminating."

"Will you at least let me be the one who deals with him?" Blue Water Woman requested.

Shakespeare stared at her and finally said, "All right. But only if I get out of milking the cow for a month."

"What?"

"It hurts my fingers. Were it up to me, I'd poke her with a knife and let the milk dribble out."

"I think you make more sense when you quote the Bard," Blue Water Woman said.

Shakespeare raised an arm. "Onward, friends! We have a beast to vanquish!"

"If I was Methuselah Jones," Winona said, "I would be very worried."

# Chapter Thirty-four

Methuselah knew they were after him. He caught the gleam of the sun off the metal in their rifles and on their belts and saddles. He wasn't worried. He had a good head start and a strong horse. He would reach the prairie well ahead of them and they would eat his dust.

Methuselah was old, but he wasn't stupid. When McNair and King made their bid to escape, he'd tried to shoot them. But he couldn't get a clear shot. The damn Se-at-co were in the way.

And when McNair got his hands on guns, Methuselah did the smart thing; he got the hell out of there.

Now, smiling broadly at how mad they must be that he had gotten away, Methuselah descended to another foothill. Another couple of hours and he would reach the plain.

He had learned his lesson. He shouldn't have gone back. He should have left the Kings and McNairs to the less-than-tender mercies of the Se-at-co and gone on east.

He was thinking of his sister and whether she might still be alive when his horse nearly stepped on a rattlesnake. He saw the snake coil and tried to rein aside, but it rattled and struck at a leg and the next thing he knew he was on the ground with the breath knocked out of him and his horse was galloping down the hill in terror.

Rolling away from the snake, Methuselah pushed to his feet.

He raised his rifle to shoot it, but thought better of the idea. Shots carried a long way. The McNairs and Kings might hear and would know how close he was. "Damn serpent," he fumed, and settled for kicking rocks at it. The rattler uncoiled and slithered away.

Methuselah turned. His horse had reached the bottom of the hill and was still going. Swearing up a storm, he set out after it. Knowing horses as he did, it would run for a mile or more before it tired. A mile he would have to cover quickly to stay ahead of his pursuers.

"If it ain't chickens, it's feathers," Methuselah groused.

He hiked over the crown of the next hill and came on a slope dotted with boulders of all shapes and sizes. He was partway into them when an idea so brilliant struck him, he stopped in his tracks.

The McNairs and the Kings were following his trail. By late in the day they would reach the boulders. There were four of them, but he had his rifle and two pistols. He could account for three of the four—say, Shakespeare, Nate, and that Shoshone, Winona, leaving Blue Water Woman for him. He cackled and studied the boulders. Below and to one side was a slab of rock higher than a horse and near enough to the trail that he couldn't miss.

It took some doing to climb up. There weren't many

handholds. But he made it and lay on his belly with his rifle next to him, and grinned.

"This will be fun."

His problem now was to stay awake. He was exhausted.

The hot sun combined with his fatigue conspired to cause him to nod off. Twice he jerked his head up, afraid that the McNairs and the Kings had gone by and he'd missed them. But no, it was too soon.

The sun climbed higher. Methuselah managed to stay awake and amused himself counting marmots and hawks and later watched chipmunks scampering about like lunatics.

Then a horse whinnied.

Instantly, Methuselah flattened. He imagined the four of them coming down the hill and soon heard the clomp of hooves.

He raised his head a fraction and there were McNair and Blue Water Woman, riding in single file. Behind them came Winona King, leading a packhorse and a bay with a saddle. He didn't see Nate King anywhere.

The McNairs came closer.

Methuselah eased his pistols out and set them one on either side. He gripped his rifle and put his thumb on the hammer to pull it back.

"I wouldn't," said a voice behind him, and something hard gouged the back of his head.

"King?" Methuselah said, his breath catching in his throat.

A hand reached over Methuselah's shoulder and relieved him of the rifle.

"Roll over," Nate King said.

Methuselah complied and stared up into the muzzle of the big man's Hawken. "Don't be hasty."

"It's not mine to do." Nate snatched up both pistols and set them and then the rifle out of Methuselah's reach. "Now, then. Nice and slow, climb down."

"I have to know," Methuselah said. "How?"

"I climbed a tree up a ways to try and spot you and see how far ahead you were, and lo and behold, here you were, lying on this rock."

"Damn," Methuselah said.

"Some mistakes cost us more than others." Nate wagged the Hawken. "Get to climbing."

The McNairs and Winona were waiting. Methuselah held his hands in the air so they wouldn't be tempted to shoot him.

"Looks like you have me."

"You miserable cur," Shakespeare said.

"The question is," Winona said, "what do we do with him now that we've taken him alive?"

"Simple," Blue Water Woman said. "He doesn't stay alive."

"Hold on now—" Methuselah tried to get a word in, but she aimed a pistol at him.

"You have no say in this. Keep quiet."

Winona brought her horse next to Blue Water Woman's. "If you shoot him in cold blood, you demean yourself."

"I can live with that."

"Did I marry Attila the Hun and not know it?" Shakespeare said.

"Who?"

"You can't just kill him. There has to be a better way," Shakespeare asserted.

"Tell me how."

"I don't rightly know," Shakespeare replied, and half grinned. "If you were white you could fight a duel."

"A what?"

"I fought one once," Nate said. "It's where two men stand back to back and take ten steps and turn and fire. It's how whites settle disputes."

"We will do that, then," Blue Water Woman said.

Shakespeare snorted. "Hold on. Nate wasn't serious."

"I am."

"You can't fight a duel."

"Why not? Because I'm a woman?"

"I just won't let you."

Methuselah listened with keen interest. He was a good pistol shot. He doubted Blue Water Woman was. Here was a straw, and he clutched at it. "If I agree to take part and I kill her, do I get to go free?"

Shakespeare pointed his rifle. "I should shoot you myself and be done with it."

"Yes," Blue Water Woman said to Jones. "You do."

"Then let's do it, squaw." Methuselah was eager to get it over with before she changed her mind. "But I want one of my own pistols. I'm used to them."

"Give him one, Nate," Blue Water Woman said.

Nate looked at Shakespeare. "I won't if you say not to."

"Give him one," Shakespeare said.

"I left them up on the boulder. I'll be right back."

Blue Water Woman climbed down. She handed her rifle to Winona and drew one of her pistols. "I am ready when he is."

Shakespeare alighted and gripped her arm. "This is insane."

"I am crazy now?"

"No. You're mad and you want revenge, and it's clouding your thinking. Just kill him if you have to, but don't do it this way."

"He will have his chance."

"Damn you, woman."

"I love you, too."

Methuselah was only interested in one thing. "I want your word, Blue Water Woman, that they will do as you say and let me ride off if I win."

"You have it. Did you hear me, husband?"

"You are the most aggravating female who ever lived." Shakespeare resorted to quotes. "Thou art the cap of all fools alive. Oh, tiger's heart wrapped in a woman's hide."

"Did you hear me?"

"Yes. He gets to live. I'll give him a day's start and go after him myself."

"Fine by me," Methuselah taunted.

"What is keeping Nate?" Blue Water Woman wondered. She glanced at Winona. "You are awful quiet."

"I don't know what to say."

Nate came around the boulder carrying all three of Methuselah's weapons. He set the rifle and one of the pistols down and brought the other pistol over to Methuselah. "Here you go."

"I'm obliged."

"Don't be."

Methuselah hefted it and ran his thumb over the hammer and grinned. "I once put a ball through an apple at twenty steps," he boasted to unnerve Blue Water Woman.

"How do we do this, Nate?" Blue Water Woman said. "You say we stand back to back?"

Nate nodded. "I'll count off the steps. When I get to ten you both turn and fire." He glared at Methuselah. "Try to shoot her on eight or nine and I'll shoot you."

"As will I," Winona said.

Shakespeare had gone pale. "Please don't do this. If I mean anything at all to you, you won't."

"If I mean anything to you, you will let me." Blue Water Woman put her back to Jones. "I am ready."

"God," Shakespeare said.

Nate moved away from them and called out, "One."

Methuselah took his first step. Inwardly, he was giddy.

The fool of a woman had let her stubbornness get the better of her. He eagerly took his second and third steps. He would shoot her in the chest. He had heard somewhere that was what duelists did. Nate King called out the fourth and fifth steps. They were halfway. Methuselah thumbed back the hammer. He took his sixth and seventh steps and nearly laughed imagining the look on McNair's face when his precious wife fell.

Eight steps now, and Methuselah focused on the pistol and only the pistol. Nine steps, and he was breathing easy and his body was loose. He had her. She was as good as dead.

"Ten!" Nate King shouted.

Methuselah whirled and brought his pistol up. He

had beaten her by a mile. He aimed square at her chest. He grinned and squeezed the trigger—and nothing happened. There was no *click*. He looked at the pistol. The hammer hadn't fallen as it should. He glanced up and saw two things—Blue Water Woman with her arm out and her pistol pointed at him, and Nate King, grinning, and Methuselah knew as surely as he ever knew anything that the reason it had taken Nate so long to return was that Nate had tampered with his pistol. He went to scream to Blue Water Woman not to shoot and heard a boom and felt searing pain.

The ground became the sky and the sky became the ground. A great weakness came over him. He tried to move and couldn't. He tried to speak and couldn't. He heard voices, as if through a long passage.

". . . didn't he shoot?" Blue Water Woman was saying. "He was quicker than me."

"Probably got a thrill out of waiting until the last moment," Shakespeare said.

Methuselah Jones whined deep in his throat as the void claimed him.

"Thank you for counting, Nate," Blue Water Woman said. "I knew I could depend on you."

"What are friends for?" Nate King said.

# Author's Note

As longtime readers of Wilderness are aware, several of Nate King's journal entries have been branded "tall tales" by some. The entries on which this story is based are an example.

It should be noted, however, that tribes of the Great Basin have handed down accounts of the "people eaters," as they were called, from antiquity.

# INTERACT WITH DORCHESTER ONLINE!

Want to learn more about your favorite books and authors?
Want to talk with other readers that like to read the same books as you?
Want to see up-to-the-minute Dorchester news?

## VISIT DORCHESTER AT:
DorchesterPub.com
Twitter.com/DorchesterPub
Facebook.com (Search Pages)

## DISCUSS DORCHESTER'S NOVELS AT:
Dorchester Forums at DorchesterPub.com
GoodReads.com
LibraryThing.com
Myspace.com/books
Shelfari.com
WeRead.com